Praise for *The Victory Club*

✷ ✷ ✷

"*The Victory Club* captured me from the first chapter and brought this time in our country's history vividly to life. A beautiful reminder of the sacrifices that were made for the freedoms we enjoy, and of the rich heritage of faith we share as a nation."

DEBORAH RANEY, author of *Over the Waters* and *A Nest of Sparrows*

"Sweet Victory! This book transported me back to 1943. Robin Lee Hatcher has again proven why she is a fiction mainstay! A fabulous read that takes you through a roller coaster of emotions! I highly recommend *The Victory Club.*"

KRISTIN BILLERBECK, author of *With This Ring, I'm Confused*

"*The Victory Club* takes readers on a heartfelt journey into the lives of World War Two's forgotten freedom fighters—the mothers, sisters, girlfriends, and wives of soldiers battling overseas. These women gave their hands, their hearts, and their prayers, facing numerous struggles themselves. 'V' stands for the victorious liberation that Christ brings, not only to the physical battles we face, but the spiritual and emotional ones also. I laughed, cried, and rejoiced with these women. I can't wait to share this story with my friends!"

TRICIA GOYER, author of the acclaimed World War II novels *From Dust and Ashes* and *Night Song*

"As an avid reader of Robin Lee Hatcher's books, I highly recommend *The Victory Club*. She has woven an intriguing story of love and war set in turbulent times. While their men fight on the battlefields of World War II, women at home fight emotional battles of fear, loneliness, and temptation. Robin Lee, in her unique masterful way, touches the heart and presents the source of peace and the ultimate victory."

YVONNE LEHMAN, author of 40 novels including *Coffee Rings*

"An exquisite portrait of sisterhood at its most touching, *The Victory Club* tells the stories of four women who wait for their loved ones to return from war while they fight their own battles on the home front. Robin Lee Hatcher captures the indomitable spirit that united this country during WWII while offering fresh hope as our country again faces war on foreign soil."

TAMERA ALEXANDER, author of the upcoming Heart of Heaven series

The
Victory Club

★ ★ ★

Robin Lee Hatcher

Tyndale House Publishers, Inc.
Wheaton, Illinois

Visit Tyndale's exciting Web site at www.tyndale.com

TYNDALE is a registered trademark of Tyndale House Publishers, Inc.

Tyndale's quill logo is a trademark of Tyndale House Publishers, Inc.

Edited by Traci DePree

Designed by Beth Sparkman

This novel is a work of fiction. Names, characters, places, and incidents are either the product of the author's imagination or are used fictitiously. Any resemblance to actual events, locales, organizations, or persons living or dead is entirely coincidental and beyond the intent of either the author or publisher.

Library of Congress Cataloging-in-Publication Data

Hatcher, Robin Lee.
  The Victory Club / Robin Lee Hatcher.
    p. cm.
  ISBN 0-8423-7666-6 (sc)
1. World War, 1939-1945—Fiction. I. Title.
PS3558.A73574V53 2005
813'.54—dc22   2004029230

Printed in the United States of America

10 09 08 07 06 05
9 8 7 6 5 4 3 2 1

To Tammy,
who kept me focused on the Victory.

How I thank God, who gives us victory
over sin and death through Jesus Christ
our Lord! So, my dear sister, be strong
and steady, always enthusiastic about
the Lord's work, for you know that
nothing you do for the Lord
is ever useless.

The Lord is my strength and my song;
he has given me victory.
Songs of joy and victory are sung in the
camp of the godly.
The strong right arm of the Lord has
done glorious things!

PSALM 118:14-15

Acknowledgments

I would like to express my appreciation to my editor Becky Nesbitt, whose patience and guidance helped this book reach completion and be the better for it. I'm thankful to be working with the Tyndale fiction team in creating novels that will, I hope, glorify the Lord and encourage His followers.

I am continually grateful for the professional partnership and the special friendship I've enjoyed for more than fifteen years with my literary agent, Natasha Kern. Thanks for believing in both me and this latest story from my heart, Natasha.

A special, heartfelt thanks goes to the members of my prayer team who weekly prayed for me and my writing, lifting my requests in prayer before the throne of grace: Anita C., Anna B., Anne W., Arlene K., Beth R., Bette B., Carol H., Catherine L., Cathie M., Deanna K., Debbie R., Dianna R., Dina M., Emily C., Ernestelle K., Frank M., Gail M., Gigi S., Grace P., Janelle S., Kay G., Kay H., Kay M., Kay W., Kelly H., Kim K., Larna P., Lauri M., Linda H., Lynne T., Marion H., Mary S., Mil-Jean B., Ola N., Paula O., Sharlet M., Shirley L., and Sunni J. Thank you, my dear and faithful friends, for standing in the gap for me.

"My response is to get down on my knees before the Father, this magnificent Father who parcels out all heaven and earth. I ask him to strengthen you by his Spirit—not a brute strength but a glorious inner strength—that Christ will live in you as you open the door and invite him in. And I ask him that with both feet planted firmly on love, you'll be able to take in with all Christians the extravagant dimensions of Christ's love. Reach out and experience the breadth! Test its length! Plumb the depths! Rise to the heights! Live full lives, full in the fullness of God.

"God can do anything, you know—far more than you could ever imagine or guess or request in your wildest dreams! He does it not by pushing us around but by working within us, his Spirit deeply and gently within us." (Ephesians 3:14-20, *The Message*)

February
1943

UNITED STAT
OF AMERICA
ar Ration Book

1

Jeb Pratt shifted into second as the lumbering bus began its ascent of the final hill. The whine of the engine sounded anything but healthy. He hoped the old girl wouldn't break down today. It was colder than all git out this morning. He didn't figure the thermostat would see twenty-five degrees. Not with this wind.

"Come on, Bessie," he muttered to the bus. "Gotta get everybody to work on time."

Jeb might not be able to serve his country in the army or the navy, being he was approaching sixty-five years of age, but he figured he was doing his part since his route included transporting civilian employees to and from the air base south of Boise.

He glanced into his rearview mirror at his four remaining passengers. These ladies were his Gowen Field regulars, and over the last few months, he felt like he'd come to know them. Not because he chatted much with them himself. No, sir. That would've been frowned upon by his superiors. His job was to pay attention to the road, especially in weather like this. But he couldn't help listening in on their conversations.

Take Margo King, for instance. Nice enough looking woman—midforties, trim figure, her brown hair worn in a short, no-nonsense style—but she was mighty reserved. Rigid, even. Rarely had he seen her smile in all the months she'd ridden his bus. She didn't wear a wedding ring, and he'd never heard her mention a husband. However, Jeb knew there must have been a Mr. King at some point because Margo had a son serving in the African campaign and the gal beside her was her daughter.

Dottie King, not yet twenty from what Jeb had gathered, bore only a slight resemblance to her mother. Her brown hair was curly instead of straight, and she wore it shoulder length. Pretty as the day was long, Dottie also had a Hollywood pinup-girl figure. If he couldn't see it for himself, he'd have known from the wolf whistles he often heard when she got off the bus. But she paid them no never-mind. She had a boyfriend, a soldier who'd shipped out to Europe not all that long ago. She was always talking about him, and she didn't try to hide how much she loved and missed him.

Ah, young love. Jeb remembered what that was like. For that matter, he couldn't see that love changed much with age, except for deepening—assuming, of course, a man was smart enough to marry the right woman. He still felt a warm glow when he looked at Martha, his wife of forty-three years.

Speaking of love, his romantic heart just about broke for Lucy Anderson, who sat across the aisle from Margo and Dottie. Lucy had celebrated her wedding day on December 6, 1941, and awakened the next morning to find the world at war. Less than a month later, her husband enlisted in the Army Air Corps and was gone soon after. She hadn't seen him in nearly a year. Even when she smiled, Lucy couldn't conceal the sadness in her light blue eyes. Must be hard for her, Jeb thought, working as a secretary at the base, hearing the news of different campaigns and wondering if her husband might be involved.

That was one thing Jeb's last passenger didn't have to worry about. Penelope Maxfield's husband was safe and secure right here in Boise. A back injury had kept him from enlisting, and he was still unable to work. With all the bad war news they'd had over the past year, Jeb would've thought Penelope would act happier that her husband was not in the military. But from what he could tell, there wasn't much that made her happy. Most of the time, she sounded more angry than anything else. But maybe Jeb was wrong. Maybe he just expected anger from the fiery-looking redhead.

The stone pillars at the entrance to Gowen Field came into view. Jeb downshifted once again, then stepped on the brake and brought the bus to a halt.

"Do you suppose we'll get to meet him sometime?" Dottie asked her mother in the sudden silence. "Wouldn't that be something if we did?"

"I wouldn't count on it, dear," Margo King replied.

After a quick verification, the guards at the gate waved the bus through. Jeb touched the brim of his cap in a semi-salute to the nearest airman before stepping on the gas.

"But he's Greg's favorite actor. If I could catch him on the way to mess, maybe I could get his autograph to send to—"

"Dottie, don't you even think of it. You could lose your job. You leave Mr. Stewart in peace."

Jeb shook his head. All this fuss over a movie actor. Seemed like everywhere a fellow went in this town, folks were buzzing about Jimmy Stewart's arrival at Gowen Field. Stewart wasn't any more important than the thousands of other young men on the base who were training to fly dangerous missions, was he? Not that Jeb didn't like Jimmy Stewart's movies. He did. Still, all the excitement seemed like a bunch of nonsense to him.

The bus finished its long trek from the gate to the bus stop, and Jeb braked to a final halt. He reached for the lever that opened the door, letting in a blast of icy air.

Margo stood and stepped toward the exit. "Thank you, Mr. Pratt."

"See you tonight," he answered as he watched her descend the steps.

The other three women quickly followed, bidding him a pleasant day as they went.

Jeb figured if the war news wasn't particularly bad today he'd have that pleasant day. Long as he could keep warm, that is.

2

Lucy waved to her friends as they left the bus stop and headed in four different directions.

As was her habit each weekday morning, she prayed silently as she walked toward the building where she worked as a civilian secretary for the Army Air Corps. She prayed first for her husband, 1st Lieutenant Richard Anderson, a pilot serving in the European theater. Then she prayed for the Allied armed forces, from the president to the generals and admirals and on down to the lowest foot soldiers and sailors. She prayed for the innocent civilians on the ground, on both sides of the Atlantic and the Pacific. By the time she whispered her soft, "Amen," she had arrived at her desk.

She returned the greetings of several coworkers while she hung her coat on a nearby rack.

"Any letters this weekend?" Alice Franks inquired.

"No. Not yet."

How Lucy hated those three little words. It seemed she was forced to say them far too often. Letters from Richard often came in bunches, and the waiting in-between was horrid.

Waiting. Waiting. Always waiting. Waiting for Richard's letters. Waiting for Richard to come home. She tried not to complain—not to the Lord, not to others. But sometimes it seemed as if she'd been waiting for him for her entire adult life.

Orphaned at eighteen by a train accident and alone in the world—she had no grandparents, no aunts or uncles, no cousins—Lucy had longed for marriage and children so she could be part of a family again. She was twenty-seven when a friend had introduced her to Richard Anderson. Tall and handsome, kind and funny, a man of both strong faith and absolute integrity, he was everything she had dreamed of and more. She couldn't have helped loving him, even if she'd wanted to. She hadn't wanted to. When she and Richard were married fourteen months earlier, two years after their first date, she'd known she must be the happiest woman on earth.

If not for this war …

Lucy sighed as she removed the dustcover from her typewriter, then looked through the stack of papers waiting in the file basket on the side of her desk. It was going to be a busy morning, from the look of things.

✳ ✳ ✳

Dottie pulled the collar of her wool coat up around her neck and leaned into the bitter wind as she hurried toward the supply depot. Most days she was thankful for her job. It was hectic and physical and it kept her from thinking about Greg too much. But this morning, she had an upset stomach and a headache—again. All she'd wanted was to stay in bed, hidden beneath the warm comforter. If not for her worrywart mother, she might have done just that.

She entered the corrugated metal building that housed the supply depot.

"Good morning, Dottie," Harriett Lewis called from behind the counter.

"Morning, Harriett." She unbuttoned her coat. "Cold enough for you?"

"Cold enough."

Dottie hung her coat on a hook on the wall. "How long have you been here? I think our bus was running late." She turned and headed toward the counter.

"Not very long."

Some days, when she wasn't careful about the direction of her thoughts, Dottie envied her coworker. Harriett drove her own car to work each day. No standing out in the cold at the bus stop for her.

"Anything wrong, Dottie?"

"No," she lied. "Why do you ask?"

"I don't know. You look a bit peaked, I guess."

As if on cue, Dottie's stomach churned. She feared she would be sick, right there on the concrete floor. She turned away from Harriett and pretended to rifle through the requisition papers on the counter. Somehow she managed to quell the nausea that roiled through her.

Please, God. Don't let me be sick. We can't afford for me to miss work right now. Money's tight.

Being short of money was nothing new for the King family. Her mother had always struggled to make ends meet while raising her two children alone. Dottie had been six and Clark eleven when their father walked out on the family. Bart King got a quicky divorce down in Nevada and never returned to Idaho. He hadn't bothered to maintain contact with his children, nor had he helped his ex-wife financially.

For years, Dottie secretly wondered what she had done wrong to make her daddy go away. Why couldn't he love her? And even once she was old enough to understand that his leaving wasn't her fault, there was a part of her heart that still felt she was to blame. She wondered if those wounds would ever completely heal.

A child needs a father, God. It isn't Your will for a father to be absent from the home. Is it?

Dottie gave her head a slight shake, as if answering for the

Lord. But shaking her head wasn't a smart thing to do—the nausea returned with force, and she had to bolt for the latrine at the back of the depot. She barely made it to the toilet in time.

Moments later, exhausted, her eyes watering and her throat burning, she sank onto the cool floor and leaned her back against the wall.

"Here," Harriett said softly.

Dottie looked up to find her coworker holding a damp cloth toward her. "Thank you."

"Want me to get your mom?"

"No. This'll pass. Besides, she'll already be in class."

"Well, you stay here as long as you need to. I can cover up front."

This will pass, Dottie repeated to herself when she was alone again. *It's just an upset stomach*. She closed her eyes and covered them with the cloth Harriett had given her. *That's all it is. Just an upset stomach*.

Only Dottie's heart told her otherwise. It was something much worse than that. And it wasn't going to go away by midmorning.

Oh, Greg. What have we done?

✯ ✯ ✯

"Heavy Allied casualties . . . northern Africa theater . . . contested sectors . . ."

The overheard words, spoken by several young officers as they filed out of the classroom, chilled Margo to the bone.

Her son, Clark, was serving in the II Corps in the African campaign. She didn't know where precisely. The V-mails people received from their loved ones in the military were closely censored, lest any classified information fall into enemy hands. Of course, the censors had little to cut out when reading Clark's letters. They were brief and revealed nothing. "I'm fine," he told her. "Thanks for the cookies," he wrote. "I miss you and Dottie," he always added. Never much beyond that.

But Margo knew his life was in danger even if she didn't know his precise location. The *Idaho Daily Statesman* had reported that a major action would soon usher in the final showdown in northern Africa. This must be the beginning.

Heavy Allied casualties . . .

She turned toward the map on her classroom wall. She often stood in this same spot and stared at that map, memorizing the names on it—Casablanca, Oran, Algiers, Tebessa, Tunis, Sfax, and Maknassy. Her job at the base was to teach French to Army Air Corps officers. Many young men who'd passed through her classroom were now in Tunisia, where many natives spoke French. She prayed she'd taught them well, for their lives could depend upon it if captured by the enemy.

And Clark? Had she taught him well? Would he be safe? Were bombs exploding around him? Was he lying injured in some rocky mountain pass or on the Mediterranean shore? Had he been taken captive? Or was he—

"Mom?"

Margo turned toward the door at the sound of Dottie's voice.

"I heard about the push at the Kasserine Pass. They're saying there are—" She broke off abruptly.

"Heavy casualties." Margo hugged herself. "Yes, I heard, too."

Dottie entered the classroom and came to stand beside her mother. Together they faced that dreaded map, staring at it, wondering what was happening on the other side of the world. It was evening in Africa now, nearly eight o'clock. Darkness had blanketed the country for some time. Had the fighting waned?

"Lord, keep Clark safe," Dottie prayed.

Yes, God. Please. Don't require me to give You my son. I'm begging You. Don't require him of me.

The sins of Margo's past, for which she deserved to be punished, had never seemed so great a burden as they seemed at that moment.

"And, Father," Dottie continued softly, "keep Greg safe, too, wherever he is."

Margo struggled to add her silent *amen*. Not that she wished harm to fall upon Greg Wallace. Not at all. He was a nice enough boy. But she was glad he'd been shipped overseas, all the same. The farther away he was from Dottie, the better Margo liked it. Without mentioning her ex-husband by name, Margo had tried to make Dottie understand how dangerous these wartime romances were—to no avail. Her daughter swore that her love for her high school sweetheart would never falter, no matter how long Greg was away.

Well, better Dottie suffer heartache from missing him than to make the same mistakes her mother had made. Margo didn't want a man to ruin her daughter's life the way her husband had ruined hers.

* * *

As had become her habit over the past two months, Lucy met her friends for lunch in the tiny break room at the back of Building B-301. They each spread cloth napkins over their laps before opening their lunch boxes, but no one seemed hungry enough to eat. So there they sat, lost in their grim thoughts, while the cold February wind buffeted the building.

It hadn't taken long before everyone on the base—and in town, no doubt—knew that a major battle for control of northern Africa was raging. The importance was clear, even to civilians. Tunisia must be taken. The Allies needed the location for a refueling stop once the bombing raids began over Europe. The previous year had seen many defeats. Each woman in that break room longed to see a victory.

Finally, Lucy could take the silence no more. "Is this what it's

going to be like for the duration of the war?" She was exasperated with herself as well as with the others. "Must we expect the
worst to happen to the people we love?" She looked from one
woman to the next. "Can't we act as if we're women of faith? I
mean, either God's in control or He isn't."

Seated across from Lucy, Margo stiffened as if she'd been
slapped. "Perhaps you wouldn't say that if your husband was in
Africa instead of England."

A different sort of silence strangled the room.

"Oh, Margo." Lucy shook her head. "I didn't mean to sound
heartless. I want to encourage us not to lose hope."

But perhaps Margo was right, Lucy thought as she lowered
her gaze to her lap. She wanted to believe she would hold on to
hope, no matter what, but she hadn't been tested. Richard had
spent a good many months stateside before he was sent, late last
year, to England. If he'd flown missions over enemy territory, he
hadn't told her so in his letters.

"You know—" Dottie folded the wax paper around her un-
eaten sandwich—"I think Lucy's right. Just about everybody we
know has a loved one serving in the military. We know people
are dying. That's a reality of war we can't escape. But we can't
give in to fear and despair. We can't. If we do, then the enemy's
already won." She held out her left hand toward her mother and
her right hand toward Lucy.

Thank God for you, Dottie. Lucy took hold of the younger
woman's hand and gave it a squeeze. Then in a similar gesture,
Lucy held out her free hand toward Penelope.

After a moment's hesitation, Penelope mirrored the action.

"Oh for pity's sake," Margo grumbled. But finally she completed the circle.

Lucy looked at each of her friends. "From this day forward, I
promise to pray faithfully for you and your loved ones. I promise
to ask God for protection and guidance and to cause us to lean
on Him, no matter how long this war takes. I promise to be here

for you whenever you need me. And I'm not just going to pray for the Allies to have victory. I'm going to pray that each of us will have *personal* victory over the enemies we face. Over our fears, our faults, and our failures. That's my promise to you."

"Me, too," Dottie said.

"So do I," Margo chimed in.

Penelope sighed. "Sure. Why not?"

✳ ✳ ✳

Penelope accomplished little that afternoon. Her thoughts were too distracted to make sense of the words and numbers on the ledger pages. She kept thinking about Lucy with her husband poised to fly into danger and Dottie with her soldier boyfriend somewhere across the Atlantic and Margo with her son in Africa—and then she thought of her husband, Stuart, sitting at home in his easy chair, expecting Penelope to wait on him because of the pain in his back.

The pain, her left foot. She didn't care what his doctor said. There was nothing wrong with Stuart's back. He was a coward, that was all. He would rather be safe at home than serving on the field of battle. He didn't have a heroic bone in his body.

"I'm going to pray," Lucy had promised, *"that each of us will have personal victory over the enemies we face. Over our fears, our faults, and our failures."*

Penelope didn't pray often. She doubted it made a difference in the overall scheme of things. But if she did believe, if she was going to pray, she would ask God to have Stuart drafted and shipped as far away from her as he could get.

3

"Good night, Mr. Pratt," Lucy said, descending the bus steps.

"Good night, Mrs. Anderson. Have a nice evening."

With a *whoosh* of air, the door closed, and the bus drove away.

Lucy walked swiftly in the opposite direction, planning to stop at the corner market before returning to her apartment two blocks away. Shortages and long lines were becoming a common sight at grocery stores these days, but thankfully, Lucy wasn't after meat or sugar. Her needs were simple since she cooked only for herself.

A few minutes later, she entered the Bannock Street Market, closing the door behind her, glad to escape the frigid night air. She shivered involuntarily. "Brrr."

"Evening, Mrs. Anderson. Cold out there?"

She turned toward the counter where Howard Baxter, the proprietor, stood. "It certainly is, Mr. Baxter. I'm more than a little ready for spring to come."

"Couldn't agree more. Need any help?"

"No, thanks. I know what I'm after."

He gave her a warm smile, then turned his attention to some paperwork.

Lucy pulled her shopping list from her coat pocket and headed down the first aisle. It didn't take long to find the few things she wanted—eggs, cheese, an onion, a bottle of ketchup, a loaf of bread.

When Lucy carried her items to the front of the store, Howard glanced at them and said, "I worry about your diet, Mrs. Anderson. You don't eat enough to keep a bird alive." He raised an eyebrow. "Would you like a couple cans of green beans? We received a shipment of them today."

"How kind, Mr. Baxter. Yes, I believe I would like some." Green beans were not among her favorite vegetables, but she didn't say so to Howard Baxter. It felt nice to have someone care about whether or not she ate right, even if that person was only the man who ran the corner grocery store.

"How was your day?" Howard asked when he returned with the beans.

"Long."

The grocer nodded in understanding. "I've kept the radio on. The news coming through hasn't been good. Is your husband in North Africa?" He rang up the purchases as he spoke.

"I don't think so." Lucy gave her shoulders a slight shrug. "Richard was stationed in England the last I heard, but I haven't received any mail from him in several weeks. He could be any-where by now."

"The not knowing is awful hard."

She nodded in agreement. The not knowing *was* hard. But, she wondered, would it be easier if she knew he was in Africa? Would she prefer to be in Margo's place, knowing someone she loved was right in the thick of battle? No. No, she wanted Rich-ard out of harm's way for as long as possible. She wanted him to live through this war and come home. She wanted him to hold her in his arms and kiss her on the lips and love her until they were both old and gray.

"Mrs. Anderson?" His voice held compassion.

She looked up through a veil of unshed tears. "I'm okay," she whispered.

"If there's anything I can ever do for you . . ." He allowed his words to fade into silence.

"No, there's nothing you can do, Mr. Baxter, but thank you for offering." Lucy lifted her shopping bag and cradled it to her chest. "Will you put this on my account?"

"Of course."

She thanked him again, then left the store, still fighting tears of loneliness.

✷ ✷ ✷

Lucy and Richard had found the apartment on Jefferson Street two weeks before their wedding day. Holding hands, they walked through the three small rooms—an apartment added on to the back of the landlady's home—and decided this was where they wanted to live. Lucy lay awake that night, thinking about how she would decorate their home, imagining all the ways she could make it perfect for her new husband. How happy she had been. How innocent and trusting that their future held only joy.

Their wedding day was all she could want. Their wedding night was blessed. Their future was full of promise.

And in the morning came the news of Pearl Harbor, and their future was changed.

After letting herself into the apartment, Lucy glanced first at the floor where the mail fell through the narrow slot in the door. No letter from Richard, and nothing else either. Not even a bill.

With a sigh, she set the bag of groceries on the kitchen counter.

"I've got to stop feeling sorry for myself," she muttered. "I've got to stop."

A soft *thump* from the living room drew her attention toward the archway connecting the two rooms. Moments later, Empress, her cat, padded into the kitchen.

"Hello, baby."

Lucy bent down and lifted Empress into her arms. She buried her face into the long, white fur of the Persian's coat and listened to the vibrating sound that declared the cat's pleasure at her company.

"It's good to be with you, too."

Meow.

Lucy scratched the cat behind the ears, then set her on the floor. "Want some milk?"

Empress serpentined between her legs, purring loudly.

"Okay. Okay. Hold your horses."

Lucy retrieved the milk bottle from the refrigerator and poured a small amount into a saucer.

"Here you go, puss."

As she watched the cat lap up the milk, she wondered if she sounded dotty. If her landlady, Elizabeth Hilburn, heard her talking to Empress, would she think Lucy was entertaining a friend, or did she already know Lucy's loneliness was driving her crazy?

Oh, Richard. Why did you have to leave me so soon? You wouldn't have been drafted right away. We had so little time together.

Richard's dad had taught him to fly when Richard was a teenager. To say he loved being at the controls of an airplane was a gross understatement. Lucy remembered the visit his parents made to Boise about six months before the wedding. Richard took Lucy up for a brief flight in his father's Cessna Airmaster. She was terrified, but the exhilaration on Richard's face was unforgettable. Watching him at the controls, she knew in her heart that her future husband was born to be a pilot.

So how could she be surprised when war made him an officer in the air corps?

She released a long sigh. "If only I'd get a letter, I'd feel better."

Lucy left the kitchen, walked through the small living room, and passed into the even smaller bedroom. She hung her coat in the closet before changing out of her dress and into a pair of slacks, thick socks, and a warm sweater. Then she grabbed a blank V-mail from atop her dresser, carried it to the kitchen table, and settled onto the chair.

V··· —MAIL

To: 1st Lt. Richard Anderson, APO, N.Y.P.E.

From: Lucy Anderson

Monday, February 15, 1943

My darling Richard,

How very much I'm missing you tonight. But then, I always miss you, my love. I stopped at the market on the way home, and Mr. Baxter asked about you. He makes sure to tell me when he has harder-to-obtain items in the store. Needless to say, it's rarely the coffee or sugar I'd love to buy. According to the secretary of agriculture, we can expect restrictions on meat later in the year. And of course, the new food rationing goes into effect on March 1. We'll receive our War Ration Book Two later this month. The coupons cover all canned and bottled soups, juices, fruits, and vegetables.

This spring, I'm going to plant my first Victory Garden. Mrs. Hilburn has given me permission to use the west corner of the backyard for that purpose. I don't know a thing about gardening, but Penelope and Margo say they'll give me pointers. With any luck, I'll be canning my own fruits and vegetables come fall. Several women at church have offered to help me with that.

I received a letter from your mother on Saturday. She said your dad's had a bad bout with a cold but is on the mend. He's feeling especially restless since he hasn't been able to fly his airplane due to fuel shortages. I wish your parents didn't live so far away. I would dearly love to spend more time with them, and maybe seeing them would help me not miss you so much. (No, that wouldn't work. I would still miss you.)

Yankee Doodle Dandy has returned to the Rialto Theater, and Dottie and I might go see it on Saturday. It won a film award last month. I wish you could be there. I miss sitting beside you in the dark, holding your hand. One of many things I miss about you, darling.

We've heard about the battles being fought in Africa, and I'm wondering if you're still in England or if you've been sent to another theater of war. I pray not. Margo King's son is in North Africa. My heart goes out to her and Dottie as they wait for news about Clark and worry for his safety.

Today I promised my friends at work that I'm going to pray for victory in a new way, rather than sitting around and expecting the worst. But I confess I haven't been successful for even one day. I simply miss you too much to keep my chin up.

I'm running out of space, so I shall close. I send this letter to you with all of my love and hope for your continued safety.

Always,
Lucy

4

Sitting at her dressing table on Sunday morning, Dottie stared at her reflection in the mirror and wondered if she looked as different as she felt.

I'm pregnant.

One time. One time she and Greg weakened in their resolve. One time they grew careless and gave in to desire. One time, and now she was alone, unmarried, and going to have a baby.

Unwed motherhood had become almost common since the war began, but that didn't make Dottie feel better about it happening to her. As Christians, she and Greg were expected to live by a higher, godly standard. They were supposed to rely on the Lord for the strength to avoid giving in to temptation. Obedience was part of their public testimony. And their disobedience?

She closed her eyes and covered her face with her hands.

Why hadn't they joined other young couples from church on New Year's Eve? Why hadn't they understood the dangers they faced that night, alone in his parents' home?

If only . . .

★ ★ ★

Greg turned the key in the lock, and as the door to the darkened house swung open, Dottie giggled nervously.

"Are you sure your folks won't mind us being here while they're out?" she whispered.

Greg flicked on the entry hall light. "Of course not." He gave her a wink. "We're not in high school anymore."

Dottie knew there were other reasons this might not be a good idea, but for the life of her, she couldn't remember what they were. And she did so want to be alone with Greg. Since his return from basic training, it seemed they constantly were surrounded by others. His leave was nearly over, and they'd had little time to talk, just the two of them.

"I'll build a fire," Greg said as he closed the front door, "and then we can pop some popcorn. Why don't you get some ice and pour us a couple of Cokes?"

"Okay."

Dottie didn't need to ask where to find the glasses or the bottles of Coca-Cola. She knew the Wallace kitchen almost as well as she knew her own.

Twenty minutes later, Dottie and Greg sat on the sofa, staring at the crackling fire, their beverage glasses on the coffee table, condensation dripping onto the coasters beneath them. A shared bowl of popcorn rested on Dottie's lap. Greg draped his left arm around her shoulders and pulled her close to his side.

Three more days. That was all that was left of Greg's leave. Just three more days, and he would report for duty and be shipped overseas. Shipped off to war.

"You're doing it again," Greg said softly.

"Doing what?"

"Thinking about me leaving."

She turned to meet his gaze. "How did you know?"

"I just know. Maybe because I love you so much." He leaned forward and kissed her.

She didn't want to cry, but she feared she might.

Greg ended the kiss but shifted his body so he could cradle her face between his hands. "I'm going to be all right, Dottie. I'll be gone a year, maybe two. It isn't forever. When I get back, we'll get married."

"Oh, Greg." Her heart thundered in her chest. "I wish we'd gotten married this week. I wish we hadn't waited just to please Mom." Despite her resolve, the tears fell from her eyes.

"Dottie." Greg kissed her cheeks, first one, then the other. When he kissed her mouth again, she tasted the salt of her own tears on his lips. "My beautiful, wonderful, sweet girl."

Something warm and dangerous coiled in Dottie's abdomen. A need. A longing. She moaned.

As if in response to the sound in her throat, Greg drew her closer to him, one hand sliding up and down her back as his kisses deepened. Dottie was vaguely aware of the bowl of popcorn falling off her lap and hitting the floor.

Leave. Leave now.

But she couldn't leave. She wouldn't listen to that small voice of warning in her head. She had only a few more days with Greg. Only three precious days and he would be gone. She needed to be with him. She wanted to be with him. What could it hurt to spend a few more minutes locked in his embrace? They hadn't done anything wrong before, and there was no reason to think they would do so tonight.

But for some reason, tonight was different. Tonight the kisses didn't stop. Tonight their resolve evaporated like a mist in the morning sunlight, and they gave in to temptation's enticing pull.

When their desperate passion was spent, Dottie and Greg knew they'd traded obedience to God for a fleeting moment of pleasure. All that remained was embarrassment and shame. And her tears.

"I'm sorry, Dottie. I never meant . . . I didn't know . . . I'm sorry, Dottie. I'm so sorry."

✷ ✷ ✷

Why didn't we join the other young couples from church on New Year's Eve? Dottie asked herself again as the memory of that night faded. Oh, how she wished they had.

"If wishes were horses, beggars would ride." That's what Grandma Turley would say if she were still living. Then she would have given Dottie a warm hug and told her God's love would see them through.

And what was Dottie's mother going to do when *she* found out? She would scowl and, as she had done before, quote John Adams: "Facts are stubborn things; and whatever may be our wishes, our inclinations, or the dictates of our passions, they cannot alter the state of facts and evidence."

This time, Mother was right. Dottie could wish she and Greg hadn't broken their vow of sexual abstinence. She could wish that she weren't pregnant. But wishing wouldn't change a thing. Dottie King was going to have a baby in a little over seven months.

"Dottie!" her mother called from down the hall. "You'd better hurry or we'll be late to church."

"I'm hurrying."

That was a lie. She wasn't hurrying. She was dragging her feet. The last place she wanted to be this morning was in church. She'd felt guilty enough for the past seven Sundays, even before she knew she carried Greg's baby. Not that where she was made a difference. Christ was with her always. God knew what she'd done, whether she hid in her bedroom or sat in the front pew of the sanctuary.

O Lord. She lifted the photograph of Greg in his army uniform and pressed it against her chest. *We didn't mean to let this happen. We didn't mean to sin. Forgive us our weaknesses and temptations.*

She closed her eyes and remembered their parting at the train depot on the third of January. Dressed in his uniform, looking both handsome and far too serious, Greg wiped the tears from her cheeks, then drew her into the circle of his arms and whispered in her ear, "If we confess our sins to Him, He's faithful to forgive us and to cleanse us from every wrong. That's what He's promised, Dottie. It may not feel like it now, but He forgave us the instant we asked Him to."

She believed that. Really she did.

"Can you forgive me, Dottie?" he'd asked, not for the first time. "I'm so sorry. It was my fault, not yours. I love you, you know. I love you so much."

Of course she could forgive Greg. She had forgiven him. She loved him, and she knew what happened on New Year's Eve was not his fault alone. She had a mind and a will of her own. She'd known what was right and what was wrong. She could have listened to the voice of warning, but she chose not to.

She looked at her reflection again. Yes, she'd forgiven Greg, and she believed God had forgiven them both. But forgiving herself was proving to be another, more difficult matter.

Dottie set Greg's photograph on the dressing table, rose from the stool, and went to her closet. She shed the robe she wore over her slip, then replaced it with a dress that was the same shade of brown as her hair and eyes. Now if only she had a pair of stockings, she might feel better. But silk hose were a luxury few could find. The material was needed by the military for parachutes.

As Dottie slid her bare feet into a pair of brown pumps, she wondered if one of those silk parachutes was harnessed onto Greg's back at that very moment. Could he be falling from some great height toward earth, only to land in a foreign, hostile country?

O God, what if he dies? What if he never lives to know he's going to be a father?

"Dorothea Ruth King, will you come on?"

"Coming, Mother. Coming."

✯ ✯ ✯

For as far back as Dottie remembered, the King family had occupied the fourth pew, center aisle, in the sanctuary of East
Boise Community Church. Not her father, of course, but the
rest of the family—mother, son, and daughter. Every Sunday,
no matter the weather or the season, they'd walked the four
blocks to church, the three of them.

In this church, one Sunday evening, Dottie first heard God
speaking to her heart, and she went forward to accept Christ
during the altar call. In this church she learned to love the Bible,
developing a hunger for the Word that was never sated. In this
church she came to understand how much God loved her and
what pleasure He took when she worshiped and praised Him.
And it was here that she met Greg.

*Father, I know You've forgiven me. I know You've forgiven us
both. But I . . . I need to tell You again how sorry I am. We never
meant to fail You, Lord.*

She stared at the round, stained-glass window above the altar,
not hearing the sermon, too lost in her own world to listen.

She needed to tell her mother about the baby, but she wanted
Greg to know first. Maybe the army would let him come home
long enough to marry her.

No, they wouldn't. She was on her own. She would have to
live with the choice she'd made and do the best she could for
herself and her child.

*Until Greg comes home. Please, God. Let him live through the
war and come home to us.*

The congregation rose for the closing prayer. Dottie followed
suit a heartbeat later, but not before her mother gave her a stern
glance.

She's going to be disappointed in me.

Dottie hated to upset her mother. Margo King expected the
absolute best from her children—just as she did from herself—
and it was hard for Dottie not to fail when the bar was set so

high. The King children were told repeatedly that they were ex-
amples to the world. They weren't to fight. They were always to
be kind and polite. They weren't to get dirty or misbehave. They
were to get good grades.

The world was watching. God was watching. They were to be
perfect as He is perfect. Their mother told them so again and
again.

When Clark and Dottie were younger, Margo had pounded
into their heads the opportunities college could afford them.
"You'll need to do well so you can get scholarships," she'd told
them. "Study hard. Don't throw your lives away. Be everything
God created you to be."

Dottie imagined the look of disappointment in her mother's
eyes when she learned about the pregnancy. *You threw your life
away, Dottie*, is what that look would say. *You threw it away.*

"Amen," the congregation said in unison.

Dottie opened her eyes, feeling all the more guilty and miserable because she hadn't listened to the prayer.

*Three weeks. I'll give the mails another three weeks. Then I'll have
to tell her.*

5

Penelope set the platter that held the pot roast in the center of the table, then walked to the living room, where her husband read the newspaper while their children played on the sofa. Today was like every other Sunday, and the staleness of the routine made her want to scream.

"Dinner's ready, Stuart. Children, go wash your hands."

Her son and daughter were quick to obey, hopping off the couch and hurrying down the hallway. Moments later, she heard Alan telling Evelyn to stand on the step stool so she wouldn't splash water all over the bathroom floor.

"Smells good, Pen." Stuart sat at the head of the table. "We'd better enjoy it while we can. Meat's going to get more scarce."

In a bored voice, she answered, "That's what they say." What did she care anyway? She hated shopping and she hated cooking, with or without meat shortages.

The children scurried into the dining room, hands still damp. Penelope helped Evelyn onto her chair.

"Did you get the new rationing book yet?" Stuart reached for the bowl of mixed vegetables.

"Not yet." Penelope sat on the chair at the opposite end of the table. "This week."

"I hope our soldiers actually get those steaks we can't buy anymore."

If you were in the army, you could find out for yourself.

As Penelope watched, Stuart dished food onto the children's plates and cut their meat into small bites.

If only you were in the army, maybe I could breathe again. If only you'd go away.

When did this happen to her? When did the predominant emotions she felt for Stuart become resentment and anger? She'd loved him when they married. At least she thought she'd loved him. She was all of eighteen, her groom nineteen, and anxious to get out from under her father's roof. The newlyweds didn't have two nickels to rub together, but they knew how to have a good time on what they did have. The arrival of the children put an end to those carefree days.

Then came the war.

"Don't worry, Pen," Stuart had said when they first learned of the attack by the Japanese. "I won't sign up just yet, and it'll take a while for the draft to get around to me. I'll be here to take care of you and the kids as long as I can. Americans'll lick the enemy in a hurry. You'll see. I may never have to go."

A few days later, he fell from a ladder in the garage. The complaints of back pain began that night, and he went to see the doctor the next day. Soon thereafter, he quit his job on the advice of his physician because he supposedly wasn't able to perform physical labor.

Only afterward did Penelope suspect he was lying. At first, she was as fooled as everyone else. But when she learned the maximum draft age for married men was twenty-six, she saw through the subterfuge. Stuart was just shy of his twenty-fifth birthday when Pearl Harbor was attacked. Another year and he would be safe. Unless the government raised the draft age, in which case heaven only knew how long he would continue his charade, sitting at home in his easy chair while she worked to keep food on the table.

Some days, she despised him.

Penelope focused her attention on the children and didn't speak to Stuart through the rest of the meal. When dinner was over, he returned to the living room while Penelope settled the children in their room for an afternoon nap. She sat on the bed between them, her back against the headboard, and read to them from *Grimm's Fairy Tales* until they slept.

With the book now closed on her lap, she turned her gaze out the window. A tree, barren of leaves, stood in the small backyard of their rental home. How like that tree she felt. Cold. Barren. Lifeless in the midst of a gloomy winter. She was only twenty-five. She shouldn't have to live a life of drudgery. She wanted to go to parties, to stay up all night if she chose. She wanted to buy things for herself instead of worrying about bills to pay.

It isn't fair. It just isn't fair.

She released a long, feeling-sorry-for-herself sigh.

At least her job at Gowen Field was a good one. And because she, Lucy, Margo, and Dottie rode the bus together every workday, the four women had formed a close bond over the past year.

Penelope sighed again.

They were friends, yes, but she sometimes felt like an interloper. The others each had a loved one in uniform, which set Penelope apart because she didn't. Oh, they never said anything to her face, but she was sure they must think it awful to have a coward for a husband. Plus they talked about God in a way she didn't understand, and that made her feel different and uncomfortable.

Oh, how she hated the way things were in her life. If only they could be different.

6

Margo sat beside the living-room window, using the last rays of afternoon sunlight for her mending. She wouldn't turn on the lamp until absolutely forced to. No point paying good money for light when the Lord provided it free.

She happened to glance up just as Frances Ballard approached the front door. "Dottie," she called. "Frances is here."

Dottie entered the living room seconds before the bell rang. As soon as it did, she pulled open the door. "Hi, Frances."

"Hi, Dot. Hello, Mrs. King."

Margo smiled at the young woman. "Hello, Frances. We haven't seen you in a while."

"I know. I've been kind of busy." Frances looked at Dottie. Lowering her voice to a near whisper, she said, "I need to talk to you."

"Sure. Come on to my room. Excuse us, Mom."

Margo nodded as she returned her attention to the mending in her lap. Whispering between them, the two young women disappeared into Dottie's room.

For the first time in a week, Margo felt a measure of peace. It was like old times, having Frances here, whispering and giggling with Dottie. Margo could half believe that at any moment Clark would enter through the back door, stomping his feet on the rug and calling, "I'm home, Mom."

The short-lived peace vanished, and tears stung her eyes. Clark wouldn't come through that back door. Her son was on the opposite side of the globe, fighting a ruthless enemy, and Margo was terrified for him. Was this the time God would require payment for the sins of her youth?

The light from the window was gone, dusk having settled over the valley. It mattered not, for Margo ceased to think about her mending. Instead her thoughts traveled back in time, back to another war, and to the foolish sixteen-year-old girl she'd been in the spring of 1917.

★ ★ ★

Bart King was the most handsome young man Margo Coffman ever laid eyes on. Four years her senior, he had chestnut-colored hair that was thick and slightly wavy. His brown eyes were flecked with gold and seemed to light up when he looked at her. His smile took her breath away. A man in uniform, he seemed sophisticated, worldly, exciting—everything Margo was not. She lost her heart to him almost the instant her best friend, Daphne, introduced them to each other.

Two months later, on a warm May night, Bart spirited her away from a party at Daphne's house. "I'll be called up soon," he whispered in her ear as they sat on a blanket beneath the stars. "I'll be going off to the war and may never see you again. I could die over in Europe. Lots of our boys already have." He kissed her, not the usual sweet touch of his lips upon hers, but a kiss that seared and demanded.

He could die. She could lose him. What if he never returned? She would die too. Surely she would die too.

"I love you, Margo. You know I do."

"I love you, too. Oh, Bart. I love you, too."

"Be mine."

"I am yours." Tears streaked her cheeks as she clung to him. "I am. I am. I am."

"Be *really* mine, Margo."

She didn't know what he meant, but that didn't matter. Margo would do anything for him. Anything he asked, she would do. Anything at all.

⋆ ⋆ ⋆

Bart King hadn't been called to war after all. Armistice Day saw to that. And when Margo turned up pregnant a few weeks later, Bart was compelled to marry her. It was either marriage or jail, her father told him. Bart chose marriage, but his love for her, if it had ever existed, proved fleeting, replaced by rancor and accusations that she'd trapped him.

What a foolish girl I was.

The two good things Bart did for Margo in those thirteen unbearable years of marriage were Clark and Dottie. And although Clark was conceived in sin, he was loved beyond measure by his mother.

Oh, God. Don't require him of me.

V··· —MAIL

To: PFC Gregory Wallace, APO, N.Y.P.E.
From: Dottie King
Sunday, February 21, 1943

Dearest Greg,

I haven't received any letters from you since you left Boise at the end of your leave. I can only pray that the address you gave me is correct and that this letter will find you wherever the army has taken you. Every day when I get home from the base, I rush to check the mail, hoping to see your familiar handwriting on an envelope.

I have something I must tell you. I wish it needn't be by letter. I wish I could tell you in person or, at the very least, by telephone. I long to see your face. I long to hear your voice. I long to know everything will be all right for us.

Greg, I'm going to have a baby. (How I hate it that the censors will read the news before you do.) I haven't told anyone else, not even Mother. Especially not Mother. She won't understand. She's never made a mistake in her life. She always does the right thing, so how could she understand something like this?

I know this isn't the way either of us wanted to begin a family. The best way would have been college and marriage and career and then children. But we didn't do things in that order. Remember how you told me at the depot that Jesus is faithful to forgive us? Well, He may forgive (He _does_ forgive), but He doesn't always remove the consequences, does He? And so now I'm asking Him to walk me through the consequences of my choices. I know He'll do it, for He's promised to always be with us.

I don't want this news to worry or distract you, my darling Greg. Be mindful to take care of yourself first. I will be fine. As disappointed as Mother will surely be, she'll be there for me. God will guide me in the weeks and months to come. "I can do everything through Christ, who gives me strength."

The war can't last forever. I'll be right here waiting for you, whenever you come home. Our baby will be waiting here for you, too.

One other thing before I close. Frances came to see me today, and you'll never guess what she had to tell me. She's joined the Women's Army Auxiliary Corps! She hopes to be posted overseas eventually. She says she wants to do whatever she can to free up men for combat so the war will get over that much sooner and we can bring everybody home. God bless her. I think she's very brave. Like you.

I'll write more soon. My prayers and love come to you with this letter.

Forever yours,
Dottie

7

Yᴏᴜ did *what*?" Penelope stared at her sister in disbelief. "Frances, you're much too young to—"

"I'm twenty, Pen. There are plenty of guys younger than me serving in the military. Just because I'm a girl doesn't mean I shouldn't do my part to help win the war."

"Then get a civilian job at Gowen Field or Mountain Home. That's all important work, too. You don't have to join the WAACs to help out." She brushed her hair back from her forehead in a gesture of frustration. "And what about your schooling? I thought you wanted a degree."

"College can wait until I get back."

Penelope wanted to throttle her sister. Frances didn't understand anything. Penelope had given up her chance to go to college, opting for a fancy wedding instead. Marriage had looked like freedom to Penelope, and she'd grabbed it with both hands. Now she wished she'd chosen college. Her life would be so different if she had.

Frances sat on the chair beside Penelope and reached out to take hold of her hand. "Who knows what I'll get to do or where I might end up serving? Think of the adventure I'm about to have. The world is changing for women. Look at the jobs we're doing while the men are gone. Never again can anyone say we aren't capable."

The world hasn't changed for me, Frances. Maybe for you, but not for me. I'm stuck in the same old place.

"Be glad for me, will you, Pen?"

"Your adventure could take you into danger," she said rather than confess her true thoughts.

"You're just envious 'cause I'll get to wear a uniform."

Penelope's smile was forced. "Yeah, that must be it. I'm envious of the uniform."

It was true. She *was* envious. Not of the uniform, but of everything else. She was more jealous than worried. Frances wasn't chained to a boring existence by a husband and children. Her sister could do anything, go anywhere.

"Hey, Pen." Frances squeezed her hand. "What is it? What's wrong? Every time I see you lately, you look like you're carrying the troubles of the world on your shoulders. Is there something going on I should know about? Is Stuart's back getting worse?"

It took great willpower not to laugh aloud. "No, his back's no worse." How bitter her voice sounded in her ears. Could her sister hear it, too? "It's nothing really. I suppose I'm just tired. You know, working at the air base all day, then trying to keep up with the household tasks after I get home at night."

"You're sure that's all it is?"

"I'm sure." Penelope slipped her hand away, then stood. "Can I get you some hot cocoa? I was warming the milk when you arrived." She walked to the cupboard and took out two large, blue mugs.

"I'd love some, sis. Do you have any marshmallows by chance?"

"Sorry. They're more scarce than sugar, I think."

"That's okay. I'm getting used to doing without those sweets I crave. I guess we can get used to anything, huh, given enough time."

"I guess," Penelope answered, but she wasn't sure it was true. She didn't think she would ever get used to the way she felt about her life. Not ever.

Her thoughts churning, she poured the heated milk into the mugs. After adding cocoa, she stirred the hot chocolate with a spoon, then carried them to the table. For a time, the sisters sat without speaking while they sipped their beverages. The kitchen was cozy on that cold February evening. From the living room came the muffled sounds of a radio program, accompanied by Stuart's occasional laughter. Otherwise, all was still. Stuart had put the children to bed nearly an hour before.

"Pen," Frances said at last, "I meant to ask you. Does Dottie King seem all right when you see her at work?"

"Dottie?" She shrugged. "Far as I can tell. Why?"

"Oh, I don't know. I dropped by to see her earlier today, and I had a strange feeling, like something was wrong."

Penelope raised an eyebrow. "Same kind of feeling you've had about me?"

"Hmm." Frances gave her a sheepish grin. "You're right. It is kind of the same thing. Guess I'm becoming a worrywart."

"I think that's supposed to be my job. I'm the big sister."

"And the best big sister any girl ever had."

"Oh, Frances." Tears welled in her eyes. "I wish I could go with you. What will I do when you go away?"

"You'll be fine. You've got Stuart, Alan, and Evelyn. You'll hardly know I'm gone before I'm back."

Her sister didn't know how wrong she was.

8

During the lunch break on Monday, Lucy received a packet of seeds from Margo.

"It'll be time to plant your peas before you know it," Margo told her. "I thought I'd give you a head start."

"But it's still winter." Lucy glanced out the window.

"The weather will break soon. You'll see. Boise goes from bitter cold to surprisingly warm before March bellows into the valley. You've lived here all your life. You should know that."

To be honest, Lucy hadn't noticed. She only knew she was glad when winter ended and the snow disappeared from the mountains. She was most definitely a fair-weather girl.

Margo patted Lucy's shoulder. "You needn't look so hesitant. There isn't that much to gardening. You till. You plant. You water. You weed. You harvest. You preserve."

"I must seem pathetic. Thirty years old and clueless about planting a garden."

Lucy supposed there was one positive aspect about Richard's departure shortly after their wedding. He didn't have the opportunity to learn how inept his bride was. By the time he returned from the war, she hoped to be a better homemaker.

Lucy's mother, Karen Grover, had known how to make a man's home his castle. She'd been the consummate hostess, an accomplished cook, had decorated her home with flair while never overspending, had maintained glorious flower beds, and had canned jar after jar of foods from her garden every fall. If Lucy's mother had lived, she would have seen to it that her daughter became as accomplished in all things domestic as she had been.

Why was it, Lucy wondered, that people put off so many things, expecting to do them tomorrow? Tomorrow too often didn't come. It hadn't come for her parents. It might not come for Richard.

Richard, I want you to have twenty thousand tomorrows. Take care of yourself. Oh, please. Take care of your todays so we can have those tomorrows.

Another week had passed without any letters. Lucy knew that didn't have to mean anything was wrong. Everyone talked about the slow mail service. People often received several letters from overseas on the same day. That had happened to Lucy before. On those occasions, she'd taken the envelopes, arranged them by date, oldest first, and then read the letters in the order they'd been written, savoring every word.

But she would settle for one letter today. Just one. She longed for news of her husband.

In a recent newspaper column by Ernie Pyle, the reporter had told of the leading American flying ace in French North Africa. Lucy had wondered if they knew Richard.

Can you tell me anything about my husband? she'd wanted to ask the pilot and the reporter. *Have you seen him, flown with him? Is he in Africa, too?*

But the newspaper had been silent about Lt. Richard Anderson.

He hasn't had all smooth sailing by any means, Ernie Pyle had written about the fighter pilot. *In fact, he's very lucky to be here at all. He got caught in a trap one day and came home with two hundred sixty-eight bullet holes in his plane. His armor plate stopped at least a dozen that would have killed him.*

Her heart nearly stopped beating when she recalled those words. Two hundred and sixty-eight bullet holes in his plane. Had Richard come under the same sort of attack in his B-17 bomber? Would a German in his Focke-Wulf 190 or Messerschmitt 109 come zooming from behind a cloud and riddle the Flying Fortress with bullets?

"Hey. Where are you, Luce?"

She looked up.

Dottie stood nearby, compassion evident in her brown eyes. "You were a million miles away."

"Not a million," Lucy answered, her voice husky. "Just an ocean."

Dottie nodded in understanding, then said, "Lunch break's over. Mom and Penelope already left."

"Oh. I didn't hear them go."

"I could tell."

Lucy rose from the chair, slipping on her coat as she did so.

Dottie hooked arms with her. "Maybe there'll be letters waiting for us both when we get home."

"Oh, Dottie. I hope so."

Outside Building B-301, the air buzzed with the sounds of airplane engines. Several Flying Fortresses, the same kind of planes Richard piloted, were headed out on their practice runs. They would fly over the desert and drop their hundred-pound concrete-filled bombs, training for the time when they would unleash real bombs on enemy targets.

But these men were safe in the good old USA while Richard—

"We've got to have faith," Dottie said above the noise of the aircraft. "We've got to, or we'll go mad."

Madness might be a kind of comfort, Lucy thought after she and Dottie parted company. If she were mad, perhaps she wouldn't think about Richard every second she was awake. If she were mad, perhaps she wouldn't dream about him at night.

Or maybe thinking and dreaming about him all the time will drive me mad.

Seated at her desk again, Lucy rolled a piece of paper into the Underwood, but her thoughts remained far, far away from the form in her typewriter.

She had waited a long time for the right man to enter her life. Alone in the world—without parents, grandparents, or extended family—Lucy had seen her friends marry and start families, and she'd wanted the same for herself. But she'd also wanted the man God chose for her. So she'd waited . . . and waited . . . and waited.

At the age of twenty-seven, she began to wonder if God was calling her to a life of singleness.

And then she met Richard.

He courted her, wooed her, won her—although, truth be told, he hadn't needed to work hard at it. She lost her heart to him almost immediately, believing he was the man God had planned as her mate. Richard's love completed her in a way she hadn't known was possible. If she were to lose him now ...

Lord, she prayed, her fingers falling idle on the typewriter keys, *keep him safe for me. And please send a letter soon. Please let me hear from him.*

V··· —MAIL

To: Mrs. Richard Anderson, Boise, Idaho, U.S.A.
From: 1st Lt. Richard Anderson
Sunday, January 24, 1943

My beloved Lucy,

It is cold and damp where we are, somewhere in England. The boys in the squadron miss their wives and sweethearts back home, especially in this gray, gloomy weather. We all wish we could hurry up and start bombing the Nazis in Berlin and get this war over with so we can come home. It doesn't help that two of our guys received Dear John letters last week. It makes every man here wonder what's going on back home. Just about every man, I should say. Not this one. I can feel and hear your love for me in every letter. I'm looking right now at the photograph from our wedding. Hard to believe it was taken more than a year ago. Seems like yesterday. I swear I can still hear the music and see you walking down the aisle in your beautiful gown of white, all smiles as you look at me. I thank God for you, my beloved wife, every day of my life. I pray that God will protect you and give you comfort, the same way He's doing for me over here. I carry the new Bible you sent in the pocket of my jacket. The small size lets me do that. Whenever I open it, I remember how God brought us together and made us one in marriage, and I rejoice. I know you're lonely, and I hate that we've spent the first year of our marriage so far apart. But this war won't last much longer. Maybe a year. Maybe two. But the Allies will triumph over evil; I promise you that. The Germans, Italians, and Japanese may not know it yet, but we do. Ask any guy in my squadron, and he'll tell you the same thing. I can't thank you enough for the many letters you write. I know you said you're afraid they must be boring, since all you do is go to work and then go home again. But they're not boring—I promise you. They help me "be there" with you, hearing about the people and places that fill your day. That's more important to me than you'll ever know. In case I haven't said this in a letter before, I want you to know, darling, that I'm sorry I'm not with you, because I miss you so much. But I can't be sorry for serving my country this way. When I come home to you and we start a family, I want my kids to grow up in a better world than the one we've got now. I know the Bible tells us there'll be wars and rumors of war right up to the time Jesus returns. Who knows? Maybe that's sooner than we think and I'll be meeting you in the air at His sudden appearing. But if He tarries, then I'm glad to do my part. I hope you agree. Well, I've squeezed in as much as this V-mail will hold. Hope the writing isn't too tiny for you to read. I love you more than I can express, my dearest Lucy.

Always and forever,
Richard

9

Well, look at you, Mrs. Anderson." Howard Baxter leaned his elbows on the counter and grinned at Lucy. "You've had a letter from that husband of yours, haven't you?"

"Yes. I got one yesterday. It was written a month ago, so I know there are others still to come. Richard's good about writing often."

"The mails are tricky things these days. No telling how many letters are sitting around in the back of a building, waiting for somebody to find and deliver them." Howard straightened. "Was he able to tell you where he is?"

"Somewhere in England as of the letter, and he didn't mention any orders. Of course, if he tried to tell me where he was or where he was going, it would be cut out by the censors. He's careful about minding those rules."

The grocer nodded. "Good thing, too. Loose lips might sink ships."

Or shoot Flying Fortresses from the sky.

As if he'd read her thoughts and wanted to distract her, Howard became all business. "I received a small shipment of beef this afternoon. Are you interested?"

"Really? You have *beef*? Yes, Mr. Baxter, I'm very interested. I still have several stamps left in Ration Book One." She placed her pocketbook on the counter and opened it. "I also need some extra heavy waxed paper and a package of gelatin."

"You're in luck. I've got both of those items. I'll get them for you. Be right back."

Funny. She was in luck because waxed paper and gelatin were in stock. Oh, for the days when *lucky* meant something far more than that!

Lucy retrieved the ration book from the bottom of her purse. "I wonder how long we'll need these," she said softly, speaking to herself.

But it was Howard who answered as he returned to stand behind the counter. "It's a long way to Berlin and Tokyo for our boys. The fighting will be fierce, and there'll be harder times for them before they get better. I remember what it was like in Europe during the First World War."

"You were there?" She didn't know why she was surprised. At forty-five—she knew that was his age because he'd told her on his birthday last December—the grocer was certainly old enough to have served in what was once called the Great War.

"I was there. In France. Twenty years old and full of myself when I shipped out. Thought I was invincible." He shook his head. "Sometimes when I read the newspaper, about the fighting going on in Africa and in the Pacific, I imagine I hear bullets zinging over my head. I remember the terror I felt when the world was exploding around me."

Lucy sucked in a quick breath. "Oh!"

Howard Baxter reached out and lightly touched her upper arm, a gesture of sympathy. "I'm sorry, Mrs. Anderson. That was thoughtless of me. I shouldn't be talking like that. Not to you."

"It's all right." She blinked back unwelcome tears. "I . . . I know what could happen to Richard." Her former good mood was forgotten. She was alone, she was frightened, and she didn't know how to keep believing that Richard would be okay.

"Let me make it up to you. I was about to close shop for the night. How about I buy you supper over at Chloe's?" His smile was gentle and somewhat pleading. "You'd be doing me a favor. I'm tired of eating alone."

Lucy was tired of it, too, and despite a little tug in her heart that told her to refuse the invitation, she said, "I'd like that, Mr. Baxter. Thank you."

✮ ✮ ✮

Chloe's was a small diner off State Street, a few blocks from Lucy's apartment.

"I'll be right back with your order," the waitress said after Lucy and Howard made their selections from the menu. "You sit tight now."

Lucy glanced around the diner. Except for an elderly man at the counter, they were the only customers.

"This your first time in here?" Howard asked.

"No. I came for lunch once, not long after . . . after I moved into my apartment." She remembered that visit. It was soon after Richard left Boise. Her sudden aloneness had overwhelmed her, and she sought comfort in the company of strangers rather than eat alone in the hollow apartment.

"The food's simple but good." Howard cocked his head toward the kitchen. "Georgia, our waitress, and her sister, Vickie, have worked for Chloe Barlow since she opened the place in 'twenty-five. They treat every customer like family." He met Lucy's gaze again. "I guess that's why I like it so much. It's comfortable, homey even. They stay busy during the dinner hour, but it's usually quiet like this by the time I close the store and come in."

"Do you eat here often?"

He shrugged. "Often enough. No fun cooking for one."

Lucy didn't want to think about cooking for one or the empty apartment awaiting her. "Have you always lived alone?"

"No. I was married once. Lost my wife to cancer fifteen years ago."

"I'm sorry. I didn't mean—"

He shook his head. "You couldn't know."

But Lucy thought she should have known at least that much, something more than his age and his profession. Howard Baxter knew that Richard was a pilot stationed in England and he knew where Lucy worked and he knew about her loneliness and what she liked to eat and even what her favorite cleaning products were. He knew because he was considerate enough to inquire and observe.

"Do you have children, Mr. Baxter?"

Again, he shook his head. "We wanted them but it never happened for us." He glanced out the window but not before Lucy saw a flicker of sadness in his eyes.

She wondered why he was still alone after fifteen years as a widower. Howard was a good-looking man. Not handsome like Richard, but pleasant to look at, especially when he smiled. While he had a slight paunch above his waistband, he hadn't gone to fat. She couldn't imagine why some woman hadn't snagged him years ago. And with the dearth of available men these days, he needn't lack female companionship. Was he, perhaps, still mourning the wife of his youth?

Will I be like that if Richard dies? Will I still mourn him fifteen years later?

"Hey, I'm sorry. I've made you sad again." Howard tapped his fingertips on the table. "Let's change the subject. Why don't you tell me …hmm …tell me what you do on your weekends?" He leaned forward, as if eager to hear her reply.

"Nothing exciting, I assure you. On Saturday I catch up with my cleaning and washing and ironing, and on Sunday I sing in the choir at church."

"And what church is that?"

She smiled. "Redeemer's Assembly, a few blocks from here. It's a lovely church. I've only been attending there for a year, but I've loved it from the start. Everyone makes you feel at home. Have you ever visited there?"

"No. Never been. I rarely go to church anyway. Christmas and Easter mostly."

Her smile faded. "Why is that, Mr. Baxter?"

"I'm not the religious sort, I guess. My mother was. So was my wife." He shrugged. "It just never rubbed off on me."

She felt a sting of disappointment. "It's about much more than religion." She shook her head. "I don't know how I would make it through the week without God's help. My trust in Christ means everything to me. And worshiping the Lord with other believers on Sundays is an important part of that."

Howard didn't reply immediately. He looked at her with an intense gaze, as if weighing the words she'd spoken against the woman he saw before him. Lucy hoped she measured up. She hoped he could see Christ in her.

After a lengthy silence, he said, "Faith can make a difference in how folks meet the hard times in life. I've seen it plenty. Just today, Mrs. Updike was in the store and she told me—" His words were interrupted by the arrival of their waitress.

"Here you go, loves." Georgia set the plates of food in front of them. "Chloe gave you the best cuts of meat she had in the kitchen."

"Thanks, Georgia." Howard gave the waitress one of his pleasant smiles. "I'm sure it'll be great."

And it was. Not only the dinner but also the company and conversation. Lucy had expected the earlier pessimistic direction of her thoughts to spoil things, but somehow Howard kept that from happening as he entertained her with lighthearted stories about his customers. She even found herself laughing a time or two.

For more than an hour, she forgot to worry, forgot to be afraid, forgot to be lonely.

It was wonderful to forget.

10

Margo stretched out a hand and touched the service flag hanging in her window. One star. One son.

God, protect him, please.

Lucy Anderson had received a letter from her husband earlier in the week, but the mails had failed Margo. She was left to wonder about Clark. Those cursed reports in the newspaper about the war in North Africa only made the waiting worse. Couldn't there be a modicum of good news for a change? Were the American generals complete idiots? They should be in control of Europe by this time.

As she turned from the window with a sigh, a song on the radio intruded on her troubled thoughts. "Don't get around much anymore," the singer crooned.

Too true, Margo thought.

She rode the bus to work. She came home again. She walked to church. She came home again. The Kings didn't own a car, and even if they did, with gasoline rationing and the serious shortage of rubber, they wouldn't have been able to go anywhere in it.

Don't get around much anymore.

She could have gone with Dottie to the canteen, but she didn't approve of those places. Oh, she knew the canteens were established by the USO to help servicemen feel at home wherever they were stationed. But the canteens also provided powerful temptations for young people, temptations that too many of them weren't strong enough to resist.

"But, Mom," Dottie had said when Margo expressed her opinion, "don't you hope Clark's able to find some rest away from the war? That's all the canteens are—an attempt to provide a sense of normalcy when nothing is normal. A place to sit and talk with somebody who isn't in the same unit. Maybe a chance to dance with a pretty girl."

Margo shuddered. She didn't want to contemplate what sort of women Clark might meet in Vichy North Africa. French women of low morals, undoubtedly. She certainly hoped he would have the good sense not to dance with them.

God demanded holiness of His children. Her son knew that. Margo had made certain he did. She'd made certain both of her children did. From the time they were little, she'd brought them up by the rod because to spare it was to spoil the child. She had devoted herself to raising them to be good Christians who walked uprightly before their God.

"Keep them from temptation, Lord," she whispered, fear surging in her heart. "Keep them safe, I pray."

11

The canteen was a lively place that Thursday night. Airmen from Gowen Field and Mountain Home and other servicemen home on leave were packed into the building. Music played, couples danced, and voices rose in conversation, making for a loud din. A haze of cigarette smoke filled the room.

"Tell me about your fiancée," Dottie said to the private sitting across from her at a corner table.

With his freckled nose and short hair that stuck out at odd angles, PFC "Mack" McDonald reminded her a little of Alfalfa of the Our Gang fame. He was probably about her age, but he seemed younger.

"Gwen's special," the private answered. "She's studying to be a nurse. Her dad's a surgeon, and she wants to work with him. We're getting married as soon as I'm home again."

"Where's home?"

"Montana. Prettiest country you ever seen." A wistful expression filled his eyes, and he glanced away, staring toward the dance floor. After a while, he cleared his throat and said, "You don't want to dance, do you? I mean, we could if you'd like."

"It's all right. I'd just as soon sit here and visit."

"Gwen says I got two left feet, but she was always trying to teach me." He sighed. "I sure do miss that."

Dottie could have told him she wasn't a good dancer either.

While their church didn't expressly forbid it, dancing was frowned upon in the King household.

She let the private's comment pass, instead skillfully guiding their conversation in a different direction, hoping to take the fellow's mind off the girl he'd left at home. For the next hour, they discussed the movies they'd seen in the past year: *Pride of the Yankees* with Gary Cooper and Teresa Wright, *Woman of the Year* with Katharine Hepburn and Spencer Tracy, and *The Pied Piper* with Monty Woolley and Roddy McDowall. Together they mourned the recent end of the *Amos 'n' Andy* broadcasts. The cancellation of the five-nights-a-week show, on the radio for the past fifteen years, had been announced in January, stunning a nation of faithful listeners. They talked about music, Dottie preferring Bing Crosby and the private preferring Gene Autry.

Finally, Mack's friends from the base came to the table and announced it was time to leave before they missed the bus.

As he stood, Mack asked Dottie, "Will you be all right getting home, Miss King?"

"Yes, thank you. I came with some others from my church."

"Okay, then. Thanks for talking with me. You've been great."

"It was a pleasure, Private McDonald. I'll pray that God keeps you safe."

"Thanks."

Then he was gone, dragged away by his army buddies, and Dottie was left alone at the corner table. She closed her eyes and prayed, as promised, for Mack's safety.

12

Penelope didn't look up from the sewing on her lap when she heard her husband's approach.

"What's that?" he asked, pausing beside her chair.

"A service flag."

Stuart moved toward the kitchen. "Who're you making it for?"

"Obviously not you," she muttered.

She heard the icebox open and close, then the sound of Stuart taking something from the cupboard. A short while later, he reappeared in the doorway, a glass of milk in hand.

She hated the sight of him.

"What'd you say?" He gestured toward the flag. "Who'd you say that's for?"

Through gritted teeth, she replied, "It's for Frances. Remember, I told you she joined the Women's Army Auxiliary Corps."

"I hope she knows what she's doing." He took a drink of milk, then shook his head. "I'd hate to see her get hurt. I think she—"

"Nobody asked what you think!" Penelope's anger boiled over. "Nobody *cares* what you think."

Stuart looked at her in genuine surprise. "What've you got stuck in your craw?"

"*You*! I've got *you* stuck in my craw. My little sister's doing something to help end this war while you sit around on your behind and drink beer and sleep. You don't have to be in the service to do something to help, you know. You could work in a defense plant. You could volunteer for rubber drives. You could do *something*!"

"For cryin' out loud, Pen. Do you think I *like* the way things are right now? Don't you think I'd rather have a job and be able to take care of my family? I feel useless, but I can't work and you know it. Not with my back the way it is."

"Your back." The words sounded like a curse.

Silence fell between them, thick and ugly.

Rather than glare at him, Penelope lowered her gaze to the service flag and the star she'd been stitching into place. She wished she were the one going into the women's auxiliary, that this star could represent her. If it weren't for Stuart and the children, she would have joined the WAACs with Frances. If she weren't married and a mother, she could have joined and been posted far away from unexciting Boise, Idaho.

I hate it here.

Tears blurred her vision.

Why did it turn out like this?

She heard the back door slam and knew Stuart was gone.

I could leave, too. I could leave Stuart for good.

Except, of course, she couldn't. Where would she go? She didn't have any money saved, and her father would never let her return to his home, even if her mother would. Her father believed once a girl married, she stuck it out, no matter what. No one in his family had faced the disgrace of divorce, and he wouldn't allow either of his daughters to be the first.

She was trapped. While Frances was free to have the adventure of a lifetime, Penelope was trapped in her ordinary, boring, uneventful life.

V··· –Mail

To: Mrs. Margo King and Miss Dottie King, Boise, Idaho, U.S.A.
From: Corporal Clark King
Saturday, February 6, 1943

Dear Mom and Dottie,

Sorry it's been so long since I wrote you. We've seen lots of action, and that hasn't left much time for correspondence. I can't say where we are, but I think you can guess.

My unit's always on the move. We set up our tents and catch some shut-eye; then we pack up what we can carry and head out. Three days in any one place is a lot. The thing I miss most is the chance to get clean. Really clean. Here, we wash when we can, and that's not often. I never knew how much I liked a hot shower until I came here.

The guys who smoke are having a hard time of it because there's nowhere to buy cigarettes. I'm glad smoking wasn't something you let me do, Mom.

We've got a couple of guys in our unit who are from Arizona, and they say this landscape is pretty similar to there. All I know is, I'll be glad when we finish our job. I miss the Idaho mountains. Right now, I even miss the snow. I'm tired of the heat and the sweat. We roast all day and then we freeze at night. (I never knew how cold it could get in the desert after the sun goes down.)

I'm doing okay for the most part. War is just what they say it is, and there are times when I'm plenty scared. But I know God's with me. If I don't make it out of here, I know where I'm going. Maybe that's small comfort to you, but it helps me when things are at their worst. Some of these boys don't have that. I can see it in their eyes, and I feel sorry for them.

You might tell the folks at church to send Bibles to me, the smaller the better since we're on the move so much. I'll be sure to give them out to the guys who don't have one. Might help some of them. You never know.

I got letters from you both last week. They sure were appreciated. It took them quite a while to catch up with me. Dottie, if you find out for sure where Greg's stationed and it's where I am, let me know. I'll keep an eye out for him. I don't know what the chances are that we'd wind up in the same place, but if that's what God wants, it'll happen.

The men here have plenty of heart. We've got good equipment, and we've had good training. I don't doubt that we're going to win. Hitler better get ready to see the red, white, and blue snapping in the breeze in Berlin, because we'll be on our way there soon. You'll see.

I love you both, and you're in my prayers.

Your loving son and brother,
Clark

13

On the last day of February, the weather turned surprisingly mild, almost balmy, and Lucy enjoyed her walk to church that Sunday morning. It was nice not to have a bitter cold wind biting her bare legs.

Arriving at church, she entered the building through a side door near the parking lot and made her way to the choir room.

"Good morning, Lucy," Ruth Norris, the choir director, greeted.

"Good morning." Lucy shrugged out of her coat and hung it on the rack. "Did you hear from Walter?" Ruth's husband, Walter, had taken a job in a defense plant in Seattle.

"Yes, he was able to call me at my brother's house last night. He found a place to stay. He says it's an attic room with enough space for the bed and a chair and that's it. But it's better than the shacks and tents many men are living in. There isn't enough housing in Seattle for them all." Ruth gave her a searching look. "How about you? Did you get a letter yet?"

Lucy beamed. "Yes. In fact, I got five of them. The first came on Monday. The rest on Friday. I didn't do much yesterday except read them, over and over and over again."

"How wonderful! Was Richard able to tell you where he is?"

"Still in England as of the letters."

"I'm glad for you, dear." Ruth came over and gave her a tight hug. "You be sure and keep us informed how we can pray for him."

"I will."

As Lucy slipped into her choir robe, she thanked God for giving her this new church family. She had been a member of her old church for so many years that she'd feared she wouldn't fit in anywhere else after she moved across town. But God had blessed her with this congregation. They'd embraced her from the start, making her feel loved.

The rest of the choir—ten people in all—trickled into the choir room. Greetings were spoken. Others asked about Richard, and Lucy asked about their loved ones, some in the military and some, like Ruth's husband, employed at defense plants along the West Coast.

A few minutes before the start of the service, the choir stood in a circle, holding hands, and prayed for God's presence to be evident during the coming hour. Then they filed into the choir loft behind the pulpit.

Lucy glanced at her hymnal. Their first song was "Amazing Grace," one of her favorites. The words often brought tears to her eyes. They reminded her of the miracle of salvation, of God's unending love, and of the trust she could place in Him. Of the trust she *must* place in Him if she meant to walk in faith and obedience.

She looked up as Pastor Osborne stepped into the pulpit. That was when she saw Howard Baxter, seated in the fourth row. He nodded and gave a slight shrug, as if to say, *Yeah, I'm surprised to be here, too.*

She was glad. She hoped he would find nourishment for his soul. She prayed that others in the congregation would welcome him the way they had welcomed her a year ago.

★ ★ ★

A little over an hour later, having removed her robe and retrieved her purse and coat from the choir room, she found Howard in the fellowship hall, visiting with Pastor Osborne.

"Good morning, Mr. Baxter," she said as she approached the two men. "What a nice surprise to have you visit this morning."

"Morning, Mrs. Anderson. I was telling the reverend here that I really enjoyed the singing. The choir was in fine form."

"And I," the pastor said with a chuckle, "was about to say I hoped he found the sermon in fine form, too."

"Yes, sir. I enjoyed it. You were plainspoken and easy to understand. I like that."

Lucy looked at Pastor Osborne. "Mr. Baxter owns the market on Bannock."

The pastor nodded. "Yes, he told me. I believe I've been in there once or twice." His gaze was drawn across the hall. "Please excuse me. I see that Mrs. Johnson needs my assistance with that coffee urn." He lifted his hand toward the woman. "Hold on, Mrs. Johnson. Let me get that for you."

After the pastor strode off, Howard stepped closer to Lucy. "I'm glad I came this morning. Thanks for the invitation. It's a nice church and nice people, too."

Lucy didn't recall issuing an invitation, but she was glad she had, whether or not she remembered. How wonderful it would be if Howard found a relationship with Christ because of it.

"Quite a change we had in the weather," he said. "Spring's gotta be just around the corner."

"I'll be ready whenever it gets here."

"May I walk you home, Mrs. Anderson? It's right on the way for me, and I'd enjoy the company."

"That would be very nice. I'd be glad for the company, too."

He helped her on with her coat. Then the two of them made their way toward the exit, pausing now and then so Lucy could introduce the grocer to members of the congregation.

A few minutes later, they stepped outside. The sky was a glorious, cloudless blue, and the sun was warm upon Lucy's face. The promise of spring, indeed.

Lucy and Howard fell into step, their pace unhurried as they moved along the sidewalk.

After a brief silence, he said, "The kids at the high school are having a scrap-metal drive from now through the end of March. They've asked if they can use the vacant lot behind my store as a collection site. I told them it was okay."

Scrap-metal drives. Rubber salvage. Newspaper and used-fat collections. Tinfoil, aluminum, and tin cans. Nylon and silk. Even junk jewelry. There was always something being collected by one group or another. Lucy thought it a miracle there was anything left to salvage.

"One of my customers, Mrs. Wright over on Washington, she took the bumpers off her Buick and replaced them with wood. You should have seen those kids lugging the metal ones down the street yesterday."

At least Mrs. Wright has a car to take the bumpers off of. Oh, for such a luxury as an automobile and the gasoline to drive it somewhere.

Lucy was immediately ashamed of her ungrateful thoughts. God was faithful to Lucy. He always had been. She didn't want for any necessity of life, and she had much more than many others.

"A penny for your thoughts, Mrs. Anderson."

A flush of embarrassment warmed her cheeks. "I was feeling envious. Of Mrs. Wright and her car. It's been so long since I've gone anywhere except on foot or by bus. I'd love to just get into a car and take a drive."

"That's understandable." He raised an eyebrow. "I don't suppose you'd care to drive to McCall with me next Saturday. There's plenty of snow in the mountains and the lake may still be frozen over, but the roads should be in good shape. We could go up, have lunch at the lodge, then drive back before dark."

"You own a car?"

"I do. I don't drive it much though. Too busy working in the store. But I've got some part-time help that could come in and cover for me for a day. What do you say?"

"I don't know."

"Come on. It'd be fun. You need a break from working and worrying about that husband of yours."

"Well . . . I—"

He grinned. "Great. We'll plan to leave at nine in the morning. How's that sound?"

She shouldn't. She had many things to do on Saturday. The laundry and housecleaning and . . .

"All right, Mr. Baxter. I'll be ready."

March
1943

14

Margo had a throbbing headache, and the atrocious pronunciations by the captain in the second row were not helping.

"Captain Denton." She closed the lesson book and pushed it to the corner of her desk. "Is it your hope to be able to speak the language like a native?"

"Yes, ma'am."

"Then I suggest you apply yourself to your studies with a bit more zeal, because as it stands right now, the Germans will shoot you the moment you open your mouth."

He frowned but answered with a respectful, "Sorry, ma'am. I'll work on it."

She rose from her chair. "That's all for today, gentlemen. Thank you."

The officers filed out of the classroom with little chatter, and a short while later, Margo was alone. Blessedly alone. She sat down again, leaned back in the chair, and closed her eyes.

However would she survive this wretched war?

Every weekday, she looked into the faces of these young men—tragically young to be facing the dangerous missions before them, boys too similar to Clark with their smooth chins and close-cropped hair and swaggering bravado—who within days, weeks, or months of these classes would fly off this base and into the gun sights of the enemy. What good would her French lessons do them then? Knowing how to speak a second language wouldn't protect them from bullets and bombs.

"I don't want another one of them to die," she whispered. "Have mercy, God."

But in that sinful, selfish corner of her heart, she knew what she meant. She didn't want *Clark* to die. She wanted God to have mercy on *her* son—even if not on others.

A soft rapping intruded on her thoughts. "Excuse me, Mrs. King. May I speak with you?"

She straightened. "Colonel. Of course. Do come in."

Colonel Vance Rhodes, her immediate supervisor, was an imposing man, well over six feet tall, with broad shoulders. His hair was sprinkled with gray, and his face was etched with the lines of both years and experience. He was the sort of officer who commanded the respect of all who knew him, including Margo.

The colonel entered the classroom, closing the door behind him.

Dread shot through her and with it a vision of Clark. The army wouldn't ask her boss to deliver bad news, would they?

"Mrs. King, I need you to take on another student."

She released a breath of relief. "Of course, Colonel. We have room in—"

"No, I need you to tutor this officer privately."

Margo raised an eyebrow in question.

The colonel nodded, as if agreeing with himself over what to do or say next. Then he turned, reached for a chair, drew it up close to the side of her desk, and sat down. "The officer is my son, Travis. He has only a short period of time to become as fluent in French as possible before he leaves for England. He took foreign language classes, including French, while in high school and college. My son's bright, and he learns quickly. That's why he was chosen to—" He stopped abruptly.

She saw the concern in his green eyes and didn't need him to say his son was being trained for some sort of secret—and dangerous—mission. She understood and empathized.

"He'll study as many hours as it takes," Colonel Rhodes added. "He'll do whatever needs done."

"I'm sure he will, sir." She glanced at her schedule. Tutoring privately meant losing the one free hour she had for lesson planning and correcting papers each day. But she wouldn't say no. "I can meet with your son at three o'clock in the afternoon. Starting today, if that's what you wish."

"I'll arrange it." The colonel rose. "He'll be here at fifteen hundred hours. Thank you, Mrs. King."

"You're welcome, Colonel Rhodes."

Margo watched as her supervisor crossed the room and disappeared into the hallway. *If only my children's father could have been a man of integrity like the colonel, a man others admire.*

She winced at the thought. Even now, all these years later, it shamed her to remember what a foolish girl she'd been. How could she have fallen for the smooth-talking ways of Bart King? Despite her youth and inexperience, she should have seen what he was—a liar and a cheat. She was forced to remember her foolish romanticism whenever she looked into the faces of her children and saw traces of their father there.

Margo sighed deeply. She feared for Clark's life as he fought in Africa, but sometimes she feared even more for Dottie. Her daughter was such a pie-eyed optimist and even more of a romantic than Margo had been. Dottie had little grasp on the realities of life. Even Dottie's faith seemed too . . . too simplistic.

Have mercy, God. Have mercy on us all.

V···—MAIL

To: Corporal Clark King, APO, N.Y.P.E.
From: Margo King
Wednesday, March 3, 1943

Dear Clark,

Your sister and I were relieved to receive your letter of February 6. I pray that you are still well, nearly a month later. The reports in the newspaper of fighting in North Africa have caused me many a sleepless night. I can only assume, since I have heard nothing to the contrary, that you are all right.

Dottie's friend Frances has volunteered to join the Women's Army Auxiliary Corps. I cannot say I approve of women serving in the armed forces, especially in combat areas. I've even heard, though I cannot vouch for the validity, that there are WAACs serving on General Eisenhower's staff in North Africa. To purposefully put women in harm's way seems wrong to me. I hope Frances will remain stationed in America. Perhaps she'll be assigned duty as a censor and will even read one of our letters.

At least I know Frances Ballard is a well-mannered and moral young woman. I suspect the same cannot be said for most women who would volunteer for the auxiliary, especially after some of the things I've read in the newspaper of late. Your sister strongly disagrees with me. She says those who join the WAACs want only to do their part to win the war. But Dottie, I fear, is naive to the ways of this world.

The grip of winter has finally broken here in the Boise valley, though there remains a great deal of snow on the mountains. I've seen yellow crocus surfacing in flower beds in the neighborhood. I'll soon be preparing my vegetable garden for planting.

I continue to find satisfaction in my employment and have reason to hope that the work I do might be helpful, even if only in a small way. (See, it isn't necessary to join the WAACs to do one's part.) Today I was asked by a superior to give private lessons to an officer who, I suspect, will soon leave the country on some special mission. My new student is your age, handsome, and very determined. I liked him immediately. I can only hope he will return to his father as he is today, just as I pray for your safe return. He is the sort of young man I would like your sister to marry when this war is over and emotions are not running so high. Dottie can be foolish when it comes to matters of the heart.

Do you remember the Wickfields on the next block? Their youngest son, George, enlisted in the navy, and last week they learned his ship went down in the Pacific and all were lost. George was only eighteen. They have two more sons in service, but I don't know which branch of the military. My heart goes out to them.

Stay close to God, Clark. No matter what else is happening, follow His laws.

You're in my prayers.
Mother

15

It hadn't been three weeks since Dottie wrote Greg about her pregnancy. It hadn't even been two. But she couldn't wait any longer to tell her mother. The weight of her secret was too heavy to bear.

"Mom?" She leaned through the doorway of the bedroom. "Is it too late to talk?"

Sitting in bed, her back propped with pillows, her mother looked up from the book in her lap. "No, dear." She removed her reading glasses and rubbed the bridge of her nose between the thumb and middle finger of her right hand. "Come in."

Dottie drew a deep breath. *God, You've forgiven me. Please help Mom forgive me, too.*

"What is it?" Her mother patted the edge of the bed. "You look upset. Is it something at work?"

Dottie sat where indicated, then stared down at her clenched hands. "I have something to tell you, Mom, and I'm afraid you'll be the one who's upset."

"Oh, heavens. You haven't joined the WAACs like Frances, have you?"

"No, Mom." Dottie smiled a little. "I haven't joined the WAACs."

Her mother was visibly relieved by that bit of news, but her relief only served to increase Dottie's misery. She was certain her mother would ten times rather have Dottie serving in the Women's Army Auxiliary Corps than unmarried and pregnant.

"Honey?" Margo covered Dottie's hands with one of her own. "What's troubling you? Tell me."

"I'm pregnant," she answered in a small voice.

Her mother withdrew her hand. "What did you say?"

"I'm pregnant." Dottie met her mother's gaze.

There was a thick, lengthy silence before her mother asked, "Whose child is it?"

That was a question Dottie hadn't expected. Her mother knew she was in love with Greg. She knew the two of them intended to get married. How could she ask such a thing?

"Well?"

"It's Greg's baby, Mom."

"Greg." She nearly spat the name. "Did he force himself on you? We could have him arrested. The army frowns on—"

Dottie stood. "You know Greg better than that. You know he wouldn't do anything that would hurt me. He . . . he wouldn't . . . he—" She turned and left her mother's room, hurrying into her own, blinking away hot tears.

Margo followed seconds later. "I'm a good deal wiser than you, young lady, and I know men will do or say whatever they need to get what they want. Greg's no different from any other man in that regard. If he was, you wouldn't be pregnant."

"I'm as much to blame as he is." Dottie stared toward her bedroom window, but it was dark outside and she saw only her reflection in the glass. She swallowed the lump in her throat. "It only happened the one time."

Her mother grunted, a sound of disbelief.

"We know what we did was wrong. We know we should have waited for marriage. It's just that . . . he was leaving soon and—"

"Spare me your excuses."

"*So now there is no condemnation for those who belong to Christ Jesus,*" Dottie reminded herself.

Only she *was* condemned. Not by God. She'd confessed her sin to Him, and as promised, He was faithful to forgive and cleanse her from all unrighteousness.

Her mother was another story.

"You'll pay for this act for the rest of your life, Dorothea Ruth. Mark my words. You won't have a moment's peace from it. Greg can't even marry you to give this child a name. Before long, everyone at church will know. Oh, the shame of it."

Dottie lifted her chin as she turned to face her mother. "It isn't *your* shame." She placed her hands protectively over her belly. "What we did was wrong. Greg and I both know it. Before he left for England, we got down on our knees and prayed for forgiveness. We didn't plan for it to happen, and we didn't plan to have this baby. But, Mom, the baby isn't a surprise to the Lord. God won't love it any less because of the circumstances of its conception, and neither will I."

"What if Greg is killed in the war? What if you have to raise this child alone?"

Dottie sank onto the bed, tears once again blinding her. "Then I'll cross that bridge when I come to it." *Oh, God. Don't let me come to that bridge. Please, Father.*

Softly, Margo said, "I should have done more to keep the two of you apart."

Dottie's heart ached. What she wanted, what she needed, was for her mother to draw her into an embrace and hold her tightly, but it wasn't going to happen.

"Do you think I was never young, Dottie? Do you think I don't understand the temptations of youth?"

Dottie brushed away her tears and looked at her mother, who stood stiffly in the bedroom doorway, arms crossed over her chest. Try as she might, Dottie couldn't imagine her mother as young or passionate or losing control of herself. She couldn't imagine her tempted to do wrong, especially not when it came to matters of the heart. Love, for Margo King, was a disciplined emotion.

"Did you love my father when you married him?" The question—one she'd never dared ask before—slipped from Dottie's lips unbidden.

The color drained from Margo's face, but she answered, "Yes. I was foolish enough to love him."

"Then can't you understand why—"

"I understand more than you know, young lady."

"Then tell me. You never talk about when you were young. You never talk about our father. You've never told Clark and me much of anything about your marriage or what went wrong between the two of you. Why did he leave? You act like he never existed, and we were too young to remember much on our own."

"It's just as well that you can't remember. I don't intend to start talking about it now." Margo turned and walked away, arms still hugged to her chest like a shield.

Pity. That was what Dottie suddenly felt. Pity for her mother, who was so afraid to let go of her heart.

✳ ✳ ✳

It had taken more than twenty-five years, Margo thought as she returned to her bedroom, but here it was. The sins of the mother had been visited upon the daughter. Despite everything. Despite all Margo had taught her children—and especially Dottie. Despite being raised in the church and studying the Word of God and being warned time and again about the sins of the flesh, still Dottie had repeated the same offense as her mother.

And this time Margo wouldn't escape the public shame by moving to a new state. This time she couldn't hide behind the lie that the baby arrived prematurely. Her daughter didn't have a husband and wouldn't have one before the baby arrived. Perhaps not ever. And everyone would know.

"Did you love my father when you married him?"

Margo got into bed, pulled up the covers, and turned off the bedside lamp, welcoming the dark, wanting to hide in it.

"Did you love my father when you married him?"

Love? This had nothing to do with love. She understood, as her daughter apparently did not, that God wouldn't be mocked. Sin had its consequences. Margo had paid for her sins with a loveless marriage to a heartless brute. She'd paid with a lifetime of struggling to stay ahead of the bill collectors. She'd paid with her guilt and her fears.

"The baby isn't a surprise to the Lord. God won't love it any less because of the circumstances of its conception, and neither will I."

Margo rolled onto her side and drew her knees toward her chest, wishing she could keen the way mourning women in other cultures did.

Foolish girl. Foolish, foolish girl. So naive. Love wouldn't feed, clothe, and house that baby. Dottie didn't know what she faced. She hadn't a clue. She didn't know anything about raising children, and she certainly knew nothing about marriage.

Wait until Greg was unfaithful to her. Wait until he abandoned her and her children.

Then she would see.

16

Lucy stared at her reflection in the mirror. She'd had a difficult time deciding what to wear today, but had finally settled on her favorite yellow sweater and a pair of light brown slacks. She hoped she would be warm enough up in the mountains. It was hard to judge the weather this time of year.

Her pale, baby-fine hair hung in a smooth fall to her shoulders, defying attempts to shape and curl it in the current fashion. Richard said he loved her hair, that it felt like silky strands of gold slipping through his fingers.

She closed her eyes and imagined he was with her now, touching her hair, kissing the back of her neck. Oh, how she ached for her husband. Sometimes she wondered if she'd imagined their wedding and their few short weeks together as man and wife. Had she truly ever known the joy of being in Richard's arms or was it merely a dream, the result of wishful thinking?

Thankfully, the doorbell drew her from her thoughts before she descended into complete self-pity. She grabbed a scarf and her jacket, then hurried to answer it.

Howard Baxter stood on the back stoop, hat in hand. "Good morning. Ready for our excursion?"

"Oh, yes. I'm definitely ready."

"Good." He motioned toward the street. "Your chariot awaits, Mrs. Anderson."

Lucy pulled the door closed behind her, and together she and Howard followed the narrow sidewalk around the side of the house. As they neared the curb, Howard stepped quickly forward and opened the passenger door of the black Ford. Lucy gave him a smile of thanks as she got into the car.

The simple act felt new and adventurous. When was the last time she'd done something out of the ordinary? Howard slid onto the seat behind the wheel. "I'm glad you agreed to come with me, Mrs. Anderson. To be honest, I've needed some time away from the store."

"I'm glad you asked me. And don't you think it's time you called me Lucy? That's what all my other friends call me."

He started the engine. "I'd like that, as long as you call me Howard." After a quick glance in the rearview mirror, he put the car in gear and pulled away from the curb. "We couldn't have asked for a nicer day for a drive."

"Perfect."

And it was. The sky was cloudless, the air warm. More like May than March. Although the trees were bare of leaves, there was a hint of green on the foothills and in the pastures.

After they'd driven a few miles in silence, Lucy glanced at Howard. "Who's watching the store for you?" She couldn't recall a single time she'd visited the Bannock Street Market when anyone other than Howard himself was working there.

"My uncle. He managed a store in the Midwest for most of his adult life. He sold it after he retired. He's in Nampa right now, visiting my three widowed aunts, his sisters. He said he'd be glad for a few hours away from all their chatter." He shook his head as he chuckled. "I don't blame him. They can rattle on about the craziest things."

"Do your parents live in the area, too?"

"No. They're both gone now. Passed away a number of years ago."

"Mine are deceased, too," Lucy said softly, feeling a wave of aloneness. "But how wonderful that you have other family members nearby."

"Yeah, I'm lucky to have 'em. My aunts are special ladies. You'll have to meet them sometime. They'd make you a part of the family right away. That's just the way they are."

Howard turned the Ford north, and they wound their way up Highway 55 through the brownish gray, elephant-backed foothills of the Boise Front. Every so often, Lucy caught a glimpse of snowy, pine-covered mountain peaks in the distance, and with those glimpses came treasured memories from the past.

"When I was a little girl, my parents and I spent one week each summer camping out. Sometimes in McCall. Sometimes in the Sawtooths. Dad and I would go fishing, and Mom would fry our catch over the wood fire in this big cast-iron skillet." Lucy looked at Howard again. "Why is it that food tastes so much better in the mountains, especially when it's cooked over a campfire?"

He grinned but kept his gaze on the twisting, winding road before them.

"Dad had a hammock that he would string between two trees, and sometimes all three of us would lie in it and stare at the sky through the branches. I love the way the lodgepole pines sway back and forth until you get dizzy watching them." She took a deep breath and released it on a sigh of pleasure. "My mom was a great storyteller. She could entertain me for hours. Dad loved her stories, too."

"Sounds like you had a wonderful childhood."

"I did. I had a perfect one. That's why Richard and I chose to live in Idaho after we married. We want our children to grow up like I did."

"Your husband's not from Boise?"

"No. Richard's from Chicago. His parents still live in Illinois. But Richard was always intrigued by the West." She smiled to herself, envisioning her tall, strapping husband who secretly wanted to be a cowboy, only in an airplane instead of on a horse.

"How did the two of you meet?"

"We were introduced at a wedding, and I made a fool of myself in front of him."

Howard cast a quick, questioning glance in her direction.

"I was the maid of honor at my friend Barbara's wedding. It was unusually hot for May, and the church was stuffy. They opened the windows in the fellowship hall, but there wasn't even a breeze." She glanced out the window of the car at the passing landscape. "We stood in the reception line forever. I think Barbara's parents invited every person in the state to see her get married. I was dying to get out of that bridesmaid dress, kick off my shoes, and sit down with a cold glass of iced tea."

Even after three years, the memory was as clear as if it happened last week. She could still feel the stifling air of that crowded room. She remembered how her cheeks hurt from smiling, how her fingers hurt from shaking hands with so many strangers. She remembered feeling relieved to see a familiar face when Annie Edwards came through the line. With a twinkle in her eye, Annie stopped in front of her and whispered that she loved Lucy's dress. Lucy considered kicking her in the shin. The floor-length gown was hideous, and they both knew it. Poofs of satin and an abundance of bows in a particularly sick shade of green. What had possessed Barbara to select it?

"And?" Howard prompted.

Lucy looked at him. "A friend and her husband came through the reception line. Richard was visiting them from Chicago, and they brought him to the wedding."

Annie's voice echoed in her memory: *"Lucy, I'd like you to meet Peter's friend from college, Richard Anderson. Richard, this is Lucy Grover, the girl I was telling you about. Richard's thinking of moving to Boise to open a business of his own."*

"I reached out to shake his hand," Lucy continued, "just as I had to dozens of other people before him. And all of a sudden, I couldn't breathe. I remember asking him what sort of business brought him to Boise, and he said he was interested in aviation. Then the whole room started to tilt and sway."

"An earthquake?"

She laughed softly. "No. Heatstroke. I almost passed out from it. Richard caught me before I hit the floor. He carried me to a chair and got me some water, and pretty soon I was all right. Except for feeling like a fool for crumbling at his feet."

Howard laughed, too. "So it was love at first sight, huh?"

Punched in the heart by the pain of missing Richard, all traces of amusement vanished. "Almost." Her voice broke on the word.

"I'm sorry, Lucy. I didn't mean to cause you sorrow by asking about your husband."

She swallowed the lump in her throat. "It isn't your fault. It's just hard sometimes, being all alone."

"I know what you mean."

Remembering how many years he'd been a widower, she thought perhaps he did, indeed, know what she meant.

✳ ✳ ✳

McCall was a small mountain town located on the south end of Lower Payette Lake. A few years earlier, Hollywood had invaded the area while filming *Northwest Passage*, but today it was its usual sleepy self.

The dining room of the rustic-looking lodge had a beautiful view of the ice-covered lake and the snowy mountains that surrounded it, making Lucy thankful for the crackling fire in the stone fireplace.

"I thought it was spring." She rubbed her hands up and down her arms, suppressing a shiver.

"Not up here," Howard answered. "Not this year anyway."

"I've never been in McCall when the lake's frozen over. It's beautiful. So serene." She turned her gaze from the window. " 'I look up to the mountains—does my help come from there? My help comes from the Lord, who made heaven and earth!' "

Howard leaned his forearms on the table. "Is that a psalm?"

"Yes. One of my favorites."

"It's very real for you, isn't it?"

She wasn't sure what he meant and told him so with her eyes.

"Your faith. The things you believe."

She felt a familiar flutter of contentment. "Yes, my faith is very real to me. *Jesus* is real to me." She wished everyone could know the joy she'd found in her Lord. She wished Howard could know it. Perhaps that was why God arranged for this day. Perhaps it was so she could share the Good News with her friend.

"You're an unusual woman, Lucy Anderson." He spoke softly. "You're special. I'm thankful for the opportunity to know you."

She blushed and lowered her gaze to the table, uncomfortable without quite understanding why. She reached for the menu and pretended a great interest in her choice of entrees.

17

Dottie knocked on Lucy's apartment door several times before giving up. Weary and disappointed that her friend wasn't home, she turned, sank onto the stoop, and started to cry. Huge tears streamed down her cheeks and plopped onto her slacks.

"Oh, God," she whispered between sobs. "I need You. I can't feel Your presence. I'm all alone."

The day had been unbearable. Her mother had scarcely spoken two words since Dottie told her about the baby last night. Every time her mother so much as looked at her, Dottie felt her disappointment and censure.

Of course, Margo King would never succumb to passion, especially not a passion that led to sin. It simply wasn't part of her nature. That was why Dottie came to Lucy's this afternoon. She needed to talk to someone who understood about the ardent, fervent, whole-hearted love of a man. She needed to talk to someone who believed that even *this* sin was covered by the blood of the Lamb.

Dottie wiped her eyes with her fingertips. " 'Let all that I am praise the LORD; may I never forget the good things He does for me.' " She released a shuddering breath. " 'You ransomed me from death, Jesus. I won't forget. I'll remember the good things You do for me. So help me, I will.' "

She took another deep breath, let it out, then stood to leave. That was when Lucy rounded the corner, smiling, her eyes sparkling with good humor, escorted by an older man.

Lucy stopped when her gaze met Dottie's. Her smile vanished, replaced by a look of concern. "Dottie? You've been crying. What's wrong? Is it . . . is it Greg? Has something happened to—"

"No. Greg's okay. I just—" Her gaze flicked to the stranger standing beside Lucy. "I need to talk to you, but I can come back if you're busy." She descended the two steps to the sidewalk.

"I'm not busy, Dottie. Stay." Lucy faced the man. "This is my friend, Howard Baxter. He was bringing me home. Howard, this is Dottie King. We used to attend the same church before I got married. I taught her Sunday school class when she was about ten or eleven. Dottie and her mother both work at the base."

"A pleasure to meet you, Miss King." Howard extended a hand in greeting.

"And you, Mr. Baxter," Dottie replied, taking it.

"Well—" He looked at Lucy—"I'll be on my way, then. It was good to visit with you today."

"Will I see you at church in the morning?" Lucy asked.

He smiled and shrugged. "You might." After a slight nod of farewell toward both women, he turned on his heel and walked away.

Lucy put an arm around Dottie's shoulder. "Come inside and tell me what's going on." She gave her a quick hug, then led the way into the apartment.

Dottie had visited Lucy's home several times since Richard joined the Army Air Corps. She loved the small apartment. Dottie liked to imagine that she and Greg would have a cozy place like this when they got married.

Lucy dropped her house key and purse onto the kitchen counter. "Would you like anything to drink? I can put the kettle on for tea."

"Only if you want it. Don't make it just for me."

"I would like some, actually." Lucy motioned to the table. "Why don't you sit there and we can talk while I get things ready?"

"Okay."

As Dottie took her seat, Lucy's big white cat entered the kitchen to welcome her mistress home. Lucy bent down and gave Empress the requisite attention. Then the cat crossed the room and jumped onto Dottie's lap, purring noisily.

"Oh, Dottie," Lucy apologized. "I'm sorry. Empress has no manners. Brush her off if you don't want to hold her."

Dottie laughed softly. "No. I like her. She's fine."

The cat turned several circles before curling into a ball of fluff and closing her eyes.

"Does Mr. Baxter go to your church?" Dottie asked as she stroked the cat.

"No." Lucy filled the teakettle with water from the tap. "But he visited last Sunday for the first time, and I'm hoping he'll come back."

Dottie glanced up. "How do you know him?"

"He owns the market where I shop. Very nice man. Everyone in the neighborhood likes him." She put the kettle on the stove and turned on the burner. Then she removed a delicate china teapot and two matching cups from a cupboard. Finally, with everything ready for when the water boiled, she joined Dottie at the table. "So tell me what's wrong."

To Dottie's dismay, her eyes teared up again.

"Oh, sweetie." Lucy leaned forward and touched her forearm. "It can't be that bad, can it?"

Dottie nodded. "It is, Lucy. It *is* that bad." She swallowed hard. "I'm pregnant."

"Oh, my." The words held a note of surprise, but Lucy's gaze was compassionate.

"Oh, my," Dottie echoed, a pitiful smile lifting the corners of her mouth.

Lucy gave Dottie's arm a light squeeze, then she straightened in her chair. She didn't say anything more. She simply waited. That was one of the things Dottie appreciated about Lucy; she was a good listener.

Why can't Mom be more like her? Why can't Mom show some compassion and forgiveness?

The kettle whistled, and Lucy rose to attend to it. By the time she returned with the teapot and cups on a tray, Dottie was ready to tell her everything.

"It happened on New Year's Eve. Greg and I wanted a romantic dinner away from everybody else. He was scheduled to ship out that next week, and we needed time for just the two of us. Later, we went to his parents' house, but they weren't home." She drew a deep breath and released it with a sigh. "We should have left right then. We knew our emotions were running high. We'd always been careful but . . ."

Her voice faded into silence as memories of that night flooded her mind. The kisses. The passion. The storm. The shame.

She covered her face with her hands. "We should have married as soon as I turned eighteen, but Mom was insistent that I wait, that I not marry as young as she had. If only we'd gotten married, this never—"

"Don't do that, Dottie," Lucy interrupted, her words gentle but firm. "Don't whip yourself with if-only-this and if-only-that. We can't undo what's already done, and we can't know what would've happened if we'd made a different choice."

Dottie lowered her hands.

"Have you told Greg yet?"

"I wrote to him but I haven't heard back. I don't even know where he is or when he'll get my letter."

"And your mother? Have you told her?"

Dottie nodded a second time. "She can hardly look at me. I've humiliated her, and it'll only get worse when everybody at church knows what I've done. I tried to tell her that Greg and I asked the Lord's forgiveness, but she doesn't want to hear it. She's too ashamed of me."

"She loves you. She's worried about you."

Dottie began to cry again. She didn't feel loved. She felt alone and scared and rejected and miserable. She was nineteen, unmarried, and expecting a baby, a baby whose father might not live to see it.

Lucy drew her chair closer to Dottie. She reached out, took Empress from Dottie's lap and set the cat on the floor, then held Dottie's hands in her own. "Let's pray, shall we? We'll ask the Lord for guidance. He knows you, Dottie. He loves you and forgives you. He walks us through everything, even the troubles we create for ourselves. You'll see."

V··· −Mail

To: 1st Lt. Richard Anderson, APO, N.Y.P.E.

From: Lucy Anderson

Saturday, March 3, 1943

My dearest, darling Richard,

It's late as I put pen to paper. There's a March wind whistling around the corner of the house. I'm wishing I had a fireplace because a crackling fire would make things seem more cozy and I wouldn't feel so alone. I miss you very much, my darling.

This morning a friend and I drove up to McCall. It was a treat to escape town for a few hours. It seems forever since I've had an outing. For that matter, it seems forever since I've ridden with someone in an automobile. I've grown so used to the bus I nearly forgot there are other modes of transportation. There's plenty of snow in the higher elevations, which means the rivers should run high this summer. North of Cascade we came upon a herd of elk in a field, and one of them had the largest rack I've ever seen. I couldn't imagine how he even lifted his head. He must have been very old.

The ice is beginning to break up on Payette Lake, but it's still mostly frozen with a blanket of snow over it. My friend and I sat in the lodge near the fireplace (perhaps that's why I'm wishing for one tonight) and ate lunch and looked at the sun reflecting off the ice and snow. We were nearly blinded by its brilliance.

When I got home this afternoon, Dottie was waiting to talk to me. She had distressing news. She's pregnant. (She gave me permission to share that with you.) She's written to Greg, but there's been no reply yet. She doesn't know if he's in England or North Africa. Regardless of where he is, it won't change her circumstances. I tried to offer wise counsel, and we prayed together for a time. She understands and accepts the forgiveness promised in 1 John 1:9, but deep down, she still feels guilty.

That's not helped by her mother's attitude. I don't mean to be unkind or to be guilty of gossip, but Margo shows little compassion for others. And not just about Dottie's predicament. Toward anyone who isn't perfect. Her faith is all about God's judgment, and too often she forgets His love, mercy, and grace. It's a joyless Christianity, and there are times I ache for her. Does she never see the beauty of Jesus?

If Greg is in England and God wills your paths should cross, please tell him that I'll do my best to help Dottie in any way that I can.

I confess, my darling Richard, that I'm a little envious of Dottie. My heart and my arms ache for you, but perhaps if I had your child to hold and to love, I wouldn't feel so alone. Stay safe, my love. Win this war and come home to me. I love you.

Forever and always,

Lucy

18

Penelope held Evelyn with her right arm, bracing the child on her hip, and clutched Alan's hand with her left one. The train depot buzzed with voices as mothers and fathers, siblings and sweethearts, said good-bye to those they loved.

The balmy weather had ended during the night. This morning, the gray sky wept.

How fitting.

Frances, looking smart and pretty in her new uniform, leaned forward and kissed Penelope's cheek. "Don't look so down, sis. I'm going to be fine. You'll see."

But her sister had misread her. Penelope wasn't sad or worried. She was resentful. Angry at Stuart. He wasn't with her today because of another doctor's appointment that he claimed couldn't be postponed. Same old story. Always the same. Penelope was twenty-five years old, but she felt decades older. Ancient, in fact. Life had passed her by. Nothing exciting would happen to her again. Not ever. She knew it.

If it weren't for Stuart and the children . . .

"Look. Here they are." Frances waved her arms above her head. "Mom! Dad! Over here. Here we are!"

When their parents reached them, Penelope watched as Frances was embraced by their mother. Julia Ballard cried openly.

David Ballard, their father, kept his usual stern expression in place.

"I was afraid you weren't going to make it in time," Frances said.

"We almost didn't." Their father's voice was gruff. "We had a flat tire, and I had a devil of a time fixing it. What I wouldn't give to own a spare tire."

Their mother offered a brown paper bag to Frances. "I made you some goodies for the train. There's plenty so you can share."

"Thanks, Mom."

Penelope could see her sister fighting to control her emotions. In a moment, Frances would be crying like their mother, and then, Penelope knew, she would cry, too.

That was when the call for boarding came, followed by another flurry of hugging and kissing across the platform.

"Don't grow too big before I return," Frances told Alan after leaving lipstick marks on both of his cheeks. "And take care of your mommy for me. Okay?"

"Okay."

Frances hugged Penelope and Evelyn at the same time. "Tell Stuart I'm sorry he's feeling bad, and thank him for the keepsake box he made me." She kissed Penelope's cheek. "I'll write often, sis. I promise. I'll tell you everything, same as I've always done."

"You'd better."

Her sister turned and bid farewell to their parents. Crying unabated by the time their mother released her, Frances picked up her belongings and hurried toward the passenger car.

"Mommy." Alan tugged on her arm. "I gotta go potty."

"Not now, honey. Mommy wants to see Auntie Frances one more time before she goes. Don't you want to see the train pull away from—"

"*Now*, Mommy. I gotta go now." As if to prove his words were true, he hopped from foot to foot.

"Here, Penelope," her mother offered. "Give me Evelyn while you take him to the restroom."

Reluctantly, she released her daughter into her mother's waiting arms.

Penelope lifted Alan off the ground, carrying him through the crowd that was surging toward the train, people saying their last good-byes, some women pressing handkerchiefs to their lips as if to hold back sobs.

Finally, she and Alan stepped through the doors of the railway depot. Penelope set her son on the black-and-white tiled floor of the vast hall, took hold of his small hand, and half pulled, half dragged him toward the women's restroom—only to find that both stalls were occupied.

"I gotta *go*, Mommy." His voice rose to a shrill whine.

"Hold on, Alan. Just a bit longer." She stared daggers at the closed stall doors while her little boy jumped and hopped and wiggled beside her. "Hold on."

At last, a woman wearing an ugly floral hat opened the door of the first stall. She barely had a moment to move out of the way before Penelope and Alan bolted past her.

That was when Penelope heard the first *chug* and *whoosh* of the train as it got underway.

"Oh, Alan." She fumbled with the buckle on his belt and banged her elbow against the wall in the process. Pain shot up her arm, from funny bone to shoulder. "Hurry, sweetie."

It was pointless to ask the boy to hurry, of course. No matter how hard he tried, they couldn't get outside before the train pulled out of the station. At least not in time to see Frances waving farewell from the window of the passenger car.

It was too late.

Too late.

Like everything else in her life.

Tears flooded Penelope's eyes. She brushed them away with an exasperated gesture.

Her sister was gone, off to see new places, foreign lands, off to fight in the war, off on an exciting exploit that was rife with danger, while Penelope was stuck in this public restroom . . .

Stuck in this lousy town . . .

Stuck in a humdrum job . . .

Stuck in a marriage gone sour.

19

For a change, the word out of North Africa was more positive. The Allies were on the offensive, and Rommel's forces had been driven back.

Margo's boss, Colonel Rhodes, said victory in the North African theater was within reach. All but assured. Soon the Allies would mop up operations in Africa and prepare for the next phase of the war in Europe.

Good news or bad, however, there was one unavoidable fact that lingered in the back of Margo's mind: Young men died in war, even when their side was winning. Clark wouldn't be safe as long as he was in the army. She wanted him home. She wanted him safe.

With her room empty between classes, Margo stood at the window, arms crossed tightly over her chest. She stared through the wavy glass at the blustery day outside. A funnel of dust spun down the road outside her building, followed by a Jeep, as if in hot pursuit.

"The baby isn't a surprise to the Lord." The memory of Dottie's words taunted her. *"God won't love it any less because of the circumstances of its conception, and neither will I."*

No, Dottie wouldn't love this baby any less. Perhaps, in some ways, she would love it more. She would love it more because she would know she didn't deserve it, that she'd never been meant to have it.

Margo remembered the look of disappointment on her father's face the day she told him she was pregnant. She remembered the mortification in her mother's eyes. And she remembered Bart King's resentment as the two of them stood before a justice of the peace in a small West Virginia courthouse, exchanging wedding vows that meant nothing to her groom.

She had been sixteen, pregnant, and desperately—foolishly—in love with a man who didn't want her and most definitely didn't want the baby she carried. Bart had forgotten he was the one who said he needed her, wanted her, would keep her memory with him every moment as he marched off to war.

From the moment that judge pronounced them man and wife, Bart had done his best to punish her for getting pregnant. She was miserable . . . and then Clark was born. He was a good baby from the start, never fussy or colicky. He loved to smile and laugh and coo. People always commented on how beautiful he was. From an early age, he was bright and adventurous, as he remained to this day.

So perfect, her son. So perfect. He made everything else in her life seem okay for a time. When Bart left her alone, night after night, while he chased other women, Margo's lonely heart found comfort in loving her son.

She didn't understand that she had no right to him because of what she'd done. That realization came a few years later, after she and Bart moved to Boise and Margo attended church for the first time in her life. There she was, a new Christian, sitting in the pew with her small son beside her and her belly large with another baby, listening as the pastor read from the second book of Samuel. No one in that church or in this town knew, of course, that she'd been pregnant out of wedlock. That was her secret.

"Then David confessed to Nathan, 'I have sinned against the
LORD.'

"Nathan replied, 'Yes, but the LORD *has forgiven you, and you*
won't die for this sin. But you have given the enemies of the LORD
great opportunity to despise and blaspheme Him, so your child will
die.'"

Even now, twenty years later, Margo remembered the terror
that had pierced her heart at those words. The fear hadn't left
her since. Not ever. Not even when Clark accepted Christ as his
Savior. Not even when she saw her son serving God by serving
others. Not even when she prayed for hours on her knees.

And why wouldn't she be afraid? If the prayers and fasting of
David, a man after God's own heart, couldn't save his son from
death, how could her prayers make a difference on Clark's behalf?

Still, she prayed. She fasted. She made certain to obey God in
every way she knew how. Yet fear was her constant companion.

And now Dottie faced the same future.

Margo turned from the window, wishing she could turn so
easily from her thoughts, wishing she could turn back time. Perhaps then she might discover something she could have done,
could have said, that would have prevented this disaster—the
sin of the mother—from visiting itself upon her daughter.

Margo had worried too much about Clark and not enough
about Dottie. Passionate, headstrong Dottie, who wore her
heart on her sleeve. How could Margo not have seen what was
coming? Dottie and Greg started dating in high school, but most
of their outings were with the youth group from church. Margo
had convinced herself that they would outgrow their infatua-
tion, even after Dottie told her they wanted to marry.

Oh, how wrong could she have been? Why hadn't she done
more to keep the two of them apart? She who knew so well
what could happen in an unguarded moment.

The sound of swift footsteps alerted her to the arrival of her pupil moments before the second lieutenant appeared in the classroom doorway.

"Mrs. King," Travis Rhodes said smartly when his gaze found her by the window.

"Good afternoon, Lieutenant."

Margo returned to her desk and opened her textbook, glad for the distraction. At least for an hour, she could think of something besides her children and the dangers that lurked in the unknown future.

20

As the bus from the base lumbered toward town, Lucy observed her three friends. Each seemed lost in thought. Disturbing thoughts, judging by their expressions.

During the lunch break, Penelope had told them about her sister's departure the previous day. "I'm going to miss her so much," she'd said, her voice breaking.

Lucy sensed there was more behind Penelope's unhappy demeanor than just Frances's absence.

As for Margo and Dottie, Lucy didn't need to guess what bothered them. She already knew. Apparently nothing had improved since Saturday. Between the two, Lucy worried about Margo the most. Dottie would rally and be okay. The girl had both a strong faith and a strong spirit. But Margo? Lucy wasn't so sure about her.

Guiltily, Lucy remembered her promise to pray for each of these women and their families and to practice a victorious Christian walk, even in the face of war and loss. She hadn't done a good job of it thus far.

Jeb Pratt brought the bus to a halt and opened the door. Margo and Dottie rose to their feet, and Margo left without saying good-bye.

"See you both in the morning," Dottie said to Penelope and Lucy, her voice soft and sad.

Lucy caught her gently by the hand. "It'll get better."

"I hope so."

After Dottie disembarked and the bus was in motion again, Penelope twisted on her seat to look at Lucy. "What's with those two? They having one of those mother-daughter spats?"

Lucy gave her head a shake, hoping Penelope would assume it meant she didn't know rather than that she couldn't say.

"My mom and I never fought much, but boy, could she and Frances ever go at it." Penelope smiled a little at that. "My sister always was the brave one. Not like me."

"Why would you say that? I think it's very brave, raising children these days."

Penelope faced forward again. "Maybe." The bus slowed, and Penelope pulled herself to her feet. "Hope you have another letter waiting for you," she tossed over her shoulder.

"Thanks, Pen. I'll see you tomorrow."

Throughout the remaining bus ride, Lucy pondered her friends' circumstances and wondered what she might do to lift their spirits. There had to be something. She'd worked at the base long enough to understand the importance of good morale, even for civilians—if for no other reason than because those same civilians wrote to the soldiers and sailors serving their country far from home.

Lord, show me what I can do to help.

For Penelope, the first step was to offer a friendly ear to listen or a strong shoulder to cry on, whichever was needed. Until she opened up about what was troubling her or asked for advice, there was nothing else to be done.

I could ask her to go to church with me again. I haven't done that in a while.

Of the four friends from the air base, Penelope was the only one who didn't attend church on a regular basis. Lucy wasn't convinced Penelope believed in God at all, even though she sometimes talked as if she did.

As for Dottie and Margo—

"Here you go, Mrs. Anderson," Jeb said.

Lucy looked up, surprised to find the bus stopped and the door open, awaiting her departure. "Thank you, Mr. Pratt." She rose and stepped toward the exit. "See you in the morning."

"I'll be here."

Walking at a brisk pace, Lucy was halfway to the market before she remembered she didn't need to shop. The food for supper was in the icebox at home.

She paused on the sidewalk, debating whether to continue on or turn toward her apartment. Finally, she decided it wouldn't hurt to stop in and say hello to Howard. He'd been so kind to give her that outing to McCall on Saturday, and since he wasn't at church yesterday—such a disappointment—she hadn't had the opportunity to thank him then.

A few minutes later, the small bell above the entrance announced her arrival at the market.

"Howard?" she called softly when she didn't see him behind the counter or in any of the aisles. "Hello?"

"Be right with you," came a muffled reply from the back. Then the door to the storeroom opened and Howard stepped into view. He grinned the moment he saw her. "Lucy."

His smile was infectious, and she returned it.

"I've been thinking about you." He walked toward her. "I wanted to say thanks again for going with me to McCall. It did me a world of good to get away from the store for a day." When he reached her, he took hold of her hand and squeezed her fingers before letting go. "I mean it. I really appreciated your good company."

"It's I who must thank you. It was a lovely day. It gave me something to write about to Richard. Something besides my job and the cat. He'll be grateful when he reads my letter."

Howard motioned with his arm toward a couple of chairs near an old potbelly stove, and they moved toward them. "How's your friend?"

"My friend?"

"The one who was waiting to see you when we got back Saturday. Miss King, wasn't it?"

"Oh. Dottie." She gave a little shrug as she sat in one of the chairs. "She's okay."

"None of my business, huh?" He joined her. "Sorry. Shouldn't have asked."

"I didn't mean—"

Howard chuckled. "It's okay. I understand about girl talk. I've got my aunts, remember? Some things men just aren't supposed to know."

Lucy hesitated a moment, then said, "To be honest, Howard, I *am* worried about Dottie. I'm worried about several of my friends from work. They seem so down lately. They have loved ones away at war, and there are problems here at home, too. Money worries and relationships and heaven alone knows what else. I want to encourage them, but I can't think how." It hadn't been her intention to unload her burdens onto anyone else, but it felt good nonetheless.

"How about this?" Howard leaned toward her, his gaze gentle and caring. "You tell me what you can without breaching anyone's confidence, and then we'll figure out something between us. Like they say, two heads are better than one."

The tension eased from her shoulders. "I'd like that. Thank you."

V···–MAIL
To: Miss Dorothea King, Boise, Idaho, U.S.A.
From: PFC Gregory Wallace
Wednesday, February 24, 1943

Dear Dottie,

I'm finally in England, but word is, we won't be here long. I suppose
by the reports in the newspapers you'd be able to tell where we're
headed. Not that we know for certain. They don't tell us GIs anything
more than they have to.

I wrote several pages to you on our way over, planning to post them
when we got here. But they got accidentally dropped in water and the
ink ran so you couldn't read them. I'm awful sorry because I know you
must be anxious to hear from me. I hope this one makes it straight into
your hands.

I got some letters from you and my folks this week. They sure did
make me homesick for all of you. But I miss <u>you</u> most of all, Dottie. I
hope you know that. I showed your picture to the guys in my unit, and
they think I'm lucky to have a girl like you waiting for me at home. I told
them, "You bet I am. Don't I know it."

The short while we've been in England has sure taught me to
appreciate the blue skies of Idaho. I'm not cut out for the rain and
gloomy skies all the time. It's a wonder these people don't have
webbed feet. I don't feel like I'll ever get warm again. This damp cold
goes right through to the bones. I shouldn't complain though. I'm in a
friendly country and am safe for the most part, not counting the
occasional bomb the Germans try dropping on us.

Speaking of a friendly country, I've got to tell you, there are plenty of
these "blokes" who aren't happy to see the Americans pouring into
England, allies or not. They say we're an undisciplined lot with too

much money in our pockets, but the truth is, English girls are falling for our guys and they can't handle it.

You don't have to worry about those English girls, Dottie. Not as far as I'm concerned. Some of the guys in my unit have taken to calling me "Preacherman." They say I'd rather stay in the barracks and read my Bible than go to the pubs with them. Truth is, I wouldn't mind getting out for a while and seeing more of the area, but I've learned my lesson about avoiding temptation. (Not that I've told anybody here that.) As long as pubs are their destination, I'll pass.

Besides, I'm saving my pay for when I get back to the States and we get married. I wish we'd done it before I shipped out, no matter what our folks said about it being better to wait until we're older. I don't think it <u>was</u> better to wait. So you start making those wedding plans so we can get married right away when I get home.

I love you, Dottie. You remember that.

Greg

21

Ready to burst with joy, Dottie waited impatiently for the bus. She longed to share Greg's letter with someone. That someone wouldn't be her mother, that was clear.

When Margo King pulled the envelope from their mailbox last night, she'd looked at it as if it were poison. Dottie had snatched it away and taken it to her room. She lost count of the number of times she'd read the letter. Enough to memorize it.

Lucy would be glad for her, Dottie thought as she stood with her back toward her mother.

She closed her eyes and replayed in her mind several lines from the letter: *I miss you most of all, Dottie. . . . They think I'm lucky to have a girl like you waiting for me at home. . . . I'm saving my pay for when I get back to the States and we get married. . . . So you start making those wedding plans. . . . I love you, Dottie. You remember that.*

"I love you, too, Greg," she whispered. "I love you, too. Hurry home."

"Does he know about the baby yet?" her mother asked, her tone low and disapproving.

Dottie didn't look behind her. "No. Not when he wrote this letter."

"Don't be so sure he'll welcome the news. He'll think you trapped him. He'll resent you for it. Mark my words."

Dottie caught her breath. *That's not true.* Pressing her lips together lest she say something regrettable, she leaned forward and stared down the street, desperately needing the bus to arrive. *It won't be like that for Greg and me. We love each other, and no matter what, we'll go on loving each other. Nothing you say will change that, Mom. Nothing.*

Even at nineteen, Dottie understood that her mother's words stemmed from bitterness over her own disastrous marriage. But why had it been such a disaster? Dottie doubted she would ever know the answer to that question. Her mother refused to speak about Bart King or the years they were married. Not under any circumstance. Not for any reason.

Dottie's recollections of her father were sketchy at best. She had only a vague image of him in her mind and had no way of knowing if it was an accurate one, especially since the man in her memory bore a strong resemblance to Gary Cooper, the actor. On the day Margo received her divorce papers, she had destroyed every photograph of him. She'd even ripped to pieces their wedding photos. She hadn't kept so much as a snapshot for her children.

Dottie felt a twinge of pity for her mother. So much anger. So much pain. Now that wall of resentment toward men was extended to Greg, and Dottie didn't know how to tear it down.

The whine of the bus's engine pulled her from her depressing thoughts. She drew in a breath, reminding herself that she had cause to be happy this morning. Greg's letter was in her purse. He loved her and he wanted to marry her. That was enough reason for gladness. If her mother couldn't understand that, then so be it.

The bus rumbled to a stop and the door *whooshed* open.

Greg loves me and we're going to get married and we're going to love this baby. We'll raise our child to know and love the Lord.

She felt some of that same joy welling up in her heart as she climbed the bus steps.

"Well, good morning, Miss King." The driver chuckled. "Going by that smile on your face, I'd say you've received good news."

She wanted to kiss him on both cheeks. "Indeed, I have, Mr. Pratt."

"Good for you."

Dottie hurried toward the empty seat next to Lucy, her smile growing with each step.

"You got a letter from Greg," Lucy said.

"Yes."

"Did he get yours?" She lowered her voice and leaned closer. "Does he know yet?"

Dottie shook her head. "Not yet."

"You'll get another letter soon."

"He was in England when he wrote this—" she pulled the envelope from her purse and ran her fingertips over the lettering— "but he was expecting to ship out soon. He didn't say where he was going, but it must be North Africa."

Lucy patted her hand. "We'll pray that your letter reaches him before he leaves England."

"I've been praying exactly that. Believe me."

Lucy's gaze moved across the aisle. "Is your mom handling things any better?"

"No. She's barely speaking to me." It surprised Dottie how much those words hurt.

"I have an idea that might help you two." Lucy looked at Dottie again, wearing an enigmatic smile. "We'll talk about it at lunch when everybody's together."

Dottie was curious but didn't ask her friend to elaborate.

Whatever Lucy's idea was, she certainly hoped it would work.

22

A watched pot never boils. Wasn't that how the old adage went?

Eager to meet with her friends on their lunch break, Lucy couldn't believe the way the second hand crawled around the face of her wristwatch, taunting her with the slow passage of time.

She had Howard Baxter to blame for her excitement. It was something he said that caused the idea to blossom. "Seems to me you'd all take your minds off your worries if you were helping others with their worries."

He was right. At least it was true for her. She spent far too many hours thinking about her own fears and concerns. She needed to *do* something. Something more than what she was already doing. First, she needed to pray more. She needed to pray in a focused, organized manner. Her prayers were too scattered, like pellets from a shotgun. Second, she needed to serve others whose hardships and heartache were greater than her own, the same way Jesus would do.

Another glance at her watch.

Another impatient sigh.

She reached for a piece of paper and scrolled it into place in the Underwood. Then she flipped open the top file folder on her desk and began to type.

One report at a time, Lucy managed to work her way toward the lunch hour. At the stroke of twelve, she grabbed the paper sack containing her peanut-butter-and-jelly sandwich and hurried across the base to Building B-301. Dottie was already there. Margo and Penelope came in together a few minutes later.

"I have an idea," Lucy announced the instant they were seated.

Everyone looked her.

"Remember a few weeks back when I said I was going to pray for victory and have a more positive attitude about things. Well, I haven't done a very good job of it. I want to do better." She clasped her hands in her lap. "Here's what I'm thinking. I'd like us to get together on Saturday mornings, to talk, to pray, to do something for others."

Nobody said anything, but Dottie leaned forward on her chair, as if eager to hear more. Margo, on the other hand, wore a suspicious frown. As for Penelope, she looked as if she wanted to bolt from the room.

Lucy continued, the words rushing out of her mouth, "We've become good friends in the months we've worked at the base. We sit together on the bus morning and night, and we eat lunch together in this little room every day. We share news about our loved ones, and we encourage one another when we're down. But we could do so much more. I read a verse in the Bible last night that says the Lord has become my victory. If I really believe that, shouldn't I be living it in practical ways?"

"I'm not sure I understand what it is you're after," Margo said. "What are these Saturday meetings for? Some sort of club?"

Lucy smiled. "I hadn't thought of it as a club, but yes. I guess that's what it would be. A victory club." She turned toward Dottie. "You know how difficult it's been for Lettie Hinkle since her husband was drafted. Those children need new clothes, the house needs a fresh coat of paint, and Lettie could use some moral support. And she's not the only one. There are many others like her." Lucy moved her gaze to Penelope and then to Margo. "Don't you see? If we were busy helping others, with our prayers and our hands, time wouldn't weigh so heavy on our hearts."

"I don't know if I could do it *every* Saturday." Penelope pushed her red hair back from her face. "I already leave the children with their father every day of the week while I'm at the base. I'm not sure I should take Saturdays away, too."

"Then come when you can, Pen. Maybe we won't want to meet every week anyway. I don't know. We haven't even tried it once yet."

"Our church already does charitable work, you know." Margo gave her head a slow shake.

"So does mine," Lucy answered. "But I see this as something more than that. Something we can do together as a group of friends. Besides, there are more needy people than there are programs to help them." It was unfair, but she decided to toss in a dab of guilt for Margo's benefit. "It's the Christian thing to do."

"She's right." Dottie took hold of Lucy's hand. "This would be good for all of us. Count me in, Luce."

✯ ✯ ✯

When Lucy arrived at the corner market after work that night, she was disappointed to find it filled with customers. She wanted to tell Howard what had happened at lunch, but the store was too busy.

It wasn't reasonable to expect him to be free whenever she wanted to talk. She realized that. He had a business to run. Obviously he'd received a shipment of some hard-to-find item because the line to the counter was a long one. She debated whether or not to join the queue, then decided against it. She would go home, put her feet up, and ponder what the Victory Club could accomplish first.

The name made her smile. She hadn't meant for these proposed get-togethers to become anything quite so formal as a club, but once the title came up, she had to admit she liked it. True, Margo's and Penelope's less-than-enthusiastic reactions left her disappointed, but Dottie had caught Lucy's vision. She hoped the other two would with time.

"Thank God for Dottie," she said aloud as she followed the sidewalk toward home.

Dear, dear Dottie. The girl might not understand it yet, but she would need the support this new "club" could offer, once her pregnancy became known. Others would condemn her. She would likely lose her job at the base. And if Greg died . . .

Well, she would make Greg's safety one of her priority prayers.

At home, Lucy glanced at the mail awaiting her. Only two pieces—a bill from the electric company and an invitation to hear a visiting author lecture at the community hall. Nothing from Richard. She dropped the two envelopes, along with her apartment key and pocketbook, onto the kitchen table.

Followed by Empress, she went to the bedroom, where she changed out of her work clothes and into a comfortable shirt and a pair of loose-fitting slacks. By the time she returned to the kitchen, her hair tied at the nape with a kerchief, her stomach was growling. She made herself a grilled cheese sandwich, then sat at the table to eat her simple supper.

And just like that, the solitude hit her, an overwhelming rush of aloneness so great it was a physical pain.

"Oh, puss." She reached for her cat and pulled the feline to her chest, needing close contact with something living and breathing. "Sometimes I don't think I can bear it. God help me, I don't think I can."

23

Penelope filled the sink with hot sudsy water while Stuart carried the last of the supper dishes from the table and scraped remnants of food into the trash can.

Setting the dirty dishes on the counter, he said, "It's okay with me if you want to go with your friends on Saturday, Pen. Lucy's idea sounds like a good one. Maybe I could help with some of the projects, too. I can still use a paintbrush."

"You'd like to help us?"

"Sure. Why not? Even the kids could help with some things." He leaned his backside against the counter. "Oh, I almost forgot to tell you. I asked the Thompson girl to watch the kids while I'm at the doctor's on Friday afternoon."

"Mary Lou Thompson?" Penelope gave him a hard look. "She isn't old enough to babysit."

"Come on, Pen. She's fourteen. That's only four years younger than you were when we got married."

Don't remind me.

"She's a good, responsible kid, and her mom'll be right across the street if anything comes up. It's only for an hour or two. I should be home before you get off work."

Penelope lowered the plates into the soapy dishwater. "What's *this* doctor visit for?"

"I think he wants to run some more tests."

"None of the other tests did any good."

Stuart placed a hand on her shoulder. "Hey, maybe this time will be different. I'm doing better than I was."

She shrugged off his hand while gritting her teeth. She didn't think this time would be different. Nothing ever changed around here. Not ever.

"What's eating you, Pen? You've been out of sorts for weeks."

She whirled toward him, sending droplets of water flying across the kitchen. "Why shouldn't I be out of sorts? You aren't working. Our medical bills are piling up. Frances has gone off to war. Evelyn has a perpetual runny nose, and Alan has grown out of most of his clothes. We're almost broke. We have a car but we can't afford to drive it, and we never do anything for fun. I'm tired of going off to work every day, then having to come back and take care of the house and you and the children. I'm tired of it all."

Stuart stared at her in stunned silence. He obviously didn't know whether to reach for her again or keep his distance.

"Just leave me alone, will you?" She turned back to the sink and resumed her dish washing with a vengeance. "I just want to be left alone."

After a few moments, Stuart said, "I love you, Pen. I'm sorry you're unhappy. I never figured I'd be laid up like this at my age. I thought I'd be a better provider. I'd change things if I could."

Would you? she wondered as he left the kitchen. *Would you become someone else, someone exciting who could give me a different life, one with some fun in it? Why didn't I see what marriage to you would be like? Why was I such a fool? Single girls are the ones having all the fun in this war, and I'm stuck here at home with you and the kids.*

Penelope let the dirty water out of the sink, then reached for a towel and dried her hands.

It would serve you right if you didn't have me around to wait on you hand and foot.

Her conscience twinged. Stuart took care of the children during the day. He did the laundry and kept the house tidy. Sometimes, when she was tired, he fixed dinner. He even went to the market on occasion, although he said standing in long lines worsened his back pain.

From the children's bedroom, she heard the beginning sounds of a squabble between brother and sister. Any second, one of them would come screaming down the hall. If they did, she would slap them silly. She was in no mood for temper tantrums tonight.

She grabbed her sweater from the peg near the back door and slipped outside. Let Stuart deal with it. She'd had it with the lot of them.

24

Lucy fell asleep in the easy chair, a book in her lap, Empress curled beside her on the armrest. She dreamed about Richard, one of those disjointed dreams filled with real and imaginary people that make little sense when examined later.

It took a few moments for the sound of knocking to work its way into her sleep-fogged brain. Awakened at last, she set the book aside and rose to her feet.

"Coming," she called, not certain her visitor would still be there.

But he was.

"Howard?" Her surprise drove away the last dregs of sleepiness.

"Sorry for dropping by this way, Lucy. I hope it isn't too late. I could come another time if it's inconvenient."

"No. Of course not." She opened the door wider. "Come in, won't you?"

He stepped past her, removed his hat, and gazed around the kitchen. "This is cozy."

"That's what I thought the first time I saw it." She closed the door. "It's always felt like home."

His gaze met hers. "I saw you come into the store tonight, but you left before I had a chance to speak to you."

"You were busy. I didn't want to be a bother."

"You couldn't be a bother, Lucy. Besides, I was eager to know about your meeting with your friends. How did they like your idea?"

"They liked it okay." She motioned toward the kitchen chairs.

"Just okay?"

They sat on opposite sides of the table.

Howard placed his hat on the empty chair beside him. "You sound disappointed."

Lucy shrugged, then nodded. "I am."

"Tell me what happened. Might make you feel better to talk about it."

"I suppose." She drew a breath and let it out on a sigh. "They weren't enthusiastic, the way I expected them to be. Except for Dottie. She was all for it. But they did agree to give it a try. We're meeting here at my place this coming Saturday. We even gave our little gathering a name. The Victory Club."

"Hey, I like the sound of that." His grin made the kitchen feel warmer. "I'd like to help, too. Perhaps I can donate some dry goods or repair a fence or something. Unless, of course, men aren't welcome in your Victory Club."

"That's kind of you, Howard. I'm sure we'll be glad for any help we can get."

From the corner of her eye, Lucy saw a blur of white an instant before Empress launched herself into Howard's lap. He leaned back in surprise as the cat made herself comfortable.

The heat of embarrassment rose in Lucy's cheeks as she started to rise from her chair. "Oh, Howard. I'm sorry. Lately she's decided all of my guests must love her, too. Here. I'll take her."

He lifted his hand like a traffic cop. "She's fine. Let her be. I don't mind at all."

"Are you sure?"

"I'm sure." Howard stroked the cat's back. "What's her name?"

"Empress."

He chuckled. "Ah. Royalty. That explains it. She rules this little kingdom."

Lucy settled onto her chair and returned his smile. "I'm afraid so." She gave her head a slow shake as she lowered her gaze to the cat. "Empress barely tolerated Richard when we were first married. She was jealous because he got all my attention." Her smile faded.

There was a lengthy silence before Howard said, "I can't say that I blame her. Lucky Richard."

A shiver moved through Lucy, starting in the pit of her stomach. She didn't dare raise her eyes to meet his. She didn't dare try to see what he meant.

V··· –Mail

To: Mrs. Richard Anderson, Boise, Idaho, U.S.A.
From: 1st Lt. Richard Anderson
Sunday, February 14, 1943

My beloved Lucy,
It's Valentine's Day. A man ought to be with his sweetheart on Valentine's Day, but instead, I'm in England, missing you. I hope someday I can bring you here and show you the places I've seen. While I don't care for the climate, there's a lot of beauty here. You can feel and see the history all around you. Makes me realize how young the U.S. is. Out West, we think something's old when it's been around a hundred years. Our squadron has flown lots of raids lately. The English prefer to fly at night, but the Americans like the day runs because we can be more precise. Between us, we're making the enemy duck for cover around the clock. We've been very successful. I'm proud of the boys I serve with. I hope you get to meet some of them when the war's over. They'd sure like to meet you after hearing so much about you. I've just about worn out your snapshot as often as I've taken it out of my pocket to look at and show it around to the guys. Speaking of the guys, I got the cookies you sent. They were a bit crumbly by the time they reached us, but they sure were good. I was the most popular guy in the barracks while they lasted. Sometimes I lie here in my bunk and remember those few short weeks we had together as man and wife, and I wonder if I dreamed them. Just like you told me you do sometimes. Lucy, I love you more than I can find words to say or write. You're a constant presence in my heart. If anything happens to me over here, I want you to know how happy you've made me. I pray God will give us a long life together, but if that's not

part of the master plan, then I'm glad for what we've had. You remember that, Lucy.

Always,
Richard

25

Margo stood at the sink, washing the breakfast dishes. The task didn't take long when she ate alone. This being Saturday, Dottie had opted to stay in bed until it was time to get ready to go to Lucy's.

Although her daughter was careful not to complain, Margo knew the girl's morning sickness had been bad all week. Dottie was developing dark circles beneath her eyes, and she was much too thin. Margo tried not to worry about her. Tried and failed.

With a sigh, she set the frying pan in the dish drain, then poured herself a last cup of coffee and settled onto a chair at the kitchen table.

"What am I going to do about her?"

Silly question. There was nothing *to* be done. Dottie was pregnant, and for most women, morning sickness was a normal part of the process. Dottie would have to suffer through.

But I could be kinder to her in the meantime.

Margo gave her head an emphatic shake, denying the thought any credence. She hadn't been unkind to Dottie. She'd simply exhibited her disapproval. Margo had to show that she didn't condone sinful behavior, didn't she?

Dottie already knows what she did was wrong.

True, but she didn't act like it. The girl seemed to think all she had to do was say she was sorry, and then all would be well. Last

Sunday at church, when they were singing a hymn, Margo glanced at her daughter and observed a look of unmitigated joy steal across Dottie's face. Even pregnant out of wedlock, even knowing Greg was overseas and might die without marrying her and giving the baby his name, Dottie was joyful in the house of God.

That knowledge frustrated Margo beyond words. Dottie had the piper to pay, and the foolish girl didn't realize it.

The creak of a loose floorboard in the hallway told Margo her wayward daughter was up at last. Seconds later, she heard the bathroom door close and the water start in the shower.

Margo lifted her gaze to the clock on the wall. Good gracious! How long had she been woolgathering at the table?

She placed her coffee cup in the sink, then hurried to her bedroom where she changed into a tan-colored dress and a pair of comfortable walking shoes. After running a brush through her hair, she applied a dab of color to her lips. Lipstick was the only makeup Margo wore. Without it, she felt invisible.

She lowered the gold cosmetic tube to the dressing table while staring at her reflection in the mirror.

Maybe I am invisible. Who sees me?

She stiffened and stepped back, not liking the self-pitying tone of her thoughts. Vanity was an unbecoming trait and not one she cared to acquire at her stage of life.

Margo turned, picked up her pocketbook from the straight-backed chair near the door, and walked to the front of the house.

Five minutes later, Dottie emerged from her bedroom, wearing a pink blouse, a burgundy cardigan, and a light brown skirt. "I'm ready, Mom." Despite the dark circles beneath her eyes, she looked pretty this morning, her dark, curly hair glistening in the light that fell through the living-room window.

"You shouldn't go out with a damp head," Margo said. "You'll catch your death."

"It isn't cold, Mom. I'll be fine."

Margo frowned. "Why must you argue with everything I say? Didn't I teach you better than that, Dorothea Ruth?" She released a heavy sigh. "Why I should be surprised, considering everything else you've forgotten, I just don't know."

Dottie stood before her for a long while without answering. Then, in a voice so small it was barely audible, she asked, "Are you ever going to forgive me, Mom?"

The question pierced Margo's heart as surely as a knife could have. She opened her mouth, surprised that she wanted to say the healing words her daughter needed to hear. But what came out was, "Let's not dillydally, Dottie. We're running late as it is."

26

Penelope accepted a cup of coffee from Lucy, then carried it into the living room where Margo sat on the sofa, Dottie on the floor opposite her. Judging by the woebegone expressions on their faces, this wouldn't be a fun-filled morning.

I should've stayed home. I can feel this miserable with Stuart and the children.

Penelope headed toward the chair nearest the window.

Lucy entered the room and sat beside Margo on the sofa. She smiled, but it seemed forced. "I appreciate that you all came." She glanced at each of the other women in turn. "Why don't we open with a word of prayer? Shall we?"

Penelope bowed her head and closed her eyes.

"Dear Father," Lucy began, "thank You for bringing us together today, to seek You and to do Your will. . . ."

Penelope wondered what it must be like, to believe in God the way Lucy seemed to believe. Sometimes the way she talked about Him—like she really *knew* Him—made Penelope envious. That Lucy believed what she said she believed was never in question. Dottie was like that, too. Unwavering in her faith.

And Margo? Well, if *that's* what religion did to a woman, Penelope didn't want any.

"You know our needs, Jesus," Lucy went on. "You know our concerns. . . ."

Did Jesus know how unhappy Penelope was? And if He did, did He care? And if He cared, why didn't He do something about it? The monotony, the sameness, the drudgery of her life was driving her insane. When was it her turn to have some fun? When did she get to be happy?

"We ask Your divine protection for our loved ones, for Clark, Greg, Frances, and Richard. Strengthen and guide them. Grant them wisdom. Give Your angels charge over them, we pray. . . ."

Frances wasn't in any danger. At least not while she was at that fort in the Midwest. Her first letter to their parents said there was a possibility WAACs would soon be posted to England. It was what Frances had hoped for when she enlisted, and now it seemed her wish would be granted. But then, Frances *always* got what she wanted. Things always went her way.

Imagine! England. London. British gentlemen with those upper-crust accents. Pubs. Music. Dancing. Life!

It wasn't fair. Penelope hadn't traveled anywhere more exotic than the Oregon coast, and her baby sister was about to go to England. It was so horribly unfair. Why did all the good stuff happen to Frances and not to her?

"Lord, let us be Your hands and feet in our community. Guide us to those You would have us help. . . ."

God, why couldn't You give me the same life You gave Frances? If anybody needs help, it's me.

V··· —Mail

To: 1st Lt. Richard Anderson, APO, N.Y.P.E.

From: Lucy Anderson

Saturday, March 13, 1943

My darling Richard,

Yesterday I received the letter you wrote on Valentine's Day. The mail is so wretchedly slow, and I am left to wonder what's happened between the day you wrote to me and the day I received your letter. Are you well? Are you whole? Are you still in England or are you somewhere unknown to me?

The newspaper says the Allies are bombing Germany 24 hours a day. When I hear of planes shot out of the sky, I'm so afraid for you. I can't help but selfishly wish you were home with me instead of in harm's way. Forgive me, love, for thinking so much of myself. I'm proud of you, my darling. I'm proud of your skills and proud of your courage.

Today was the first meeting of the Victory Club. I believe it went rather well. Much better than I expected, to be honest.

Margo, who seemed so resistant before, had several good suggestions for ways we can reach people in our community with acts of love.

Dottie was reserved when she first arrived. I think she and her mother had been quarreling earlier. But by the time we finished praying, she overflowed with enthusiasm. Dottie has a huge heart for God and His people. It puts me to shame. I wonder if I could have such peace and joy if I were in her shoes.

As for Penelope, I'm not convinced she'll return after today. She seemed very distracted, and I know she views the rest of us as peculiar. (Isn't that what 1st Peter says we Christians are—a peculiar people, set apart for God?) I pray that God will use us to somehow lead her to a heart-changing faith in Christ.

We decided our first official project will be painting Lettie Hinkle's house and tidying up her yard. Dottie and I will call for volunteers from our respective churches. I know Mrs. Hinkle will be surprised, and I hope our efforts will leave her uplifted and encouraged.

Spring has come early in Boise. We're enjoying much warmer temperatures. If today was any indication, I may be planting my first Victory Garden sooner than expected. My friends say I mustn't plant before the snow is gone from Schaefer Butte. Some years that isn't until late May, but weather prognosticators are predicting this year will be different.

Oh darling, how I wish you could be home to see this garden grow or at least to see it harvested. Wouldn't that be something, if you were home by September? I close my eyes and imagine the two of us together, plucking ripe tomatoes from the vines. How ordinary. How wonderful. I miss you so very much, my dear husband.

Stay safe for me, my love.

Forever and always,
Lucy

April 1943

27

By the time the Victory Club—including Penelope, to the surprise of the others—and a small band of church volunteers gathered on a Saturday to paint the Hinkle house, April had arrived with glorious promise. Trees were in bud up and down 17th Street, lawns had patches of green, and tulips and daffodils lifted colorful faces in many a flower bed.

Dottie welcomed the signs of the changing seasons. Spring was a time of hope and renewal, and she felt in need of both. She hadn't received mail from Greg in over a month. She hadn't received a response to her letter about the pregnancy. In her weakest moments—during the dark hours of the night—she wondered if her mother was right, if Greg resented what happened and didn't want to marry her after all.

Those doubts were banished today. On this Saturday, with its bright sunlight, blue skies, and warm, gentle breeze, Dottie felt hopeful again. She would hear from Greg soon. She knew she would.

Standing on the back porch of the Hinkles' house, she pried open another can of yellow paint, then stirred the thick liquid with a stick. She didn't worry about splatters at this point; after several hours of work, the front of her coveralls were already covered with yellow and white paint flecks.

"Hey, Dottie," Bobby Crawford, one of the volunteers from

East Boise Community Church, called from atop a ladder. "Want some help?"

With a hand shielding her eyes from the sun, she looked up. "No thanks. I can handle this."

She would much rather be up there where Bobby was, working on the trim beneath the eaves, than down here painting the spindles of the porch railing. However, she'd received strict instructions, first from her mother and then from Lucy. She was to stay off ladders and avoid heavy lifting. She wasn't to stray from the porch. Period.

She knew they were right. Still, it was frustrating. She felt fine. In fact, she felt better than ever. This past week, she hadn't been sick in the mornings, and her appetite had returned. If she kept eating the way she had lately, she would weigh a ton by the time Greg came home.

She smiled, imagining herself, round as a beach ball, and the surprised expression Greg would wear if he saw her that way. Then he would laugh, and he would hug her close and—

"Dottie?"

She looked up to find Greg's parents standing on the back lawn, their expressions grim. Her mother and Lucy stood right behind them.

Did her heart stop beating at the sight of them? It seemed to.

"No," she whispered, her voice paper thin. The paintbrush slipped from her grasp. "No, not Greg."

Nancy Wallace spoke with haste. "He's hurt, honey. He isn't dead."

Her knees like rubber, Dottie sank to the porch floor.

In an instant, her mother was crouching beside her, an arm around her shoulders. "Did you hear what Mrs. Wallace said, Dottie? Greg's alive. When he's able to travel, he'll be coming home."

Her heart flipped. "Home?" Dottie raised her eyes, first to her mother, then toward Greg's parents. "They're sending him home?"

Elation flowed through her. Greg was coming home. Home to her. They could be married. He would be here to see his child born. He wouldn't be in danger any longer. Everything would be all right now.

Then reality set in. The army didn't send a soldier back to the States for minor injuries.

She stared at Greg's father. "How bad is it, Mr. Wallace?"

"They didn't tell us much."

Dottie sensed that Ken Wallace was hedging, that he knew more than he wanted to say. "How bad?" she asked again.

Greg's father drew a deep breath. "He's blind. They aren't sure he'll recover his sight."

"Oh, God." Dottie hugged her arms to her abdomen and began to rock slowly, forward and back . . . forward and back . . . forward and back. "Dear God, don't let it be true."

28

Hours later, tears spent, heart sore, Dottie sat in a chair by her bedroom window, watching dusk settle over the earth. She was alone at last and grateful for it. Although her mother meant well—staying nearby from the moment they returned home, asking over and over again what Dottie needed or wanted—her hovering only made things worse.

Peace. Dottie needed and wanted peace.

She looked at the open Bible in her lap. Softly, she read aloud. "'You are my Master! Every good thing I have comes from You.'"

She paused, allowing the words to sink deep into her heart. *You are my master, Jesus. Everything good in my life is from You.*

"'You guard all that is mine. The land you have given me is a pleasant land. What a wonderful inheritance!'"

I put Greg into Your hands, El Elyon, God Most High. I will trust You with him, no matter what.

"'I know the LORD is always with me. I will not be shaken, for He is right beside me.'"

Dottie closed the Bible and pulled it close to her chest.

I will not be shaken. I will not be shaken. Oh, Jesus, help me keep from being shaken.

✯ ✯ ✯

Lucy lay on her living room sofa, the curtains closed, the lights off. Her chest ached, and she felt cold to her core. The image of Dottie, collapsed on the porch of the Hinkle home, wouldn't leave her. Worse still was knowing that her first thoughts hadn't been about Dottie or Greg or their unborn child. First Lucy had thought about herself, about her own fears, about her loneliness and her aloneness.

"I don't think I can bear it," she whispered into the darkness. "I can't bear it."

Richard could die. Richard could be blinded or crippled. Richard might never father children.

Tears fell from her cheeks onto her arms. Large tears. Slow tears.

Splat . . .

Splat . . .

Splat . . .

Someone rapped on her apartment door.

She didn't move. She didn't want to see anybody. Odd really, since she was lonely.

Whoever it was rapped again.

"Leave me alone," she commanded softly.

And rapped again. Harder this time. Persistent.

Why didn't people go away when it seemed no one was home? Didn't they have anything better to do than stand on her stoop and knock?

Lucy rose from the sofa and walked from the living room through the kitchen, not bothering to turn on the lights. She touched the knob with her right hand while pressing her forehead against the door. "Who is it?"

"It's me. Howard."

She opened the door an inch.

"Lucy, I heard what happened. About Dottie's fiancé."

She wondered how he'd heard. Bad news carried fast, but still—

As if he'd heard her thoughts, he said, "A couple of the volunteers from your church who helped you paint that house were in the store. I overheard them talking about Dottie."

"Oh."

"I came as soon as I could. I knew you'd be thinking about your husband. Anybody in your shoes would."

"Would they?" she whispered.

"Of course." He leaned toward the crack in the door. "I thought you might need a friend. I...I don't mean to intrude, but I'd like to help if I can." He hesitated, then asked, "Can I help, Lucy?"

She didn't invite him in. She simply turned and made her way back to the sofa. Seconds later, the door closed with a soft *click*, followed by the sound of footsteps. It seemed a natural thing, having him sit beside her and gather her into his arms.

"You go on and cry." He patted her back. "You've got a right. Nobody's gotta be strong all the time. Not even you."

She choked back a sob as she turned her face into his chest. "Oh, Howard. I'm so tired. I'm so scared."

"Of course you are. Of course."

She let herself give in to the pent-up storm. It felt good to let go, to hold nothing back, to have strong arms around her and a kindly male voice comforting her. It was good not to be alone with her thoughts and fears. She'd been alone too long. Too long.

But when the tears were spent, when her sobs subsided and her mind finally cleared, Lucy knew something had shifted in her friendship with Howard Baxter. She knew from the way he held her—more like a lover than a friend.

A soft voice in her heart told her to flee from it, but she didn't. She couldn't. Not yet. Not quite yet.

Lucy drew a shaky breath as she pulled back from Howard.

His arms loosened but didn't release her. She lifted her eyes to look into his. Only the room was too dark to see.

"Better?" His voice sounded husky, strained, as if he'd been the one crying.

"Yes."

"Good. If it were up to me, Lucy, you'd never be sad again."

Her pulse quickened. "I think I'd better put some water on my face." She stood.

His fingers trailed down her arm until he gently clasped her hand.

Softly, she said, "I . . . I'll only be a moment."

"Take your time." He squeezed her fingers before releasing her.

Lucy hurried into the bathroom, pushing the door closed at the same time she flicked on the light switch. The sudden brightness was almost blinding. She stepped toward the sink and stared at her reflection in the mirror. Her eyes were red and puffy, her cheeks tearstained, her hair disheveled.

"What are you doing, Lucy Anderson? What in the name of heaven and earth do you think you're doing?"

Nothing.

Don't play with fire.

I'm not. I'm upset and a friend came over to comfort me. What's wrong with that? Howard's just a friend.

Is he?

Of course. I'm a married woman. I love Richard, and Howard knows that. That's why he came. Because he knows I'm afraid for Richard. Because he's concerned about Richard, too.

Be wise, Lucy. You're a sheep among wolves.

He's been nothing but a gentleman with me. He's kind and thoughtful. He's a friend.

He's a man.

I know what I'm doing.

✳ ✳ ✳

From the hallway, Margo looked inside Dottie's room. Her daughter lay on the bed, her back toward the door. She hadn't moved since the last time Margo checked on her—which wasn't all that long ago. Perhaps fifteen minutes at most.

Her heart ached for her daughter, ached more than she'd expected it would. And she *had* expected it. She'd predicted there would be a price to pay. Hadn't she tried to tell Dottie that?

But being right didn't lessen the sorrow she felt.

With a sigh, she returned to her bedroom, removed her robe and hung it on the closet door, then sat on the edge of her bed. She closed her eyes and pressed her folded hands against her chin.

"O God, I know what Dottie did was wrong." How could she not know when her own sin had cost her dearly? "But please, Lord, don't make Dottie pay the same way I have. If You must exact a price for their sin, let her regret and his blindness be enough."

She reached over, turned out the light on her nightstand, and slipped beneath the blankets.

Greg would come home now. Did he know about the predicament he'd left Dottie in? Had he received Dottie's letter telling him she was pregnant before he was injured? If so, he hadn't bothered to answer. What did that mean? He would *have* to do the right thing by Dottie. Margo would see to it.

At least a blind man won't be so easily unfaithful to his wife, the way Bart was to me.

She felt a sting of regret for the cruel nature of her thoughts. And yet, wasn't it true? Greg would be dependent upon Dottie in many respects. He wouldn't be able to sneak out and run around on his wife. That might be one heartache Dottie would be spared.

✳ ✳ ✳

Penelope listened to her husband's steady breathing and knew he finally slept. Thank goodness. He'd been more restless than usual tonight—sighing, rolling from one side to the other, sighing, fluffing his pillows, sighing again. If Penelope hadn't wanted Stuart to think she was asleep, she would have told him to go spend the night on the couch and leave her in peace.

Carefully, she pushed aside the covers and got out of bed. She reached for her bathrobe, one she'd had since before Alan was born. The terry-cloth garment was faded and a bit shapeless, but it was warm and comfortable. She felt in need of comfort tonight.

Tiptoeing on bare feet, she made her way out of the bedroom, down the hall past the children's room, and into the kitchen. Soft moonlight fell through the window, drawing her to it.

Outside, the children's swing set looked oddly still. The tree with its new leaves seemed more crooked than it did in the daylight. The clothesline, empty but for the bag of clothespins that hung at one end, appeared longer than it really was.

Penelope turned from the window, leaned her backside against the sink, and reached for the packet of cigarettes tucked behind the toaster. She'd started smoking about a year ago. Stuart hated it, but she didn't care. Maybe that was one reason she kept smoking—because she knew he hated it. She took perverse pleasure in irritating him any way she could.

As she lit the cigarette, Penelope wondered if Dottie would one day feel the same way about Greg. She wondered if Dottie would resent her husband for who and what he was.

Penelope often heard how quickly a person went from being young to being old. The elderly were always saying that time passed in the blink of an eye. She felt it slipping away from her now. Today she was pretty and slender and youthful, but she wouldn't be forever.

She took a long drag on the cigarette, feeling the nicotine burn the back of her throat. With a sigh, she blew out the smoke, watching it curl upward, silvered by the moonlight.

If ever there's been a time to live my life to the fullest, it's now. I can't wait until it's too late. I can't. I've got to do something or I'll go crazy.

29

Lucy went through the motions of singing with the rest of the choir, but her heart wasn't in it. Nor were her thoughts. She didn't hear the sermon or the Scripture reading or the announcements. In her mind, she was far, far away, lost in a cloud of confusion.

After the service ended, Lucy started for home, then changed her mind. She didn't want to be alone this afternoon. It alarmed her, how much she dreaded being by herself. She used to like her times of quiet reflection. But lately . . . lately everything was different.

Since the day was pleasantly warm, she decided to pay a call on the Kings. The four-mile walk would do her good.

Lucy hoped Dottie was doing better than when they parted yesterday afternoon. She'd looked so lost, so distraught, so young and vulnerable.

But at least Greg's coming home.

It was a selfish thought, but she couldn't help it. She couldn't help envying Dottie. Soon Greg would be home. Lucy wanted Richard to come home, too.

And yet, as she followed the sidewalk through the center of town, it wasn't Richard she thought about. It was Howard. It was the tenderness in her friend's voice and the gentle strength of his arms as he'd cradled her and let her cry. He'd done many kind things for her since they'd become acquainted. He was a good man. A good, good man.

Sometimes when he looked at her, it was as if he . . .

She felt a nervous, pleasant-unpleasant sensation in the pit of her stomach. Her mouth went dry, and she stopped walking.

Howard had wanted to kiss her last night. She'd known it at the time. He'd wanted to but he hadn't. He'd held back for her sake. She'd known that, too.

But I didn't want him to hold back. I wanted him to kiss me.

She gasped, trying to deny the truth but unable to do so. She'd wanted him to kiss her. She'd wanted him to take her back in his arms as they'd stood in her kitchen, saying good night, and kiss her, the way a man kissed a woman.

That's impossible. I love Richard.

Impossible, perhaps, but still true.

Oh, God. I never meant to let this happen. Why didn't I see it coming? Why wasn't I more careful?

God didn't have to speak to her. Lucy knew the answer. She *had* seen it coming. She'd simply pretended she didn't.

Playing with fire, a girl can get burned.

"What do I do now?" she wondered aloud. "What do I do about Howard?"

30

We are pressed on every side by troubles, but we are not crushed and broken. We are perplexed, but not driven to despair..."

When the minister read that passage of Scripture in the morning service, Dottie had known it was God speaking straight to her heart.

Pressed but not crushed.

Perplexed but not despairing.

Even now, more than two hours later, she could close her eyes and recall the way she felt when she heard those words. It was as if God reached down and cradled her in His hands, the same way one catches and holds a fragile butterfly. Oh, how tenderly He held her. How safe and loved she felt, despite the storm.

As Dottie washed the lunch dishes, she stared out the window over the sink and saw her mother watering the flower beds. She wished her mother could feel as safe and loved by God as she did. And why Margo King didn't feel it was a mystery. Dottie knew her mother was a believer, and yet . . .

The door chimes rang, followed by the sound of Lucy calling, "Anybody home?"

"In the kitchen. Come on in." Dottie reached for the dish towel and dried her hands as she turned from the sink.

A moment later, Lucy appeared in the kitchen doorway. "I hope you don't mind me dropping by like this."

"Not at all. I'm glad to see you." She tossed the towel onto the counter. "Would you like a cup of tea?"

"No thanks. But I would like a glass of cold water. It's surprisingly warm out today."

"Have a seat. I'll get it for you."

The two women had barely sat at the table, Lucy with her water glass in hand, when the front door chimes sounded again.

"Goodness," Dottie said. "We don't usually have this much Sunday company." She rose from her chair. "Excuse me." She walked down the short hallway, surprised to see Stuart Maxfield on the other side of the screen door.

"Dottie, is Penelope here by chance?"

She shook her head as she opened the screen. "No. I haven't seen her today."

"Oh." He gazed toward the street. "I was hoping she would be. Maybe she's over at Lucy's."

"I doubt it. Lucy is here."

He looked at her again. The desperation in his eyes was unmistakable.

"What's wrong, Stuart?"

There was a long, painful silence before he answered, "She's left me."

"Oh, no." Dottie pressed the flat of her hand against her chest. "Stuart, are you sure?"

He pulled a slip of paper from his pocket. "I'm sure. She left a note. I was hoping . . ." He let his words fade into silence.

"Come inside. You don't look so good."

"I don't want to bother—"

"Come on." She took hold of his arm and gently drew him down the hall to the kitchen. "Have a seat, Stuart. I'll get you a glass of water." To Lucy, who watched her with a curious gaze, she added, "He's looking for Pen. Have you spoken with her today?"

"No. I came here straight from church."

"She's gone." Stuart covered his face with his hands, his elbows braced on the table. "She's gone."

"I don't understand," Lucy said. "Gone where?"

Dottie gave her head a slight shake, then took a glass from the cupboard. She turned on the tap and let cold water run into the sink for a few moments.

Lord, what should Lucy and I do? Dottie inquired. *What should we say? Give us wisdom, please.*

She filled the glass with water and carried it to the table. "Here, Stuart. Have a sip of this. Maybe it'll help." She sat next to Lucy.

He didn't move, and Dottie wondered if he'd heard her. But finally, he lifted his face from his hands and looked at her, then at Lucy, before he pushed the note across the table.

It was Lucy who lifted the slip of paper, holding it so both she and Dottie could read it.

Stuart,

I don't want to live like this anymore. I'm sorry. I need some fun and excitement before I'm old. Maybe I'd feel different if you were away at war, but the way things are, I'm not ever going to be happy. I'm tired of working all the time and having nothing to show for it.

I don't love you, Stuart. Maybe I never did or maybe those feelings died somewhere along the way. But what does it matter now?

Tell Alan and Evelyn that Mommy will write to them when I can, as soon as I know what I'm going to do and where I'm going to live. I know you'll do your best by them. You're a good father.

Penelope

Dottie gasped. Could it be true?

But after a moment of reflection, she realized that Penelope leaving her husband wasn't a complete surprise. She'd suspected something was wrong between the two of them.

"When did she leave?" Lucy asked gently.

"Some time during the night, I guess. She didn't say much after she got home yesterday. I knew she was upset, but I never imagined she'd do anything like this." His eyes flicked toward Dottie. "She told me what happened to your fiancé. I'm real sorry. I hope he'll be okay."

Dottie acknowledged his words with a nod.

Stuart raked the fingers of one hand through his hair. "I don't know where she'd go, if not to you two. Except for her sister, she doesn't have anybody she spends much time with. With Frances gone off to her WAAC training . . ." He left the sentence unfinished, punctuating it with a shrug. "I called her folks but she wasn't there. I knew she wouldn't be. She'd rather choke than tell her dad what she's doing, and I sure didn't tell him. I'm hoping she'll come back before he finds out."

"We'll help any way we can, Stuart." Dottie reached across the table and patted his arm. "Give Penelope a few days. Once she's had a chance to think things through, she'll come to her senses."

Dottie didn't believe what she said. She didn't believe Penelope would come back. Penelope had left her husband and children the same selfish, uncaring way Dottie's father had left his family . . .

Without a backward glance.

Without a second thought.

Her heart broke for Evelyn and Alan even more than for Stuart. Dottie knew what it was like to be deserted by a parent, to feel unloved, unwanted, and guilty of some unknown wrongdoing. She wished she could gather those precious children into her arms right now. She wanted to tell them that this wasn't their fault.

Anger, hot and bitter, swept through her like a fire. She wanted to slap Penelope Maxfield. She wanted to slap Bart King. She wanted to hurt them both for the hurt they caused others, for the wreckage they'd left in their wake.

31

On Monday, the three remaining members of the Victory Club joined one another for their lunch break. Since the day was pleasant and bright, Lucy suggested they sit outside.

"Do you suppose Stuart's heard anything from Pen yet?" Dottie asked.

Lucy had wondered the same thing. "I hope so. He looked awful when he left your house yesterday." She removed the sandwich, dill pickle, and cookie from her lunch box and placed them on the bench beside her.

"You're assuming she'll bother to contact him." Margo's words were laced with disgust. "What sort of woman walks out on her family that way?"

"A lost one," Dottie answered. With a look of chagrin, she added, "When Stuart told us she'd gone, I remembered how I felt when my father left us, and it made me angry. So angry I wanted to—"

"It's worse when it's the mother," Margo insisted.

"Is it?" Dottie asked. "I don't think so, Mom. The pain is the same."

Realizing she had no appetite, Lucy returned her still-wrapped food to the lunch box, leaned her head against the building at her back, and closed her eyes. "We should have seen how unhappy she was. Maybe we could have helped."

Margo harrumphed. "You can't rescue the world, Lucy."

"Maybe not, but Penelope's our friend. We could have tried to do *something* if we'd known."

"She didn't want us to know." Dottie sighed. "I wonder how much any of us actually knows about another person. We keep secrets, even from ourselves."

Lucy was glad her eyes were closed. Otherwise, Margo and Dottie might have guessed *her* guilty secret.

Oh, God. How do I stop my thoughts from turning to Howard instead of Richard?

She loved her husband. She wanted nothing more than to have Richard home with her, for them to build a life together, to have a family together. So what were these feelings she had for Howard Baxter? It couldn't be love. Yet it was something more than friendship.

Lust?

No. Impossible. She didn't think about Howard in *that* way. Not at all. Still . . .

"Lucy? Are you listening?"

She opened her eyes. "I'm sorry, Dottie. I guess I drifted off. I didn't sleep well last night." She yawned, giving her words credence.

Besides, they were true. She hadn't slept. She'd spent the night tossing and turning, punching her pillow, getting up, pacing the floor, going back to bed. She'd tried to pray, but her prayers rose no higher than the bedroom ceiling.

Dottie stared at her, as if trying to ascertain the cause of Lucy's restless night.

Afraid her friend would see the truth in her eyes, Lucy straightened abruptly. "Do you mind if we talk about this later?" She grabbed her untouched lunch and stood. "I really need to get back to my desk."

I'm pathetic. I'm no better than Penelope. I'm running away, too.

With a halfhearted wave, she hurried toward the two-story wood-framed building that housed her office.

But I'm not like Pen. I haven't left Richard. I write him almost every day. I pray for his safety. I'm anxious for him to come home. Oh, God, let him come home soon.

She arrived at her desk, slid her lunch box into the bottom drawer, then reached for the top form in the In basket and rolled it into the typewriter. Better to keep busy. Better to fill her mind with dates and numbers, requisitions, and military jargon rather than her own untrustworthy emotions.

Does Richard have a woman friend in England?

Her fingers stilled above the keys.

Is he holding another woman in his arms while she cries because the man she loves is away at war?

Of course not. Of course he hadn't. He was there to fight a war.

But he wasn't always in the air. He might work with some of the WAACs stationed in England. Or he might have met one of the local women who lived near the base.

If he had a woman friend, did he feel guilty about it? Did he *need* to feel guilty about it?

If it could happen to me . . .

She swallowed a hard lump in her throat and resumed typing.

V··· –MAIL

To: Mrs. Margo King and Miss Dottie King, Boise, Idaho, U.S.A.
From: Corporal Clark King
Thursday, March 18, 1943

Dear Mom and Dottie,

I hope this letter finds both of you well and in good spirits. I guess you know from the newspapers that the fighting was bad in northern Africa last month, but everybody believes we've shown the Nazis what we're made of. Finally. None of the guys I serve with will be surprised if we're in Italy before the end of summer. I sure hope so.

You'll never believe who I got to see a couple of weeks ago. General Eisenhower. A few of us were sent by our commanding officer to Algiers on military business, and that's where we saw him. I'm mighty glad he's the man leading this army. The men over here trust him. We don't feel that way about every officer, but we do about General Eisenhower.

I got a letter a week ago from Anna Crawford. Do you remember her, Mom? She's Stella Crawford's daughter. The Crawfords live over on Walnut. We went to school together, and sometimes her family came to church. Not often, but sometimes.

Well, Anna went to college over in Oregon, and then she got a job in Portland after the war started. Her little brother, Bobby, got my address from Dottie (thanks for doing that, sis), and when she found out he was writing to me, she decided she would, too. She sent me her picture so I'd know what she looks like now, and all I can say is, Wow! Amazing what five years can do for a girl! You wouldn't recognize her. I'll guarantee that.

I've been on the lookout for Greg, but if he's in Africa, he's nowhere near where we are. I'll keep watching for him, Dottie. If he gets here, I'll take good care of him.

The weather's improved some in the last month, but I still wouldn't give you two bits to live here. Give me the mountains of Idaho any day of the week.

I love you both, and you're in my prayers, just like I know I'm in yours. Give my best to the folks at church and be sure and thank them for their prayers, too. There have been some dark times since we got over here, and that's when I'm the most aware it's the prayers of the saints that are getting me through.

Clark

32

Stuart Maxfield sat in the dark, sipping beer from a bottle and listening to the *tick-tick-tick* of the kitchen wall clock.

Five days. His wife had been gone five days, and not a word from her. He'd called all her friends. No one had seen her. No one had heard from her. He'd visited every place she liked to go—the park, the movies, the soda shop, the five-and-dime. Nothing. At last, he'd gone to see her parents, as much as it pained him to do so.

It hadn't been easy to stand before her coldhearted father and admit that Penelope had left him.

"So, she finally ran off, did she?" David Ballard had scowled as he leaned back in his chair. "That girl never had much sense."

"Sir, I was hoping you or Mom Ballard might know where she is." Stuart had looked from his father-in-law to his mother-in-law.

"She hasn't called us," Julia Ballard answered softly.

"Well, I promise you, if she does, she'll get a piece of my mind." David had muttered a foul curse. "She won't get a dime from us, Julia. Do you understand me? Not a dime if she comes crawling to us for help."

Stuart figured Penelope would rather chew glass than ask her father for help. He couldn't blame her. He felt the same way. Besides, he didn't think Penelope was coming back.

Man, it hurt to admit that. Hurt in his chest and all the way down to his gut, as if he'd been sucker punched. Hurt worse than the constant pain in his back that he'd lived with since falling off that ladder more than a year ago.

He'd never loved anybody but Penelope. From the first time he saw her, he was a goner. Sure, he had been only a teenager at the time, but it didn't matter. He loved her, and that was that.

He'd thought she felt the same.

He'd thought wrong.

Stuart expelled a deep breath, then drained the last of the beer. Afterward, he rose from the chair, walked to the trash container near the back door, and dropped the brown bottle into it.

"What now?" he asked the darkness.

He had two confused little kids to take care of and no idea how he was going to do it. He needed a job of some sort, but that wouldn't be easy to find. Not with his physical limitations. He couldn't stand for long periods of time, and he wasn't supposed to lift too much weight. Not yet.

"You're coming along nicely," his elderly physician had said last week. "Give yourself time, Mr. Maxfield, and I believe you'll be able to do everything you used to do."

But Stuart didn't have time. He had kids to feed and bills to pay.

He rubbed his eyes with the heels of his hands, cursing his fate. Since the day of his accident, he'd felt less than a man. He'd felt it whenever Penelope looked at him. He'd felt it whenever he heard about one of his old school friends or work buddies going off to war. He'd felt it whenever he went out during the day, and the only other males in sight were old men and small boys.

But half a man or not, he couldn't—wouldn't—fail his children. He'd do whatever he had to do to take care of them.

"I just never thought I'd have to do it alone, Pen," he whispered. "I thought we were in this together."

V··· –Mail

To: Miss Dorothea King, Boise, Idaho, U.S.A.
From: PFC Gregory Wallace
Friday, April 2, 1943

My darling Dottie,

I guess you must have heard the news by now that I was wounded. I'm going to be all right, so I hope you're not too worried. I don't want you to worry, Dottie. I love you too much for that.

If you don't recognize the handwriting on this letter, it's because my eyes are bandaged, so I asked one of the nurses here in the hospital to write down what I want to say. I bet you wish I did that more often. You can probably actually read this one.

They've taken real good care of me since I came here from the field hospital. The army doctors are the best, and the nurses try to make things easier on the guys, making us laugh even. I hear there was some movie star who came through here last month, but I forget now who it was. Who knows? Maybe somebody else will come before I leave.

They tell me I'll ship out for the States in another week or two. Can't be soon enough for me. I'm eager to get back to you. Your letter, the one where you told me something real important about our future, caught up with me just before I was wounded in battle. It's hard, knowing what you must be going through there on your own. But you aren't really alone. We both know that. When I get back to the States, we'll get married. I'm more sorry than I can say for causing you hurt because of my actions. I know, even when we're forgiven, we sometimes have to live with the consequences of our actions. Still, I wish you weren't having to deal with this without me by your side.

I'm praying this letter won't take as many weeks to reach you as yours took to reach me. I'm praying it'll get to you before I get there myself. I hope when you read it you'll understand all the things I don't have the words to say or don't want somebody else writing for me. I think you will. You've always seemed to know my heart even before I know it myself.

Dottie, I love you. I think about you all the time. Thinking about you is what's getting me through the long days in this hospital and through the sleepless nights when I'm wondering about tomorrow. Sometimes the wondering about the unknown tomorrows is worse than any fear I felt in battle. I know we're not supposed to do that. I know it doesn't add one second to our lives. Funny, how I tell you not to worry and then do it myself.

I'll be home soon.

Love,
Greg

33

"Lucy! Lucy, are you home? It's me. Dottie."

Lucy hurried to answer the persistent knocking, not sure if Dottie's voice sounded alarmed or joyous. When she pulled open the door, she had her answer. *Glowing* was the only word to describe her friend. Absolutely glowing.

"He's coming home," Dottie said, tears in her eyes and a smile on her lips. She clutched a V–Mail in her left hand.

"Come in and tell me."

Dottie slipped past Lucy, making a beeline to one of the kitchen chairs and sinking onto it as if her legs wouldn't support her another instant. "He wrote this letter on April 2. Can you believe it? It got here in three weeks. He said he was supposed to ship out in a week or two. That must mean he's already on his way back to the States." Her eyes twinkled with happiness. "He must be on a ship right now."

"Oh, Dottie. I'm glad for you." Lucy leaned down to hug her friend, then sat on the chair next to her and rested her forearms on the table. "I'm so, so glad."

"Do you suppose they'll send him to another hospital before they let him come to Boise?"

"I don't know." She hesitated before saying what Dottie must already know. "I suppose it depends on the extent of his injuries."

"I've prayed that God will amaze the doctors and nurses by healing him completely. Especially his eyes. I've asked God to give him perfect vision when they remove those bandages."

"I hope God will heal him, too. For both your sakes."

Dottie's smile faded. "And for the baby's sake, Lucy. I want Greg to be able to see his son or daughter."

"Of course you do."

Dottie placed a hand on her abdomen. "It'll break my heart if he can't see the baby." Worrying, her lower lip between her teeth, she gazed out the window. "Why do you suppose God allows evil things like war to happen?"

I wonder, too, Lord. Why do You allow it? Why do You allow the wicked to do harm to the innocent? Why don't You stop them?

If God spoke, Lucy couldn't hear.

"That's a question people have wrestled with for ages, Dottie. I certainly don't know the answer." She rose from her chair, feeling restless. "Would you like some tea?"

"You needn't bother. I—"

"It's no bother. I'd like some myself."

As Lucy bustled about the kitchen—filling the teakettle with water and setting it on the stove, taking down the cups and saucers from the cupboard—her thoughts churned.

There was a small, ugly corner of her heart that remained jealous of Dottie. Greg was coming home. He might be blind, but he would be home with her. Before very long, Dottie wouldn't be alone. She would have Greg's arms to embrace her. She would have the comfort of his presence in the morning when she awoke.

I want the same. I don't want to be alone anymore. Why must I be alone?

She *didn't* have to be alone. Not completely.

Howard . . .

Did the devil smile as that name whispered in her mind?

For two weeks, Lucy had shopped at Safeway instead of the

Bannock Street Market. For two weeks, she had carefully avoided walking anywhere near Howard's business. For two weeks, she'd done what she thought—no, what she *knew*—was the right thing to do. And for two weeks, she'd felt more lonely than ever before. For two weeks, she'd been too tired to read the Word, her thoughts too disjointed to pray. She'd felt alone and abandoned—by her husband and by her God.

The kettle whistled, the sound sharp and piercing. Lucy pulled it from the burner.

"What's troubling you, Luce?"

"Nothing." She glanced over her shoulder, trying to look serene. "Nothing out of the ordinary, at least."

She should ask Dottie to pray for her. She should ask God to keep her from temptation.

But she didn't.

✳ ✳ ✳

Lucy entered the market a few minutes before the store closed, knowing it was less likely any customers would be there. She was right.

Howard stood behind the counter, writing in a notebook. He looked up as she approached. She suspected he'd been about to tell his last-minute customer that it was closing time.

His eyes widened when he saw who it was; then he straightened, laying down the pen. "Lucy."

"Howard."

There was a world of unspoken sentiment in their greeting, a confession of right and wrong, temptation and resistance, longing and regret. It wasn't until then that Lucy realized Howard wouldn't have pursued her if she stayed away. He wanted her— that she knew—but he would let her go.

Turn . . .

Run . . .

Resist . . .

Oh, that wretched voice of warning. She wanted it to be silent.

"I've missed you." His smile was tentative. "Did you find a better place to shop for groceries?"

She shook her head. "No."

"How've you been?"

Lonely. I've been lonely, Howard, and I don't want to be lonely anymore.

He untied his apron, removed it, and laid it on the counter. "I'm hungry. Would you care to join me for supper?"

Resist . . .

Flee . . .

"I was headed for Chloe's," he said, "but we could go somewhere else if you want."

"Chloe's is fine."

He stared at her for a long while before he said, "Give me a few minutes to close things up, and then we'll go."

Richard . . .

She nodded. "I'll wait."

34

Margo glanced up from Greg's letter to look at Dottie, who was seated on the sofa across from her. "At least he seems ready to do the right thing by you."

The hurt showed instantly in Dottie's eyes.

Her conscience tweaked, Margo said, "I didn't mean that quite as it sounded." Except she *had* meant it that way. Exactly that way.

"You mustn't think the worst of Greg, Mom. He's going to be your son-in-law, and he's the father of your grandchild." She drew a deep breath and let it out. "And I love him."

"It was love that got you into this predicament."

This time, Dottie pulled back, as if Margo had struck her.

What was it the Bible said about the tongue? It's a small thing, but it can do enormous damage. Well, perhaps that was true, but at least Margo was honest. Didn't truth count for something?

Truth with love.

She looked at the letter again. "I suppose we need to get ready if there's to be a wedding. We can have it here at the house. Considering the circumstances, the church would be inappropriate."

"Or maybe, *because* of the circumstances, the church would be the *most* appropriate place for our wedding to take place."

Margo stiffened. "What on earth do you mean?"

"Jesus gathered the sinners. He ate with them and walked with them. The Pharisees didn't like it, but Jesus did."

"Dottie, you cannot possibly—"

"Our Lord said every sin and blasphemy can be forgiven except blaspheming the Holy Spirit. Don't you believe Him?"

"Of course I do. But you—"

"Don't you think He's forgiven me?" Dottie stood. "I do. I believe I'm forgiven. I know I am. And after Christ forgave me, He told me to go and sin no more." She stepped forward and took the letter from Margo's hand. "But we've said all these things before, haven't we, Mom?"

"Yes," Margo answered with a heavy sigh, feeling weary. "We have."

"So I'm left to wonder this—what is it you think *you're* not forgiven for?"

She gaped at her daughter, stunned into silence.

"Think about it, Mom." Dottie turned on her heel and left the living room.

"What is it you think you're *not forgiven for?"*

How dare Dottie ask her such a thing! Whatever happened to young people respecting and honoring their parents? Dottie had no business taking that tone with her.

"What is it you think you're *not forgiven for?"*

Nothing. Of course she was forgiven. She'd followed God's laws unswervingly for years. She wasn't like many others who called themselves Christians. No, she'd stayed the course from the moment she gave her heart to God, and she'd done everything she could to make certain her children did the same. God was holy and He demanded holiness of His children.

I want you to show mercy, not offer sacrifices.

The unexpected whisper in her heart caused her to shiver. It was almost as if she'd heard an audible voice.

Oh, for pity's sake. How absurd! God spoke to people

through His written word. She was not about to become emotional like her daughter. Christianity wasn't about *feeling* good. It was about adhering to God's laws. It was about *being* good, *being* righteous, *being*—

Your righteous deeds are nothing but filthy rags.

Margo massaged her forehead with the tips of her fingers, wanting to rub away the troublesome words in her mind and heart.

I want you to show mercy, not offer sacrifices. . . . Your righteous deeds are nothing but filthy rags.

Unsettled, she rose and hurried into the kitchen. She needed to get busy with the remainder of her Saturday chores. Margo had no intention of allowing her misguided daughter's strange notions about God Almighty lead her astray. She had followed the Lord much longer than Dottie had. Her daughter still had a lot to learn about God's holy judgment. Much more.

35

Howard asked Georgia—the same waitress who served them the other time they came to Chloe's—to seat them in a booth in the back of the diner. "It's too windy near the door."

But it wasn't windy outside, and the diner wasn't hopping with activity on this Saturday evening. Lucy knew there was another reason for his request.

She was the reason.

Because we shouldn't be here together. Because I'm a married woman, and Howard has become more than a friend.

Avoiding Georgia's gaze, she felt color rising in her cheeks as she slid into the booth.

"I'll get some water and be right back," the waitress said.

As soon as Georgia was out of earshot, Howard leaned forward. "Are you all right?"

Lucy looked up, swallowed hard, and nodded. "Yes."

The look in his eyes said he didn't believe her. "We don't have to stay if you're uncomfortable."

"I'm not uncomfortable." She was a poor liar; she flushed hotter. "I'm fine. Really."

He lowered his voice. "I wouldn't do anything to hurt you."

I know, she mouthed, though no sound came out.

Georgia returned, and Lucy wasn't sure if she should be relieved or sorry for the interruption.

After another quick glance in Lucy's direction, Howard said, "Georgia, please bring us two of tonight's special, whatever it is. I've found the special is always a good choice."

"Sure thing, Mr. Baxter." Georgia pointed with her pen at the glasses she'd set on the table. "Either of you want something besides water to drink?"

"No, thank you. Water will be fine."

"Okay then. I'll have those specials right out."

Lucy reached for her glass and drew it toward her, although she didn't lift it to take a drink. Instead, she traced her finger around the moisture on the rim.

"I'm in love with you, Lucy."

Her heart thudded, then threatened to stop as she looked across the table at her companion.

"You must know I never meant for that to happen. You're married, and I'm fifteen years your senior. Those are just two reasons it shouldn't have happened." He looked as disturbed as she felt. "But it *did* happen, and I can't deny it. These last two weeks, not seeing you, it nearly killed me."

"Oh, Howard. You've been so kind to me. But—"

He lowered his voice even more. "I'm not asking you to do anything that would go against your beliefs. I know you're a religious woman, and I'm not looking for a mistress anyway."

At that word, Lucy felt the color drain from her face.

"I just want to be near you, Lucy. I just want to be able to spend time with you, and help you when you need help, and listen to you talk about your day, and offer a shoulder to cry on if you need one." He leaned forward, his gaze searching hers. "I'd never ask for more than you could give. I promise I wouldn't. We'll draw that proverbial line in the sand, one we won't cross. How's that?"

He made it sound so simple, so easy. Could it be?

"You're lonely, Lucy, and so am I. What's the harm in the two of us easing our loneliness in each other's company? Who would we be hurting?"

Lots of harm. Plenty of reasons. They could all be hurt—Richard the most. Or maybe not. Was it possible she and Howard could be together and never cross that line in the sand?

You've already crossed it, Lucy, her conscience warned. *You're already sitting where no married woman should be sitting.*

But she didn't want to hear that warning. She had a right to friendship and companionship, didn't she? Besides, she would *never* do anything to hurt Richard. Never.

Richard wouldn't want you to be lonely, a darker, uglier voice whispered. *He wouldn't mind you making new friends. It isn't wrong.*

"Lucy?"

"I love my husband, Howard."

"I know you do."

"But I . . . I care for you, too, and I want us to remain friends. As long as you understand that friends is all we can be. . . ."

"I understand."

She shook her head. "You mustn't say you love me again."

Howard slid his hand across the table and took hold of hers. "All right. If that's what you want. I'll do whatever you ask, Lucy. I won't say I love you. We'll just be friends. I won't require anything more than that."

There was something in his gaze and in his touch that belied his words. Something that made her heart *rat-a-tat* a frantic warning in her chest.

Resist . . .

Flee . . .

But there was nothing to resist, no reason to flee.

It's not wrong to be friends. He's alone, and I'm alone. What harm can there be in spending a little time together? None. None at all.

Glad that the matter was settled, Lucy slipped her hand from Howard's grasp as Georgia approached the table, carrying two large dinner plates on a tray.

Friends they would be. No one could object to that.

36

On Monday, Dottie left work at noon after telling her supervisor she had a doctor's appointment. Of course, she didn't tell the man the reason for it, nor did she tell him she had another appointment immediately afterward, that one with her minister.

As she sat on a hard wooden chair outside Pastor Danson's office, she silently repeated a line from a psalm she'd memorized.

"Your right hand supports me; Your help has made me great."

How contrary was that truth to what the world thought. It was God's gentleness that made a person great. He was a mighty God, but it was His compassion that led to strength.

She was thankful for His grace, grateful for His unmerited mercy and love.

"Dottie."

She looked up.

"Sorry I kept you waiting." Kevin Danson smiled at her from his office doorway.

Nerves exploded inside her. She had great respect for this humble man, a faithful shepherd for the small family of God who met here. And now she needed to confess her failures to him.

"Come in, Dottie."

She stood, and when Pastor Danson motioned for her to precede him, she did so, clutching her pocketbook with both hands.

Father God, help me.

The pastor's desk was set against a wall, leaving space on the opposite side of the room for a compact sofa and two old but comfortable chairs that faced it. Dottie sat on the sofa.

Pastor Danson sat on the chair closest to her. With a glance at her coveralls, he said, "You must have come from work."

"Yes."

He leaned back in the chair. "So tell me. What brings you to see me?"

Dottie drew a deep breath. "There's something I need to tell you." She looked at her hands, clenched in her lap. Oh, how she hated this. But it had to be done. "I . . . I'm pregnant, Pastor Danson." She waited for him to say something. When he didn't, she looked up again. "It's Greg's baby. We . . . we plan to marry as soon as he returns to Boise. We . . . we hope you'll let us get married in the church."

The man's gaze was filled with compassion, leaving no room for condemnation. "I see."

Those two simple words and the kindness in his eyes were enough to open the floodgates.

Dottie poured out the story of that careless night with Greg and of their repentance afterward. She told the pastor things she'd kept bottled up inside for weeks—the shame, the regret, the fear, the dread, even the pain of her mother's unwavering censure. As she spoke, she felt the balm of God's love touching wounds she hadn't known were still open and bleeding.

The words spent, Dottie fell silent at last.

Pastor Danson gave her an encouraging smile. "Dottie, you have given me hope."

"Hope?"

"Yes." He nodded. "When I see how you have taken responsibility for your wrong choices, it gives me hope. Too many people today are simply sorry when they are caught in their sin. They are not sorry for the sin itself. But you, dear girl, have shown me true repentance."

She returned his smile with a tentative one of her own.

"When Greg returns to Boise, the two of you come to see me so we can talk about your wedding."

"Then we can have it here? You'll perform the ceremony for us?"

"I'd be honored."

"Thank you, Pastor Danson," she whispered, her smile blossoming.

He leaned forward and patted the back of her right hand. "Give your mother some time. She loves you dearly. Perhaps I can have a word with her that might help."

Please, Lord. Let it help, Dottie prayed. *I don't want us to continue this way. I love her, too.*

To: *Penelope Maxfield, Boise, Idaho*
From: *PFC Frances Ballard*
Sunday, April 18, 1943

Hi, Sis.

I got your last letter a couple of weeks ago, but it's been hard to find time to write.

I completed my four weeks of basic training (I'm now officially a WAAC) and was immediately posted to an Aircraft Warning Service (AWS) unit in Massachusetts. I hope it's a temporary assignment! I still want to go overseas.

Be sure and note the new mailing address for me because I want to get lots of letters from home.

Here at the AWS, fifteen of us operate what they call a filter board. We track the paths of aircraft flying in the area. I'd love to tell you the work is exciting, but the truth is, the hours stretch out in endless boredom while we wait for something to happen. There just aren't that many aircraft flying around, and there certainly aren't any German ones to fight. Still, this isn't exactly what I had in mind when I enlisted. They say the army's learning that there are a lot more positions WAACs are capable of filling than the standard clerks, typists, stenographers, and motor-pool drivers. I sure hope that's true.

Did you know there are five WAAC officers serving Lt. Gen. Dwight D. Eisenhower at the Allied Forces Headquarters in North Africa? When they were en route from Great Britain, their ship was torpedoed. Two of them were rescued from the burning deck of their sinking ship by a British destroyer, and the other three made it into a lifeboat and were later rescued by another destroyer. Eventually, the WAACs were delivered to Algiers, but they'd lost everything—their uniforms, supplies, and all personal items.

*I probably shouldn't have told you that. You'll worry
something like that could happen to me. Don't worry.
Okay? Nothing's going to happen to me in Massachusetts.
Unless I die of boredom, that is.*

*I've requested a transfer to the 149th Post
Headquarters Company, the unit that's serving in Algiers.
They're sending more WAACs over there next month, and
I want to be one of them. It's doubtful I will be sent this
soon after completing my training. But you never know.
Doesn't hurt to try.*

*I'm not going to tell Mom and Dad about my transfer
request just yet. Dad wasn't crazy about the idea of
England as a possibility. He'll <u>hate</u> this. You know how he
is. "A woman's place is in the home" and all that. As far
as he's concerned, I should be married and having babies
at the ripe old age of 20. Where does he think I'm going to
find a husband when all the young men are off fighting?
That doesn't seem to occur to him. Besides, maybe I'm not
ready for marriage. And if I was, what better place to find
a husband than where just about the whole US Army is
posted. Right?*

*Speaking of marriage, I got a letter a couple of days ago
from Dottie King. She tells me Greg was wounded and is
being sent home. She said they're getting married right
away and that she'll have lots more to write me about
soon.*

*That sounded mysterious. Do you still see her out at the
base? What's going on? Can you tell me?*

*There's a girl in my unit that reminds me of Dottie. Her
name is Midge. She gets up early to read her Bible and
pray and never misses chapel on Sundays. In my
experience, there are plenty of folks who go to church and
they're no different than me. But Midge is different, same
as Dottie. Some of the other girls in the unit razz her about*

*what a goody-goody she is, but I haven't felt like joining in
their teasing. It's like she (and Dottie) have something I
haven't got. That bothers me. It never used to, but it does
now.*

*Know what I mean? Do you ever feel that way when
you're with Dottie? Or am I just crazy?*

*You'll never guess what I bought last week. A pair of
silk stockings! Can you believe it? I didn't ask if they were
from the black market. I hope not. I don't want to end up
in jail or anything.*

*Well, I've gone on long enough. Give Stuart my love
and give Alan and Evelyn a hug and a kiss from their
Auntie Frani. I love and miss you all.*

XXXX
Frances

37

After reading Penelope's letter from Frances for the third time, Stuart refolded the soft green stationery and slipped it into the matching envelope. Then he placed it on the night-stand and turned off the light. He lay down on the bed, one arm bent over his forehead, and stared through the darkness at the ceiling.

Maybe he should feel guilty about reading his wife's mail, but he didn't.

Where could Penelope be? She had no money to speak of. Perhaps a few dollars left from the weekly grocery fund. She'd packed only a small bag. Could she have joined the WAACs like Frances?

"Help me, God. Help me find her."

Stuart wasn't a religious man, but he would change that in an instant if it helped bring his wife back.

He thought of Penelope's friends, all of them churchgoing women. Penelope often made sarcastic remarks about the things they believed and the things they wouldn't do and the places they wouldn't go. But like Frances said in her letter, there was something different about them, especially Dottie King and Lucy Anderson. They didn't act like they were better than any-body else. In fact, just the opposite.

In the past two weeks, Lucy and Dottie—and Margo King,

too—had dropped by with hot casseroles and loaves of fresh-baked bread. More importantly, they'd listened as he'd gone on and on about how he missed Penelope and wondered where she'd gone. Dottie had offered to watch the children while he searched for his wife, and she'd said she could take care of them after he found a job, too.

That was more than his in-laws had done when they found out about Penelope. His mother-in-law might have wanted to help, but his father-in-law would never let her. He didn't believe in handouts to anybody, including his own family.

David Ballard had never liked his son-in-law. That hadn't mattered to Stuart in the early years of his marriage, but later it grated on him. It got worse after he injured his back and couldn't work. Ever since then, his father-in-law had looked at him as if he were a bug that needed smashed underfoot.

Kind of like the way Pen looked at me before she left.

He groaned softly.

Why had his marriage gone sour? He'd known Penelope was unhappy, but he hadn't realized it was so bad that she would leave him. Worse, she'd left her kids. How could she do that? He didn't understand.

If there was a God, why didn't He stop something like this from happening?

May 1943

38

Out of habit, Margo awoke before dawn. She tried to make herself go back to sleep. There was no reason to get up early on this Saturday. Lucy had cancelled today's meeting of the Victory Club.

"I'm working on a few ideas for future projects," she'd told Margo and Dottie, "but I don't have particulars yet."

Margo had nearly mentioned that one of their reasons for meeting was to pray, and there were plenty of people who needed prayer. Dottie and Greg, to start with. The needs of those two were too numerous to think about. Then there was Penelope, who hadn't been heard from in three weeks; and Clark, who was fighting in Africa; and Richard, who was flying missions over enemy territory. They could pray for 2nd Lieutenant Rhodes, her private pupil, who'd left this past week for Europe on some secret and undoubtedly dangerous mission. There were parents and wives in their churches who had lost sons and husbands in battle.

Needs. So many prayer needs.

But something in Lucy's demeanor had stopped Margo from saying any of that.

Margo frowned as she shoved aside the bedcovers and sat up.

This was unlike Lucy. She wasn't a quitter. Yet Margo had the distinct impression that was what the younger woman was doing—quitting. Perhaps without admitting it to herself. Lucy had lost heart and not just about her precious Victory Club. It went deeper than that.

Margo rose, put on her bathrobe and house slippers, and headed for the kitchen. If she couldn't sleep, she intended to treat herself to a rare cup of real, honest-to-goodness coffee.

Despite it being the first day of May, the house was chilly. Still, Margo didn't touch the thermostat. No point running the oil furnace when the sun would warm things up eventually. In the kitchen, she took her treasured Hills Brothers tin of rationed coffee from the cupboard and spooned out enough grounds to make two cups.

Clark had written that the army issued instant coffee in their rations kits. An abominable brew, in Margo's opinion, but apparently the soldiers were thankful for it. She supposed they were grateful for a good many things that she would find second-rate.

As she set the coffeepot on the burner, the shrill ring of the telephone broke the early morning silence. Margo spun toward the offending object, her heart hammering, her eyes wide. No one called at 6:00 AM unless it was bad news. Was it about Clark or Greg?

She hurried across the kitchen and picked up the receiver. "H-hello."

"Mrs. King?"

"Yes."

"It's me. Greg Wallace."

She leaned against the wall, willing her pulse to slow. "Greg?"

"Yes, ma'am. I'm back in the States. I was hoping I could talk to Dottie. Is she there?"

Margo was about to ask him if he had any idea what time it was.

"Mom?" Dottie—now standing in the hallway—sounded as fearful as Margo had felt moments before. "Who is it?

Margo held out the receiver. "It's Greg."

Her daughter's expression went from anxiety to ecstasy in an instant. She grabbed the handset and pressed it to her ear, holding it with two hands. "Greg? Greg, is it really you?"

Feeling the intruder, Margo returned to the stove. But she couldn't help overhearing one side of the conversation.

"Where are you? . . . I love you, too. . . . When will you be home? . . . Are you sure? . . . Oh, I love you, too. . . . I'm fine. Honest . . . yes . . . no . . . Thank God. Oh, thank God. . . . I talked to him last Saturday. . . . Yes, he said he would. . . . Did you tell your parents? . . . Greg, you shouldn't wait. . . . Well, I suppose that's a good idea. . . . Oh, honey, God's been merciful to us. . . . "

Margo didn't have to look to know her daughter was crying.

"His grace is sufficient," Dottie whispered. "His power works best in our weakness."

You no longer live under the requirements of the law. Instead, you live under the freedom of God's grace. The words of Scripture whispered in Margo's heart as she reached for a cup and filled it with the freshly brewed coffee, her hand shaking. *God blesses those who are merciful, for they will be shown mercy.*

"I love you, too. . . . Yes, I'll be there . . . yes . . . yes . . . I won't. . . . I love you, too. . . . I'll be waiting . . . Okay . . . I love you, Greg . . . yes . . . Good-bye, honey . . . I love you . . . me, too. . . . I love you. . . . Bye."

Holding her coffee cup with both hands, Margo turned around.

Dottie dried her eyes on her pajama sleeves. "He's coming home, Mom. He'll be here on Thursday's train."

You no longer live under the requirements of the law . . . freedom of God's grace . . . they will be shown mercy.

Those beautiful words, so simple, so gentle—known by Margo for years but never fully understood—echoed in her mind as she stared at her daughter.

Unexpectedly, she felt a hard place in her heart begin to soften.

39

Lucy shifted the telephone receiver from her right ear to her left. "I'm disappointed, too, Ruth, but I don't see any way around it. Mondays are always bad, but this one was the worst yet. My supervisor doubled my workload today. I won't be able to come to practice most weeks, and that's unfair to everyone else in the choir. I simply must resign for now."

"I suppose it can't be helped," the choir director replied with a sigh. "We all have to make sacrifices for the war effort."

"Maybe I'll be able to rejoin in a few months, if you'll let me."

"Of course we'll let you. You're welcome back at any time, dear. You know that."

Guilt knotted Lucy's stomach. "Thank you, Ruth. I appreciate your understanding." A headache pounded in her temples.

"Everyone will miss you. The choir won't be the same without your lovely voice. I do hope things at work will ease up soon."

"Thanks, Ruth. I appreciate your understanding more than you know."

"It's quite all right. Good-bye, dear."

"Good-bye."

I didn't lie, Lucy thought as she set the receiver in the cradle. *Things* are *hectic at work, and I* am *working longer hours.*

But that wasn't why she'd resigned from the choir. The truth was, she felt uncomfortable sitting in the loft with the other choir members, singing hymns to the Lord. She felt like . . . like a fraud.

I haven't done anything wrong, God. Why do I feel this way?

Oh, the silence was deafening.

"Well, I haven't," she argued aloud. "What's a few suppers with a friend? What harm is there in that? Can't a married woman have a few friends who aren't also married women?"

"Let us strip off every weight that slows us down, especially the sin that so easily trips us up."

But she hadn't sinned. She *hadn't*.

Restless and needing immediate activity, Lucy opened the back door and headed for the corner of the yard that would soon become her Victory Garden. Yesterday afternoon, Howard had tilled that section of the lawn with a borrowed rototiller, exposing the rich clay soil beneath.

Howard. Her friend. Any friend would have helped her as he had. Any friend.

"Remember," her pastor had said during yesterday's sermon, "you must not use legal cover or technicalities to mask moral failure."

A garden hoe leaned against the fence where she'd left it. She grabbed it and attacked the freshly tilled soil as if it were an enemy spy. Chopping, chopping, chopping.

Moral failure . . .

Technically, she'd told Ruth Norris the truth about her workload and why she'd quit the choir.

Just as, technically, she hadn't been unfaithful to her husband with Howard Baxter.

Who am I hurting? Nobody. Richard won't know, and besides, I haven't done anything wrong. Howard is my friend. Howard listens to me. He cares about me. He understands me. Who can it hurt?

Lucy choked back a sob as she released the hoe and let it fall. Then she dropped to her knees, weighed down beneath the truth.

Me. It's hurting me. And it's hurting Richard.

Howard wanted much more than to be her friend. He denied it with his mouth, but he said otherwise by his actions. He was a man and she was a woman, and something churned beneath the surface whenever they were together, something volatile and dangerous.

"Let us strip off every weight that slows us down, especially the sin that so easily trips us up."

"Oh, God," she whispered. "Help me."

V··· –Mail

To: Mrs. Richard Anderson, Boise, Idaho, U.S.A.
From: 1st Lt. Richard Anderson
Monday, April 12, 1943

My beloved Lucy,
It's with a heavy heart that I pick up this pen and write to you tonight.
On our bombing raid today, we lost XXXXXXXXXXXXXXXXXXXXX.
Good men. Good airmen. I've served with most of them since the first
week I arrived in England. They won't be easily replaced. I guess that's
true of all the Americans dying in this bloody war. It's hard not to get
discouraged. One morning I sit down to breakfast with a bunch
of guys who are my pals, and the next morning one of them isn't at
breakfast. Or two aren't there or three or five or ten aren't there. You
know what's hardest for me, Lucy? Not hating the Germans. I know,
as a follower of Christ, I'm not supposed to hate another person, but
how can I not hate the enemy? How, when they're killing innocent
people? That's something I keep asking God to tell me or show me,
but I haven't found the answer yet. Maybe it <u>helps</u> to hate them a little
as my plane roars down the runway on its next mission, those red
lights on the ground whirring past me as we lift off the ground. Once
we're in the air, all's quiet except for the drone of the B-17's engines
and the comforting whisper of the radio coming through my ear-
phones. That's what I've always loved about flying, that quiet when
I'm up above the earth. But now it's different. Now I know the lives
of the crew behind me depend on my skills, on the choices I make, on
my reactions when we come under fire. Now I know we're headed
where there'll be guns aimed right at us, and the Luftwaffe will be trying to knock us out of the sky, and if I don't make the right choices,
these boys could die. I could die. I know we need to be here,

Lucy. I know this war has to be fought and it has to be won. I just wish I was back home with you, holding you in my arms, loving you. I just wish things could be different.

Always,
Richard

40

Tuesday evening, Lucy waited across the street from Howard's store until she was certain the last customer had left. Then, in the gathering dusk, she crossed the street and entered the market.

Howard was walking toward the front entrance, keys in hand. He stopped when he saw her, and his face lit with a smile. "Lucy. What a nice surprise." His voice was like warm honey, sweet and tempting. "I wasn't expecting to see you tonight." He moved toward her.

Lucy stretched out her right arm to stop his forward momentum—and the embrace she knew would follow—by placing the flat of her hand against his chest.

His smile vanished, replaced by a frown. "What's wrong?"

"I . . . I can't see you anymore, Howard."

"What?" He placed his hand over hers, holding it to his chest. "Why? What's happened?"

"It isn't right for me to . . . to be with you. It isn't fair to . . . to Richard."

In the beginning, when Howard was just the owner of the corner market and Lucy was just his customer, he'd asked about Richard. In the beginning, Lucy had answered his questions, telling him many things about her husband. Lately, they'd avoided mentioning Richard altogether.

"Howard, I've tried to tell myself you and I are good friends and we're not doing anything wrong, but that's a lie. It *is* wrong, and it would hurt Richard if he learned about our . . . about us." Lucy slipped her hand from beneath Howard's and took a step backward. "I'm sorry. I never meant to mislead you or hurt you. I never meant to—"

"You can't do this, Lucy. I need you. You're like the air I breathe. You're essential for life. I love you."

"Howard, stop." She shook her head slowly. "You agreed not to say that again."

"Say it or not, it's true. You know that I love you, Lucy. Don't you? Don't you believe that I love you?"

She sighed in despair. "Yes. Yes, I believe you do. But, Howard, I'm not free to be loved."

"Then get free," he said, sounding gruff. "Divorce Richard and marry me. I'm here. I'll take care of you."

Lucy caught her breath. "I could never get a divorce." She braced her shoulder against the doorjamb for support.

"Why not? People do it all the time."

"Other people might," she whispered, feeling shame wash through her, "but I couldn't. I don't want a divorce. It goes against everything I believe about marriage. I forgot what I believed for a while. I ignored what I knew was true because I was lonely. I can't do that any longer."

"Lucy, that's—"

"I was selfish." Her voice grew stronger. "I was so selfish I refused to see I wasn't being fair to Richard. And it wasn't fair to you either. I love my husband and I don't want to divorce him. I want to be his wife and I want to have his children. I want to grow old with him. It's Richard I love. It's Richard I will always love. Until the day I die."

Silence fell between them.

A range of emotions flickered across Howard's face—anger, frustration, sorrow, defeat. After a long while, he opened his mouth, as if he might try to change her mind with a new argument. But then he pressed his lips together, gave his head a slow shake, turned on his heel and walked away, disappearing into the storeroom at the back of the store.

Lucy straightened away from the doorjamb, uncertain if she should follow him.

But for what purpose? she asked herself. Did she think she could make him feel better with more words? Did she think she could undo the harm she'd already done?

She couldn't. She had wronged Howard at the same time she'd wronged Richard. Perhaps not to the same degree, but she had wronged him all the same.

"I'm sorry," she said softly as she opened the door.

The chimes jingled overhead, a tuneless, empty, fitting sound.

41

As a Flying Fortress barreled westward down the Gowen Field runway, Dottie joined Lucy on a bench on the north side of Building B-301.

"Where's your mom?" Lucy asked when the roar of the B-17 had faded to a hum in the distance.

"She had a dentist appointment." Dottie opened her lunch box but didn't remove the food inside. She wasn't particularly hungry. Softly, she said, "I think my supervisor's guessed I'm pregnant."

"Are you sure?" Lucy asked. "You don't show. If I didn't already know, I don't think I could tell."

"You could if I wasn't wearing these coveralls. None of my clothes fit right." She knew she would be dismissed from her position as soon as her pregnancy was confirmed. Should she quit now or wait it out? *I'll wait. Greg will be home soon. He'll know what I should do.* Thinking about Greg and their upcoming nuptials made her feel better.

Lucy unwrapped her sandwich. "Will your mother be able to go with you to meet Greg's train?"

"No. She has exams to give. Greg's parents will take me."

"Do they know about the baby?"

Dottie shook her head. "Greg wants to tell them in person. I thought they should know before now, but he insisted."

Lucy stared toward the mountains, and her voice grew as distant as the look in her eyes. "That's good. He wants to take responsibility for his choices. We all have to do that, sooner or later."

"Luce, what's bothering you?"

Her friend drew a deep breath. Tears glittered in her eyes but they didn't fall. She looked brittle, as if she would shatter if touched.

Dottie wanted to comfort Lucy, but she wasn't sure how to go about it. Lucy was the strong one, the one who reached out and comforted others. It felt awkward to have the roles reversed.

Setting aside her lunch box, Dottie asked, "What is it? What's wrong?"

"Oh, Dottie." Lucy covered her face with her hands. "I've made such a mess of things. I . . . I almost had an affair." She whispered the words, but her pain was audible. "I've been unfaithful."

"*What?*" Dottie could imagine this of many people but never Lucy Anderson. "I don't believe it."

Her face still hidden, Lucy nodded. "I betrayed Richard."

"But you didn't actually *do* anything. Right? You said *almost*."

For a long while, Lucy was silent, unmoving. So still, Dottie wondered if Lucy had heard the question. But then, at last, she spoke.

"I was unfaithful in my heart, and that's more than enough. 'From the heart come evil thoughts, murder, adultery.... These are what defile you.' That's what the Word says. It's my heart that's the problem." Lucy lowered her hands but kept her eyes closed.

Dottie nearly asked who the man was. Then she remembered that Saturday in March when she went to Lucy's apartment. She remembered the man—Mr. Baxter—who was with Lucy. She remembered the sparkle in Lucy's eyes and the way the two smiled at each other.

"The grocer," she said softly, answering her own unspoken question.

"Yes." Lucy met her gaze. "Last night I told him I couldn't see him anymore. If we kept on the way we were, I . . . I would have . . . my sin wouldn't have been only in my heart. I know it." Her breath caught on a sob. "Oh, Dottie, it hurts. It hurts so bad."

Dottie felt way out of her depth. What should she say? What counsel could she give?

"I never meant to hurt anyone. I love Richard and would never . . . I didn't mean . . . I . . . I—" She broke off suddenly and let the tears fall. "I haven't been able to pray. Not really. When I do, I don't feel like my prayers go anywhere. I quit the choir because I felt so guilty." Her tone grew harsh. "It was easier to quit the choir than to quit what I was doing. I feel so far from God. I feel more alone than ever before."

This was something Dottie understood. "If you ask God, He forgives you. No matter what we've done, our Father forgives when we ask and repent. He's right here beside you. He hasn't gone anywhere. He's here."

"I know." Lucy choked back a sob. "I know."

"You did the right thing, Luce. It wasn't the easy thing, but it was the right one. It'll get better. You'll see. It'll get better."

Dottie slipped an arm around her friend and drew her close. Together, they wept.

42

"*You did the right thing, Luce. It wasn't the easy thing, but it was the right one.*"

As a moonless night fell over Boise, Lucy sat on the stoop of her apartment, wrapped in a bulky sweater to ward off the chill. Her eyes were puffy and her nose stuffed from her latest round of tears.

"*It'll get better. You'll see. It'll get better.*"

Would it? Would she stop hating herself for her weakness, for her wrong decisions, for her sinful nature? Would her guilt ever ease? Would a night come when she slept once again in peace?

She hugged her legs to her chest and looked upward. Stars pinpricked the black canopy of sky. It was four-thirty in the morning in England. Perhaps Richard was up, beginning his day, and looking at the same sky. Perhaps he could see that same bright star she stared at now.

"If you can see that star, darling, please know I'm sorry. Please know I love you."

Ah, but those were just words. Anyone could say "I love you" and still be unloving. Real love was an action, a day-in and day-out way of living. A conscious choice. Had she shown love for Richard when she'd given her thoughts, her attention, her affection, to another man?

"No."

Father God, I'm a fraud. How will I face Richard when he comes home again? Why didn't I listen to Your voice of warning? Why did I choose momentary comfort over doing what's right? Why did I listen to the enemy's lies instead of Your truths?

Satan was a liar and the father of lies. She'd heard that from the beginning of her Christian walk. But only now did she understand what it meant. The devil took the truth and twisted it, making it palatable while lacing it with poison. He'd taken a friend—and that's what Howard was in the beginning—and then told her to ignore the warning signs when things began to change between them. He'd taken her loneliness and told her she deserved something better, something different—different from what tens of thousands of other wives, girlfriends, parents, siblings, and friends felt.

Pride. Selfishness. The pursuit of happiness rather than the pursuit of righteousness.

"You did the right thing, Luce. It wasn't the easy thing, but it was the right one."

Looking again at the bright star above the eastern horizon, Lucy stood.

"Richard, if you can see that star, I hope you'll know I'll never be foolish like this again. I hope we'll have many years together so I can prove my love for you in a thousand ways. I don't expect I'll be a perfect wife, but I promise I'll never again betray you with my heart."

V··· —Mail

To: Corporal Clark King, APO, N.Y.P.E.

From: Margo King

Wednesday, May 5, 1943

Dear Clark,

Today the mailman brought us four of your letters. You can't imagine how wonderful it feels when I see your handwriting on those envelopes. After dinner, Dottie and I sat in the living room and took turns reading them aloud to each other. We had to guess what you wrote in a few places because the censors had been busy with their scissors. It used to be they never cut anything you said. Are you being more open in what you say, or are they being more careful about what gets through?

You'll be pleased to know that Dottie and I have become creative in the kitchen. We observe meatless Tuesdays and Fridays and have invented several new casserole dishes that we intend to feed you when you return to the States. We eat lots of eggs. Those are never in short supply at the market. But we do miss having coffee, butter, and sugar on a regular basis. Neither of us cares much for fish, but we make do when we have to, usually on Fridays. We've even started having creamed chipped beef on toast once a week. I understand you GIs call it SOS. A cry of distress seems applicable since I find it, at best, merely tolerable. But Dottie likes it.

No one has heard a word from Penelope Maxfield in the weeks (almost a month) since she left town. Stuart is still looking for a job that he can physically handle, but hasn't found one yet.

The big news here, of course, is that Greg is scheduled to arrive in Boise tomorrow. He's been honorably discharged from the army and is coming home for good, Purple Heart in hand. Dottie and Greg plan to marry as soon as they get their blood tests and the marriage license. It will be a small affair at our church with Pastor Danson officiating. I'm sure Dottie will write you all about it when she can.

Your sister doesn't know yet where she and Greg will live after they're married. I've invited them to stay with me. God alone knows what Greg will do for a living if he doesn't regain his eyesight. Dottie seems oblivious to the difficulties that await them.

But perhaps I'm wrong about that. Perhaps your sister understands how hard it will be but has a greater understanding of God's mercy and grace than I do. You and Dottie have always been joyful in your faith, and it has occurred to me lately that I've often tried to steal that joy away from you because I didn't share it.

Pastor Danson said something in his sermon on Sunday that has stayed with me all week. In the book of John, Jesus told the Pharisees, who were accusing Him of breaking the Sabbath rules, that He does only what He sees the Father doing. "Jesus lived His life to please the Father," Pastor Danson said, and then he added, "The Pharisees followed the law in such a way that they missed God's heart."

Clark, I think that's what I've done all these years. I've been a believer who followed every dot and tittle of the law but who missed God's heart. I hope you and your sister will forgive me for the mistakes I've made because of it.

I'm out of space and must close. I pray for you every day, Son, and I love you dearly.

Mother

43

It had been a gray and frigid January morning when Dottie last stood on this depot platform, saying good-bye to the man she loved. Four months ago. That was all. Only four months, and yet enough time for a young soldier to go to England, to Africa, to be wounded and hospitalized, and finally to sail back to America again.

Four months that seemed a lifetime.

On that Thursday afternoon in May, the day of Greg's much anticipated return to Boise, the sky was dotted with puffy, white clouds, and the sun was warm on Dottie's shoulders. The trees sported green leaves that waved gently in the breeze. Other people crowded the platform, but Dottie paid no attention to them. She had eyes only for the bend in the railroad tracks where, any moment, she expected to see the train come chugging into view.

Hurry, Greg. Hurry.

She pressed her pocketbook against her abdomen—and the child her body nurtured within—and hoped the full skirt of her dress would conceal the evidence of her pregnancy for a short while longer. It felt dishonest to stand here with her future in-laws and not say anything about her and Greg's wedding plans. His parents knew, of course, that the two planned to marry. They just didn't know how soon, nor the reason for their necessary haste.

Dottie wished her mother was with her. A few weeks ago, she wouldn't have wanted it, but something had changed between them. Dottie had a hard time defining what that *something* was. Was it because Margo King at last accepted her daughter's pregnancy and plans to marry or was it something more than that?

Last night, the two of them had sat in their living room, reading Clark's letters aloud. Her mother had smiled—even laughed a few times—at some amusing incidents Clark related. She'd seemed . . . *peaceful?* Margo King peaceful?

Dottie was pulled from her reverie by the longed-for sounds of the approaching train. The yellow engine rolled into view, and Dottie's heart leapt for joy. Nancy Wallace, her future mother-in-law, took hold of Dottie's right arm, the touch both giving and taking comfort.

Amid squeaks and clanks, the *whoosh* of escaping air, and voices rising in expectation, the train rolled to a stop. Dottie looked from one railcar exit to another as passengers disembarked.

The waiting, the watching, was agony.

Soldiers and sailors and airmen. Those arriving. Those departing. Mothers with young children in tow. Old men with gray hair and bent shoulders. People embracing. People laughing. People crying.

Scarcely able to breathe, Dottie covered Nancy's hand on her arm and held on tight.

What if Greg wasn't on this train? What if something had gone wrong? What if he'd fallen ill on his way to Boise and had been taken back to that hospital in the East? What if . . . ?

Then she saw him, standing on the step of the last car, a thin figure in a too-large, light brown uniform. Her chest tightened at the angry scar that sliced the left side of his handsome face from forehead to jawline and the white bandages that covered his eyes.

As a fellow soldier helped Greg from the train, Dottie's heart went to its knees.

Oh, Father. Oh, Jesus. She broke free of his mother's grasp and pushed her way through the crowd on the platform. "Greg!"

He turned his head at the sound of her voice. A smile—oh, that wonderful, familiar smile—curved his mouth.

"Greg!"

A moment later, she was in his arms, pressed close against him, her tears dampening his uniform.

"Hey, princess," he whispered near her ear.

She breathed in, his scent both familiar and foreign. "Oh, Greg. Oh, Greg. It's really you. You're home at last. Oh, darling. You're here. Oh, Greg. Oh, Greg."

"It's me, sweetheart. I'm home. Let's get married."

Dottie hadn't expected to become a blubbering fool, but she couldn't help herself. All she could do was cry and say his name, over and over again.

He pressed his face against her hair, and she felt his warm breath on her scalp. "It's okay, Dottie. It's okay. I'm home. Everything's going to be all right."

"Greg, darling."

"Son."

At the sound of his parents' voices, Greg lifted his head away from Dottie's. "Mom. Dad."

Dottie withdrew from his embrace and watched through tear-blurred eyes as Greg was hugged by his mother, then his father. She hated to admit it, but she didn't want to share him with anyone. Not even with his parents. Not even for a few moments. She wanted him all to herself. She was greedy for his touch, for his kisses, for the sound of his voice in her ears. Greedy to be reassured that he was real and not a dream.

"How was your trip?" his mother asked.

"Long." Greg's voice was laced with fatigue, saying far more than his one-word reply.

"Let's get you home," his father said.

"Sounds good to me."

The soldier who'd helped Greg from the train stepped forward. "This is his gear." He passed a duffel bag to Ken Wallace.

"Thanks, Dan," Greg said. "You've been a big help."

"Glad to do it, buddy. You take care of yourself." The soldier leaned toward Greg and, in a stage whisper, said, "Your girl's every bit as pretty as you said she was. You're one lucky guy." He gave Dottie a nod and a wink as he spoke. Then he climbed onto the train, disappearing into the passenger car.

Greg extended his hand, as though searching for something, a tellingly helpless gesture that brought tears back to Dottie's eyes.

"I'm here, Greg." She took hold of his hand and squeezed his fingers. "I'm right beside you."

I'll always be right beside you.

44

Margo was supposed to be grading the tests on her desk, but she found it impossible to focus her thoughts.

She glanced at her watch. Unless something delayed the train, Greg had arrived in Boise by now.

She rose from her desk chair and walked to the window. Young airmen moved about the base, some in Jeeps, some on foot. So young. How many, after they left here, would come back like Greg, wounded, broken? Worse, how many would never return at all?

Margo envied Nancy Wallace having her son back. She was sorry Greg was blind, but at least he was alive. At least he was home. Clark was still over there, fighting, in danger.

But Clark wouldn't want her to be envious, would he? Clark would want her to trust God—for this day, for each tomorrow.

You and Dottie have always been joyful in your faith—she'd written last night. *I've been a believer who followed every dot and tittle of the law but who missed God's heart.*

Grace. Mercy. Trust. Faith. They were words she had known, heard, read, and repeated for many years. But she suspected her son and daughter understood their meanings better than she.

She drew a deep breath and released it slowly.

God, I don't want to miss Your heart. Reveal it to me. Help me to understand.

She hesitated. This kind of prayer was foreign to her. It was so
. . . personal and . . . intimate. Yet she had to go on. She didn't
want to go back to her old ways.

*Father, I don't want to be a Pharisee, caught up in the rules and
the law. I want to obey You out of love, not fear. I want to love You
like the woman with the expensive perfume. With extravagant
abandon. Help me to be extravagant in my worship.*

She turned and leaned against the windowsill, her gaze moving about the classroom. She thought of the many different
men—boys, really—who had sat at these desks during the past
year. How many of them might she have impacted for Christ
had her attitude been different?

*So now there is no condemnation for those who belong to Christ
Jesus.*

How was it possible, she wondered, to be a Christian—to belong to Christ Jesus—for so many years and miss the meaning of
that verse? No condemnation. None. Not for getting pregnant
out of wedlock. Not for being so unlovable that her husband di-
vorced her. Not even for being an imperfect mother.

How had she managed to recognize God's holy nature but
miss the expansiveness of His love?

She recalled another Scripture, the one Dottie alluded to a
couple of weeks before. Jesus asked the woman caught in adultery, "Where are your accusers? Didn't even one of them condemn you?" And when the woman answered, "No, Lord," He
said, "Neither do I. Go and sin no more."

Jesus didn't condemn the adulteress, and He didn't condemn
Margo King. Amazing!

A soft tapping drew her gaze toward the classroom doorway.

Lucy stood in the opening. "Ready?"

Ready for what? Margo straightened away from the windowsill.

"It's five o'clock. We'd better hurry if we don't want to miss
the bus."

Incredulous, Margo looked at her watch. "Is it that late already?" She went to her desk and gathered the exam papers, then shoved them unceremoniously into an old leather briefcase. From the bottom drawer, she retrieved her lunch box and purse. "It's a good thing you came by," she said as she walked toward the door. "No telling how long I would have stood there woolgathering."

"Thinking about Dottie and Greg?"

"Yes. And other things besides."

Lucy lifted her eyebrows in question, waiting for elaboration. Margo shook her head.

Her friend graciously accepted the refusal by changing the subject. "I hope Dottie will be able to come with you to the Victory Club meeting on Saturday."

"We're going to continue?" Margo glanced at her companion. "I thought you'd lost heart about our little club. Ever since Penelope left, I—"

"No," Lucy interrupted softly. "I haven't lost heart. I just got off track for a while. We're told that where two or three are gathered in Jesus' name, there He is. Well, there are still three of us and still many things we can do to help others."

Margo might have asked what their next project would be, but they were joined by several other women headed for the bus stop, and the opportunity vanished.

45

Hands clasped, Dottie and Greg sat beside each other on the top step of the Wallaces' front porch.

Greg faced forward, as if staring at the street through the bindings that hid his beautiful brown eyes from Dottie's view. He'd lost weight since she last saw him. His uniform was a size or two too large. His coal black hair was mussed on the crown of his head, poking up at odd angles above the white gauze.

Dottie longed to unwrap the bandages from his beloved face. She longed to smooth his disheveled hair. She longed to stroke his cheeks with her fingertips and to kiss the scar with her lips and tell him how handsome he was. No scar would change that. Being sightless wouldn't change that. Nothing would ever change that.

"Let me stay," she pleaded softly.

"No, Dottie. I need to do this alone. It's my responsibility."

"But—"

"I *need* to do it." He brought her hand to his lips and kissed the back of her fingers. "Let's not argue. Okay? You go on home. I'll tell my folks everything after you're gone. I need to do this alone."

She wanted to ask why, but he answered before she could.

"I don't want you or my parents feeling like you've got to take care of me. I don't know if I'll be blind forever 'cause even the doctors don't know yet. But if I am, I've got to know how to take care of myself so I can take care of you and our baby. That needs to start now, with me accepting responsibility for what's happened and what's going to happen. I've got to make my parents understand that, and I don't think I can if you're here. Maybe that doesn't make sense to you, but it's the way I feel."

He was right. It didn't make sense to her. But she wouldn't argue. "I love you, Greg."

"I love you, too." He stood, drawing her with him. "Want me to ask Dad to drive you home?"

She shook her head, then remembered he couldn't see her silent answer. "No. I'll walk. It's a beautiful evening."

"I'll call you later." Greg rested his hands on her shoulders. "Did you arrange for tomorrow off?"

"Yes."

"Good. In the morning we'll go downtown, get our blood tests, and apply for our license. Afterward we'll see Pastor Danson to make arrangements for next week." He smiled—the same smile that always caused her heart to skip a beat—and leaned down to kiss her cheek.

Dottie wrapped her arms around his chest and pressed her face against his shirt. "I'm afraid to leave. It's like I'm afraid something will go wrong and when I get up in the morning you won't be here or you'll have changed your mind and not want to marry me."

"That could never happen, princess."

"What if your parents try to talk you out of it?"

"They won't."

"But what if—"

He buried his face in her hair. "They couldn't talk me out of it even if they tried." His voice deepened, a husky caress on her heart. "But they won't try. They love you, Dottie, and they know we love each other. They might not be happy about the circumstances, but they won't be sorry about our marriage."

A thousand more worries popped into her head all at the same time: *Where will we live? What kind of work will you do? When should I give notice at the base? or should I wait until they let me go because I'm pregnant? Will your veteran's disability pay be enough to support a family?*

" 'Don't let your heart be troubled,' " Greg whispered, as if reading her heart. "Don't be fearful. He's told us He'll take care of us, and He will."

Dottie believed what God said was true. She loved Greg, and they both loved the Lord. So why wouldn't the fear and worries go away?

After saying her good-byes to Greg and his parents, she started for home. She didn't hurry. Her mother would be waiting with lots of questions, but Dottie needed time to reflect, to pray, and hopefully, to find answers.

She hadn't realized, until Greg stepped off that train this afternoon, how much her life was about to change. Nor had she realized that change, even when it was something she'd wanted for a long time, could be scary.

Why is that, Lord?

Strange, how confident she'd been in the weeks since she realized she was pregnant with Greg's baby. Even when her mother condemned her, Dottie hadn't wavered in her convictions about God's love, forgiveness, and divine control. Yet today, all her assurance had turned to ashes. Why? Why now, when she had less to be afraid of than before?

"When I am afraid, I will put my trust in You. I praise God for what He has promised. I trust in God, so why should I be afraid? What can mere mortals do to me?"

She stopped walking, closed her eyes, and allowed peace to flow through her.

"I trust in God, so why should I be afraid?"

She was going to hold on to that truth for all she was worth.

V··· —Mail

To: 1st Lt. Richard Anderson, APO, N.Y.P.E.
From: Lucy Anderson
Saturday, May 8, 1943

My darling Richard,

I received a letter from you this week that was less than a month
old. Sometimes it's hard, reading what you wrote while knowing so
much more has transpired since you wrote it. In this most recent
letter, you reported the loss of some men, and my heart broke over
the pain I felt in your words.

I've had some emotional and spiritual struggles of my own, and
someday, when we are together, with your arms around me and we
have all the time we need to talk and talk and talk, I will tell you about
them. It's enough for now for me to say that I am well and God is
watching over me and I love you. You needn't worry about any of that.

Word reached us of the American and British victories in Tunisia
with the taking of Bizerte and Tunis. The general belief is that the
North African campaign will end before another week is out. One of
the officers at Gowen Field told me our forces should be in Italy by the
end of summer. He says that's thanks to Allied bombing. If I've learned
anything in the months I've worked for the armed forces, it's that pilots
and their crews believe wars are won from the air. Without exception.
You're a brash lot of braggarts! (And I say that with all my love.)

Greg Wallace arrived in Boise on Thursday. He and Dottie plan to
marry next week. I went by to see him yesterday after work. I confess I
was thankful that he couldn't see my shock. He is painfully thin, and his
face bears an ugly scar.

I couldn't help but think of you, darling. How would I feel if you were
seriously injured? Be safe, Richard. Be careful. Please. Ask God to
set angels on the wings of your Flying Fortress. Ask the Holy Spirit to

guide you through the skies. That's what I'm doing. Right now as I write this, that's what I'm praying for you.

Our little Victory Club met again this morning after a two-week respite. I can't say we've been <u>victorious</u> lately. It's just the three of us now that Penelope is gone. (Still not a word from her or about her. It's as if she disappeared off the face of the earth.) We decided today that it's Pen's family who we'll strive to help for the foreseeable future. Stuart found employment at one of the movie theaters and begins work next week. We're going to make sure there's always someone available to watch the children and to prepare meals.

Before I run out of space, I must share something I read in Philippians this morning: "Fix your thoughts on what is true, and honorable, and right, and pure, and lovely, and admirable. Think about things that are excellent and worthy of praise. Keep putting into practice all you learned and received from me—everything you heard from me and saw me doing. Then the God of peace will be with you."

Richard, I lost sight of that for a time this spring. My thoughts weren't fixed on the right things. They were selfish thoughts. I forgot that my faith has to be <u>practiced</u>. It isn't stagnant. It's active. I have to live it each day anew, just like I need food and water each day. I hope I never lose sight of that again. With God's help, I won't.

I love you, darling.
Lucy

46

Stuart tugged the sleeves of the pink sweater over his daughter's pudgy arms, then turned her on the stool to face him while he attempted to fasten the top pearl-like button. Attempted and failed.

"Whoever invented these tiny things should be hanged," he muttered.

"Pretty." Evelyn rubbed one sleeve against her cheek.

That simple word in his little girl's cherubic voice erased the scowl on Stuart's forehead. "Yeah, you're right, Evy. It is pretty." He kissed the tip of her nose. "And so are you."

She giggled.

"Ah, forget the button." He took her hand and helped her down from the stool. "Alan," he called in the general direction of the children's bedroom, "let's go."

"Comin', Daddy."

Minutes later, with both of his children sitting in the backseat of the Buick, Stuart drove out of the detached garage and into the alley. Gas rationing and limited income had made driving the automobile a rare experience, but he figured a wedding was a good excuse. Especially since he was scheduled to begin his new job the next day.

A month ago, Stuart would have found a reason to stay home. He was never comfortable in church settings; he felt like an outsider. Besides, a month ago he'd known the bride and her mother only slightly and had met the bridegroom once. But things had changed since then. Dottie and Margo King had been kind beyond words, babysitting and making meals for him and the children. They had proven to be true friends, giving without asking for anything in return. When Dottie had given him the invitation to her wedding, he knew—church or no church—that he had to come and offer his congratulations.

East Boise Community was a small, wood-frame building. The welcome sign out front announced the times of the Sunday and Wednesday services in fat black letters. Stuart parked the Buick on the street near the sign, then walked with his children to the front entrance. The door was propped open, letting in fresh spring air. Stuart paused in the narthex. It was empty, but he heard voices coming from the sanctuary.

He'd been told this would be a small, private wedding, but he hadn't realized how small. Dottie, wearing a soft blue dress and a matching blue hat with netting that covered her forehead and eyes, stood near the altar with Greg. The two of them talked with the pastor. Lucy Anderson, the matron of honor, stood on the bride's left. Stuart didn't know the best man, who stood on the groom's right. Margo King sat in the front pew with people he presumed were Greg's parents.

Dottie smiled when she saw Stuart enter the sanctuary. "Here they are." She left Greg and the others at the altar and came to greet him. "I'm so glad you came." She glanced at the children. "Hello, Alan. Hello, Evelyn."

"Are we late?" Stuart asked.

"No, but now that you're here, we can begin." She led the way up the center aisle, pausing long enough to motion for Stuart to join the three family members in the front pew.

As her daughter had done moments before, Margo gave him a welcoming smile, then slid to her right to make more room on the pew. She held out her arms for Evelyn, drawing the little girl onto her lap. Alan sat beside his father, looking uncomfortable in his suit, tie, and polished shoes. Stuart knew how he felt.

"Dearly beloved," the pastor began, drawing all eyes toward him.

Stuart and Penelope had been married at the country club by a judge who was a friend of David Ballard. The wedding ceremony was followed by a reception with lots of fancy food and fine champagne, an orchestra, and dancing. Eight million Americans had been unemployed in 1936, but no one would have known it that night. The Ballards spared no expense. The guest list ran into the hundreds and included the names of prominent members of Boise society—lawyers, state senators, bankers, and business owners. Even at the age of nineteen, Stuart understood the affair was a production meant to impress others, not something Penelope's dad did out of love for his eldest daughter.

Poor Pen.

Stuart had believed his love could make up for what Penelope's father held back from her. He'd thought Penelope was as happy as he was. Stuart never made much money, but they did okay. He loved being a husband and a dad. He had been planning to start his own landscaping business when the war came along and threw a monkey wrench into his plans.

If he had to pick a point when things started going wrong for him and Penelope, it would be right after the Japanese attacked Pearl Harbor. Things went from bad to worse after he fell off that cursed ladder.

Swallowing a sigh, Stuart shook off his thoughts and focused his attention on the bride and groom. Only it hurt to do that. Dottie was radiant. She looked at Greg as if he'd hung the moon and the stars.

Lucky guy.

When was the last time Penelope looked at me like that? Stuart couldn't remember. Seemed forever. He hoped things would work out better for these two. It wasn't as if they didn't have a strike against them, what with Greg being blinded in the war.

Blind, but still lucky.

As he watched, the couple bowed their heads in prayer above their joined hands. United. The two of them were united in love, united in faith.

Maybe it was their faith that would make the difference. Stuart hoped so, for their sake. Love hadn't been enough for Stuart and Penelope Maxfield, and they sure hadn't had any faith in God to unite them.

47

Standing to the left and behind the bride, Lucy wiped her eyes with a handkerchief. Her feelings throughout the ceremony had been bittersweet. Sweet with gladness for the bride and groom, understanding the joy they felt, memories of her own wedding day so clear in her mind. Bitter because of the way she'd failed Richard, failed herself, failed her Lord.

You were running the race so well. Who has held you back from following the truth?

The verse from Galatians pierced her heart, as it had when she read it a few days ago. Who'd held her back from her walk of faith? She had. She'd held herself back. She'd given in to her selfish nature, her willfulness, her pride. She wanted to hang her head in shame.

"I now pronounce you man and wife."

Hearing the pastor's words, Lucy shook off her guilty thoughts. This was not the time to dwell on herself and her mistakes. This was a day to think of others and to celebrate with them.

When it was her turn to congratulate the newlyweds, Lucy embraced Dottie and whispered in her ear, "God bless you both."

"He already has." Dottie drew back and met Lucy's gaze. Her smile was breathtaking, innocent, stunning. "God's grace is so amazing, isn't it? Thanks for being my matron of honor."

"I'm honored you asked me." Lucy turned toward the groom, put her hands on his shoulders, and said, "God bless you, Greg. May your marriage be filled with joy."

"Thanks, Lucy."

She kissed his left cheek, below the white gauze bandage. "Stay close to the Lord and you won't go wrong."

This wasn't the sort of wedding where people lingered for punch, cake, and the opening of gifts. The newlyweds weren't going away for a honeymoon, and there was no tossing of the bouquet. Within half an hour, everyone dispersed.

"Can I give you a lift home?" Stuart asked Lucy as he and his children followed her outside into the gathering dusk.

Lucy glanced at the automobile parked in front of the church. She wasn't looking forward to the solitary walk home. "Are you sure you wouldn't mind, Stuart? I know how precious gas is."

"I don't mind. It's a treat for the kids to go for a ride. Haven't had the Buick out of the garage in ages."

"All right, then. I accept."

Stuart walked to the car and opened the front and back passenger doors. Alan climbed onto the backseat, then Stuart lifted Evelyn into place beside her brother while Lucy slid onto the front seat. A minute later, Stuart was behind the wheel and pulling away from the curb.

"Do you think they'll make it?" he asked after a short silence.

Lucy stared out the window. "Yes, I'm sure they will."

"What makes you so sure?"

It was a fair question. Hadn't Penelope loved Stuart when they married? And yet she left him. Didn't Lucy love Richard? And yet she betrayed him with her heart. How could she be certain Dottie and Greg would succeed where others failed?

Stuart didn't wait for Lucy's answer. "Dottie's pregnant, isn't she?"

"She didn't tell you?" Lucy looked over at Stuart. "I thought she might have."

He gave his head a slow shake. "No, she didn't tell me. But something about her appearance tonight made me remember Pen when she was expecting. That and their hurry to get married as soon as Greg got back from the war. It wasn't hard to put two and two together and come up with four. If she wasn't expecting, I figured they'd have waited at least a couple more weeks so they could plan a wedding with all the frills."

"You're very astute."

"Not really. If I was, I'd've known what Pen was planning."

Hearing the pain in his voice, Lucy's heart went out to him. "Still no word of her whereabouts?"

"Not to me, but I suspect her mother's heard something." He cast a quick glance in Lucy's direction. "Last time Julia came by to see the kids, I could tell she wasn't as worried about Pen as she was before."

"But surely Mrs. Ballard would tell you if she knew where Penelope is."

Stuart's laugh was tinged with bitterness. "I doubt Pen told her that. She most likely called to say she was okay. She wouldn't want her dad to discover her location. She'd be afraid he'd come after her. He's never liked me, but he hates failure in his children more."

"I'm sorry," Lucy said softly. Sorry that Penelope's father was harsh and cold? Sorry Stuart's marriage had faltered and his heart was broken? Sorry for bringing up a tender subject? Even she wasn't certain which it was. Maybe all three.

"Yeah. Me, too."

They fell into silence, the remainder of the drive accompanied by the hum of the Buick's engine and three-year-old Evelyn's singsong voice as she chattered in the backseat.

It wasn't until Stuart stopped the car in front of her apartment that Lucy looked at him again. "Perhaps I shouldn't ask this. It isn't any of my business, and you're welcome to tell me to stay out of yours if you want. But I . . . I'm curious. Would you take Pen back if she wanted to return?"

Would Richard take me back if he learned how I failed him?

Stuart sighed heavily as his hands tightened on the steering wheel. "I don't know."

His response made her wince on the inside. When the day came—as it most surely would come—that she confessed her sins to her husband, she hoped Richard would respond more positively than Stuart just did.

48

Dottie stood in the bathroom of the bridal suite, staring into the mirror above the sink. But it wasn't her reflection she saw. Instead, she remembered the night she and Greg gave in to their desire, breaking their vow of chastity.

Oh, Father. Help me put that night behind me.

On that night, they hadn't dined on room service while the lights of Boise came alive outside.

You've removed my sin as far as the east is from the west. Help me never to forget that.

On that night, Dottie hadn't excused herself, gone into the bathroom, and donned a pink negligee, a gift from her mother.

Let us build something new together, Greg and me, something wonderful based on our love for You rather than something tainted by our past sins.

On that night, she'd been introduced to intimacies that were rightly shared between a man and wife, something that was meant to be beautiful. Her experience had been one of darkness, furtive whispers, and belated shame.

Please, God. Don't allow shame to become part of this night as we begin our marriage.

Drawing a shaky breath, Dottie turned from the mirror—and the memories—and opened the bathroom door. Greg waited where she'd left him, at the small round table near the window overlooking Main Street. He straightened in his chair as she approached.

He's nervous, too.

The realization surprised her. He'd seemed confident since his return home. He'd been strong with his parents, strong with her mother, strong with the pastor. But now . . .

It's because he can't see me.

With sudden clarity she understood, and her heart tightened like a fist in her chest. Greg couldn't see his bride, and because of it, he felt less than whole, less than a man, less than her husband.

She took his hand and drew him up from the chair. With tender fingers, she touched the bandage that wrapped his head and hid his blinded eyes. "May I?"

For a moment, he didn't respond. She feared she'd made a mistake, but at last, he nodded.

Slowly, carefully, she removed the gauze binding. His skin was pale and pasty where it had been bound, his thick hair matted against his scalp. He kept his eyes closed, and she wondered what she would see if he opened them. Whatever it was, it wouldn't make any difference to her. He was beautiful.

She rose on tiptoe and kissed his closed eyes, first one eyelid, then the other. Next, she traced the scar down the length of his face with her fingertips, following with her lips upon the damaged flesh. Finally, she pressed her cheek against his chest. "I love you, my darling husband."

His arms tightened around her. "I promise to never again make you regret loving me."

"Oh, Greg." She lifted her head and stared at him. "I've regretted many things. I've regretted the wrong choices we made. But I've never, ever regretted loving you."

"I'll be a good husband, Dottie. I'll do everything I need to do to take care of you."

"I know you will. I've never doubted it."

He framed her face between his palms and smiled before leaning down to kiss her forehead, the tip of her nose, her lips. Straightening, he whispered, "I may not be able to see you with my eyes, Dottie, but I can see you with my heart. I'll always be able to see you with my heart."

With those words, her fears were wiped away.

49

It was nearly midnight before Margo closed the novel she was reading, set it on the coffee table, dimmed the lamp, and headed for bed. Her nighttime routine was completed in short order—hanging her clothes in the closet, slipping into her cotton nightgown, brushing her teeth, washing her face.

Then, by the pale light of a quarter moon, she slid beneath the covers on her bed and willed herself to sleep.

It didn't work. She kept thinking about Dottie.

Her daughter's wedding had been simple, heartfelt, beautiful. As she observed the ceremony from the front pew, Margo had felt Dottie's joy. The dour thoughts she'd entertained about men and matrimony only a few short weeks before were banished for good, and she was able to love her son-in-law with a full heart.

Tomorrow, Dottie and Greg would return from their one-night honeymoon and take up residence in Dottie's girlhood bedroom. For how long? That would depend on Greg's recovery. He was fiercely determined to be a productive member of society.

She sighed and rolled onto her side, drawing her knees upward as she hugged a pillow to her chest.

Her daughter married.

Her son away at war.

Her world turned upside down.

For more than twenty years, Margo had poured everything into raising her children well. Despite herself, despite her mistakes, her wrong attitudes, and her bitter heart, she'd succeeded. Clark and Dottie were wonderful children who'd become wonderful adults. They were bright and hardworking. They were caring and giving. Most important, they were strong in faith, having a love for God that anyone could see.

So what now, Lord? What's next?

She was forty-three. Was that too old to have a life beyond the one she'd had thus far? Was there a new path the Lord wanted her to travel?

Dottie would make her a grandmother in the fall. Perhaps that would be the next important role she had to play.

Is it, Lord?

Margo rolled onto her other side and stared toward the window.

The branches of the tall spruce at the corner of the house were idle on this calm night. Between the tree limbs, she saw stars twinkling against the backdrop of an ink black sky, the sliver of moon already having traveled beyond her view.

Forty-three and fast approaching her next birthday. Not old, but no longer young either. She'd heard more than one preacher say from a pulpit, "God has a plan for your life." What did that mean now that her children were grown?

What's Your plan for my life, Lord?

Margo sighed again, sat up, plumped the pillows at her back, and turned on the bedside lamp. She reached for her Bible, and when she opened it, a slip of paper fell onto the bedspread. On the paper she'd written Romans 9:31-32, altering the words slightly by putting her name into the Scripture, making it personal, wanting never to forget the meaning for herself.

She read it aloud. "'But Margo, who tried so hard to get right with God by keeping the law, never succeeded. Why not? Because she was trying to get right with God by keeping the law instead of trusting in Him. Margo stumbled over the great rock in her path.'"

Her restlessness dissipated. God had it all in control.

Father, You set me free from a bondage of my own making. Thank You. I've caught sight of Your grace at last. Now please show me what to do with my newfound freedom. What is Your plan for me?

She drew the Bible to her chest and closed her eyes, waiting, hoping to hear His voice speaking to her heart.

Dottie won't need me any longer. Not really. She has Greg, and that's as it should be. Clark is a grown man now. He won't come home to live with me when the war is over. That's as it should be, too. So what about me? What does my future hold?

As if in a dream, she saw herself standing on a diving board, high above a large swimming pool. No, it was more like the sea, stretching to the horizon. She felt the wind in her hair and the sun on her cheeks. She glanced down ...down ... down at the water so far below. One step would take her beyond the board. One step, and there would be nothing to stop her fall into the crystal blue sea of her unknown tomorrows.

Nothing except You, Jesus.

She threw wide her arms and took the plunge.

June & July
1943

UNITED STAT
OF AMERICA
ar Ration Book
WARNING

To: Stuart Maxfield, Boise, Idaho
From: PFC Frances Ballard
Tuesday, June 1, 1943

Dear Stuart,

I've lost count of the number of times I started this letter. I've wasted a lot of paper, trying to get the words right. Only I'm not sure what the right thing to say at a time like this is. Maybe I shouldn't even be writing to you, but it seems unfair not to.

I talked to Penelope a few days ago. She's in San Diego, working in a clothing store. She tried to pretend things are going great for her, but I don't think that's true. Perhaps at first she had a good time, being on her own and doing as she pleased. I don't think that's the case any longer.

Stuart, I may be the baby in my family, but I'm old enough to know my sister can be plenty selfish. This isn't the first time she's done something without thinking it through. Penelope's always been a bit reckless. I love her to death, but my eyes are open.

I guess she's got a few good reasons for being the way she is. I don't have to tell you our dad's a hard man, and all his girls have paid for it, one way or another. Mom, she just pretends things aren't the way they are. She's made up some fantasy family. Penelope, she just tries to prove she doesn't care, even though she does. Me? I don't know. It's easier to figure out people other than myself. Maybe I ran away, too, only I joined the WAACs.

I'm not trying to make excuses for my sister leaving you

and the kids the way she did. Really, I'm not. She was dead wrong to do it, and I told her so.

I've got a question for you. I don't want you thinking she asked me to ask you this, because she didn't. Maybe she won't. But if she did ask, would you let her come home?

I told her she needed to at least call you, that she couldn't just disappear the way she did. She didn't say she'd call, but I think she might.

I don't know how much longer I'll be stationed here on the East Coast. I've applied again for an overseas posting, and I think there's a good chance my transfer will come through this time. Before that happens, if there's anything I can do to help, I hope you'll let me know.

Your loving sister-in-law,
Frances

50

Would I take her back? Stuart laid aside the letter from Frances. *Would I let Pen come home if she wanted to?*

It was a tough question, one he'd been asked before and still didn't have the answer to. He wasn't sure what he felt for his wife now. Loathing? Longing? Yes, both of those. And regret. Loads of regret.

"Hey, kids. Come on. It's time to leave for Miss Dottie's."

In seconds, Alan and Evelyn scurried down the hallway, carrying their overnight things in small canvas bags.

It was a huge relief to Stuart, knowing his children enjoyed being with Dottie, Greg, and Margo. It made it easier to leave them each afternoon before he went to work at the movie theater. He couldn't say his job was exciting—taking tickets at the door; selling popcorn, drinks, and candy; cleaning up the mess left behind after the moviegoers went home—but at least he was earning his own way again.

Stuart winced as he lifted Evelyn and her bag and held her in the crook of his left arm. Then he grasped Alan's hand in his right, and the three of them left the house. The day was warm and sunny, a perfect summer day, the kind that brought families outdoors on a Saturday afternoon. Dads played baseball with their sons. Little girls sold lemonade from their homemade stands on street corners while their mothers kept a careful eye on them.

It made him think of Penelope and what they and the children might have had.

One thing Stuart's work afforded him was lots of time to think, especially between the hours of midnight, when the last show was over, and two in the morning, when he was done mopping up. During those hours, he thought a lot about his wife, about their marriage, about his mistakes and her mistakes, about the sad-funny turns life took.

Penelope, he'd come to realize, didn't believe there was any-thing wrong with his back. She thought him lazy . . . and worse.

"My little sister's doing something to help end this war while you sit around on your behind and drink beer and sleep." The memory of her voice as she hurled those angry words at him rang pain-fully in his ears. *"You don't have to be in the service to do something to help, you know. You could work in a defense plant. You could volunteer for rubber drives. You could do something!"*

Why didn't he understand before? Penelope believed that he faked his injury. She thought him a coward. The evidence was there—in her attitude, in her words, in her response to him—but he hadn't seen it. Maybe he hadn't wanted to see it. For that matter, maybe she'd had cause to think it.

Stuart had been an avowed supporter of the Neutrality Act. He'd spoken against Roosevelt's Selective Service and Training Act. He'd wanted the U.S. to stay out of Europe's problem. That was truly how he had viewed the war in the beginning. It was Europe's problem. Even Pearl Harbor hadn't changed his mind immediately. He'd thought guys like Lucy's husband, who enlisted right after the attack, were idiots, and he'd said so to his wife. Wait to be drafted, was the position he'd taken.

Now he thought differently. Now he realized there were times a nation had to draw a line in the sand and stand up for those who couldn't stand up for themselves. But Penelope didn't know he'd changed.

He looked at his daughter. Evelyn grinned as she watched the activity all around them—the birds in the trees, a neighbor mowing his lawn, a dog chasing a squirrel. Stuart shifted his gaze to his son, who walked with gusto at his side. His children were happy, cared for, loved. Yet, for all Stuart did to fill the empty place Penelope had left behind, they were without their mother, and they missed her.

Do I want her to come back?

Sometimes Stuart hated Penelope for what she'd done, running out on her kids. He might have failed in plenty of ways, but he hadn't left his kids. He hadn't deserted his wife and left her to cope on her own. He hadn't disappeared without a word, leaving her to wonder if he was alive or dead.

Yes, sometimes he hated Penelope. But sometimes he loved her, too. How was that possible? To love and hate at the same time.

What would I do if she asked to come back?

He wished he knew the answer.

51

Lucy tied a ribbon around a small jar of preserves and placed it into a box beside a crocheted baby blanket and a pretty yellow apron. The box also held a Bible and a collection of meatless recipes from the ladies' circle at East Boise Community Church.

"That's the last one," Lucy told Margo, Dottie, and Greg as she surveyed the ten boxes covering the tabletop and counters of the King kitchen. "When did you say Bobby Crawford's coming for them?"

Dottie glanced at the clock above the stove. "In about an hour. He and some of the other kids from church are taking the boxes straight from here to that shelter west of Twenty-Seventh Street."

"Alone?" Margo asked, her expression disapproving. "That's not a safe area of town. All those drifters living in tents and shacks. I'm not so sure—"

"Pastor Danson's going with them, Mom." Dottie placed her hand over her mother's. "Bobby and the others will be perfectly safe. Besides, those drifters are the people who need these things the most."

The frown on Margo's forehead eased. "You're right. May God help me stop judging others."

Lucy smiled. Whatever God was doing in Margo's heart, it

made a world of difference. There was a new softness in her appearance. She smiled more easily. She seemed more patient, with herself and with others. Even when she let irritation show, as she had a moment before, she was quick to acknowledge her error.

There's always hope for change, isn't there, Father? You're always working on us because You love us.

Greg touched Dottie's arm. "I'm going to tag along with Pastor Danson, if he doesn't mind."

"He won't mind," Dottie replied, smiling at him even though he couldn't see the smile for himself.

The past month had done wonders for Greg. His wife's and mother-in-law's good home cooking had added much needed weight to his waistline. The bandages had been removed from his eyes two weeks ago, and the absence of the white gauze made him appear less injured, less fragile. Although the doctors at the VA hospital weren't optimistic that his sight would return, Greg wasn't discouraged by the news. At least not that Lucy could tell.

Rising from the chair, Lucy placed her hands on the small of her spine, arching backward, stretching her tired muscles. "I don't know about the three of you, but I'm exhausted."

"Lucy?" Dottie looked up. "Have you realized how much good you've accomplished with the Victory Club?" She pushed her chair away from the table and rested both hands on her rounded belly. "Do you realize how much hope you've brought into the lives of others?"

"I didn't do it alone."

"But it was your idea. All of this was your idea."

The doorbell rang, and Lucy turned toward the sound. "Maybe Bobby's early."

"I'll get it," Greg said as he stood. He left the kitchen, moving with more confidence than he had upon his return to Boise.

It wasn't long before Alan and Evelyn barreled through the

living room and into the kitchen. Alan headed for Margo and an anticipated goodie. Evelyn launched herself into Dottie's waiting arms. In the children's wake came Stuart, Greg right behind him.

Dottie spoke her husband's name softly, something she'd done often throughout the afternoon. He stopped behind her chair, put his hands on her shoulders, and leaned down to kiss the side of her throat.

Watching the tender scene, Lucy was swamped by those old, troublesome feelings of aloneness.

Dottie had her husband home from the war and he was never going back. Stuart's children adored her, and she would have a baby of her own soon. Dottie wasn't orphaned. Her mother was alive to talk to when she needed advice. She wasn't alone. She was surrounded by love.

I'm so jealous I could scream.

Feeling small and petty, Lucy looked away so Dottie wouldn't see the raw emotions on her face. "I'd better get home. Empress is going to think I've deserted her, as much as I've been gone lately."

"Are you sure?" Margo said. "You're welcome to join us for supper."

Lucy was in danger of bursting into tears of self-pity. "Thanks, Margo. That's kind of you, but I need to get home."

Oh, Lord. Get me out of here. I don't want them to see me feeling sorry for myself when I have so much to be thankful for.

As if in answer to her prayer, Stuart said, "If you're headed home, Lucy, I'd be glad to escort you as far as the theater. Just about every airman from the base seems to be in town today, looking for a good time. You shouldn't have to make that long walk home alone."

Lucy wasn't overly concerned about randy young airmen bothering her. She'd learned in the past year and a half how to deflect their less-than-subtle overtures. However, Stuart's offer gave her the excuse she needed to leave quickly, and she took it.

"That would be nice. Thank you for offering." She gathered her pocketbook and sweater while he said good night to his children.

After leaving the house, they walked in silence for three blocks before Stuart spoke. "You seemed upset back there."

She glanced his way and gave him a brief, sad smile. "I miss Richard. Sometimes, when I see Greg and Dottie together, it hurts."

"Yeah, I understand what that's like."

Empathy squeezed her heart. "Any word?"

"I heard from Frances." He shoved his hands into his pant pockets, his gaze locked on the sidewalk a few steps in front of him. "She says Pen's in San Diego."

"What do you intend to do? Will you go down there, try to convince her to return to Boise?"

"I don't know. What do you think I should do?"

"I'm not the right person to ask. I've made too many mistakes of my own."

And I forgave you, beloved.

Her heart fluttered at the soft voice in her heart, and it made her wonder if Stuart didn't deserve a chance to hear it, too.

"Stuart, why don't you ask God what He wants you to do?"

He released a humorless chuckle. "I don't think God would listen to me. I'm not the religious sort."

Lucy stopped walking. "It isn't about religion. It's about a relationship with Jesus."

"What's that supposed to mean?"

"Too often, religion is just a set of rules to live by or rituals to observe. But that isn't what Jesus wants from us or for us. Jesus wants us to *know* Him, to love Him."

Stuart shook his head.

"He wants us to delight in Him so He can give us the desires of our hearts. He wants to make you His child."

Stuart's expression changed from skepticism to puzzlement. "You really believe that, don't you?"

"Yes."

"So, then what? If I believe all you're telling me, then is everything supposed to go right from then on? I get what I want from God. Is that what you're saying?"

"No, that's not what I'm saying." She leaned toward him, willing him to understand. "We get what *He* wants, and that's always what's best for us."

His face darkened. "What if He wants Pen to stay in San Diego and never be a mother to our kids?" Challenge sharpened his voice, hinting of anger. "What if God wants your husband to die in Europe?"

His words hit Lucy like a fist. She sucked in a gasp of air, at the same time pulling back from him.

"I'm sorry," he said—but he sounded more frustrated than sorry. "I can't accept the whole Jesus-loves-me-this-I-know thing. Maybe it works for you and your friends, but it won't work for me. I'm not saying there's no God. Maybe Jesus did die on the cross and all that. But when I see the stuff that's going on in the world, it's hard to believe He cares all that much about any of us."

Lucy knew he was wrong. God cared, infinitely more than she would ever understand. But she had no reply, not with Stuart's question ringing in her heart: *"What if God wants your husband to die in Europe?"*

"Look—"Stuart motioned with his hand, indicating they should resume walking—"let's change the subject. I don't suppose you care about the Dodgers' eight-one loss to the Cubs?"

"Not really." Lucy fell into step beside him.

"What if God wants your husband to die in Europe?"

God knew the number of their days from birth to death. No

one could snatch a life out of His hands. No one. So *was* it His will for Richard to die in the war? She'd never let that question surface before. She'd known he *might* die, that he *could* die, and she'd prayed that he wouldn't.

But was it possible Richard wouldn't come home because it was part of God's plan?

A headache pounded behind her eyes. She pinched the bridge of her nose between thumb and index finger in a futile attempt to stop it.

"I'm sorry, Lucy," Stuart said in a low voice. "I shouldn't've said what I did. It was thoughtless. You've been a good friend to me and the kids since Pen left, and I should be more careful what I say."

She lowered her hand. "It's okay. Really it is."

But it wasn't okay, because now the question continued to ring in her heart: Was it possible Richard wouldn't come home because it was part of God's overall plan?

☆ ☆ ☆

When Lucy arrived home twenty minutes later, she dropped her pocketbook on the stoop without going inside and crossed the backyard. Nine straight rows ran the length of her Victory Garden, and at each end were tiny stakes wearing empty seed packets, a reminder of what produce to expect come harvest-time.

How long would it be before the first shoots broke through the soil? Sunshine and water had begun the growing process, though there was no evidence of it yet. Germination and growth happened underground first.

People were like that, Lucy thought. So much going on beneath the surface. Growth that could take days, weeks, months for others to see.

God, do You see growth in me? I don't want to be dormant. I want to be fruitful. I want a harvest of faith and obedience.

She squatted and touched the loose soil, warmed by the sun. God, when He created the world, had made the earth fertile. He designed it to grow food to sustain man and beast. He looked on His creation and called it good. If not for sin, she thought, there would be no weeds, no thorns.

You could remove weeds and thorns from the earth, Lord. You could remove evil, too. She drew a slow, deep breath. *You could end this war and stop the killing. Why don't You?*

Wasn't it a paradox that God, who was good, allowed evil to remain?

"If we understood everything," her pastor once said, "then we would be God. We will never understand everything. God's riches and wisdom and knowledge are too wonderful for full comprehension."

But I want to understand, Lord.

The questions churned in her mind. If God was firmly in control of events, if He truly held the future, then what about free will? Was what happened completely out of her control? Had she no choice, no say? She'd read in the Bible that God changed His mind in response to an act of man. So did that mean her actions could change God's plans?

Lucy stood, raised her eyes toward heaven, and said, "I want to understand the whys, Lord, of what happens in the world. Is that possible? Is it wrong to want to know?"

52

Dottie awakened slowly. Through closed eyelids, she became aware of morning sunlight falling onto her face, accompanied by a feeling of decadence for having slept late, something she got to do only when Stuart Maxfield had the night off from work and his children stayed at home with him.

Smiling, contented, she moved her arm across the sheet, but discovered Greg wasn't beside her. She opened her eyes.

The bedroom curtains were pulled open wide. Greg stood at the window, his face toward the sun. If she didn't know better, she would have thought he saw the world outside—the morning light, the dew on the roses in her mother's garden, the green grass, the birds in the willow tree near the back fence. But she *did* know better. His beautiful eyes saw nothing.

A sharp ache pierced her heart. *Oh, God. His beautiful brown eyes. Will he never see our child with those eyes? I want him to see our child.*

As if she'd spoken the words aloud, Greg turned toward her. "Hey there, sleepyhead."

She sat up, leaning her back against the headboard. "How did you know I was awake?"

"You make a funny sound in your throat when you first wake up."

"I do? I didn't know that." She yawned as she glanced toward the alarm clock. "I can't believe the time. How long have you been up?"

"Not long. Your mom already left for work." He stepped toward Dottie and sat on the edge of the bed near her hip. "I've been thinking I should get a Seeing Eye dog."

He's giving up on regaining his sight.

"It would mean going away for a few weeks of training."

Dottie placed a hand on her abdomen. "How soon would you go?"

"I don't know." He covered her hand with his own. "Don't worry. I'll make sure it's not when the baby's due."

She smiled. How well he knew her.

"The fellow I talked to at the hospital last week told me there's a waiting period to get a dog. I'm not sure how long that period is. Weeks. Months, maybe."

"But what . . . what if you regain your sight? The doctors haven't ruled out the possibility. Maybe you should wait a little longer before you get a dog. They said—" Seeing his expression, both patient and pained, Dottie swallowed the remainder of her argument.

Greg linked fingers with hers. "Princess, we make plans, but the Lord determines our steps. Let's see where those steps take us."

But it seems unfair that you should never again see the sky, never again be able to play baseball with your friends, never hold your firstborn in your arms and see his smile.

After a period of silence, Greg whispered, "Our steps *and* our stops?"

"What?"

His smile was pensive. "There was a Christian in my unit. Bryant. We used to talk about our faith and the Bible a lot. Bryant told me a story about a man in England named George Müller." Greg spoke softly, yet with an undercurrent of strength in his voice. "Müller lived in the 1800s, and he saw how bad things were for the orphans there so he decided to do something about it. He wasn't a man of means. He didn't have any money. But by faith, he opened an orphanage for a couple dozen girls. Over the years, God kept answering Müller's prayers of faith for the needs that arose, and by the time Müller died, his orphanages had helped more than ten thousand orphans."

Dottie listened to her husband, knowing he told her the story for a purpose. Yet she wondered what a man from another century had to do with Greg regaining his sight or getting a guide dog.

"Psalm 37 has a verse that says, 'The LORD directs the steps of the godly.' The story goes that George Müller added two words to it. He changed the verse in his Bible to read, 'The LORD directs the steps *and stops* of the godly.' " Greg squeezed her fingers. "Do you see, Dottie? God orders every detail of our lives, both the steps *and* the stops. Maybe this blindness of mine is one of our stops because He loves us. We can trust Him with it."

"But didn't you say this Müller prayed and had his needs met? 'The earnest prayer of a righteous person has great power and wonderful results.' Right? If we prayed harder—"

"Dottie." His grasp tightened on her hand. "God delights in every detail of our lives. He's holding our hands like I'm holding yours now. He's holding on tight. He won't let us fall. We might stumble, but He won't let us fall."

"But—"

"Princess, I'm not afraid of being blind if that's what God allows." With that, Greg slid closer and drew her into his embrace. "Let's see where He's taking us." His breath whispered through her hair. "We may find we're on the greatest adventure we can imagine."

To: Mrs. Richard Anderson, Boise, Idaho, U.S.A.
From: 1st Lt. Richard Anderson
Wednesday, May 19, 1943

My beloved Lucy,

*I'm sending this letter through a buddy of mine instead
of using a regular V—Mail. I have too much to say for a
single V—Mail. And maybe this will get to you
uncensored. My friend says it will.*

*There's a full moon tonight. I'm sitting on the bank of a
river while writing. I come to this spot a lot, to think, to
meditate on God's Word, to pray. For a change, the sky's
not overcast with low-hanging clouds. No rain is weeping
through the trees. Instead, it's clear, and I can see a
million stars overhead. The air is sweet. The airfield's not
far off, but it's quiet for now. No roar of engines to disturb
the night.*

*"Be still, and know that I am God! I will be honored by
every nation. I will be honored throughout the world."*

*I wish that time was now, Lucy. I wish the whole world
would honor God, that they knew who He is and would
worship Him. I'm ready for Christ to return.*

*We had a close call on our bombing run today in the
Boise Babe. (That's what the boys in the squadron
dubbed our Fortress. Did I tell you that before?) First we
ran into flak and ground fire. We were flying at about 60
feet at the time. Low enough to see the men who were
shooting at us. Then there were German fighters coming at
us from every direction. A cannon shell exploded beneath
my seat after coming through the aircraft, just missing
Eddie Caldwell, my navigator. Could have torn off his
legs, it came so close. My mid-upper gunner was nearly hit
in the head with another shell, and he got a nasty burn on
his hand. The whole aircraft was shot up from end to end.*

*I wasn't sure we would make it back from this mission.
Had some tense moments.*

*But we did make it, and I'm thankful for another night
on this earth, another chance to write and tell you how
much I love you. Do I tell you enough, Lucy? I'm not sure
I do. These letters and too few memories— that's all
you've got of me. Are they enough?*

*It was about 3:30 when we landed in England. Glad to
be alive, all of us. Eddie and I headed for the hut for a
quick shower, and the chaplain met us on the road. He
had a yellow envelope in his hand. Eddie grabbed my
arm. I think he was more scared to see that wire than he
was when that shell ripped through our plane. But it was
good news. He's got a son! Eddie Jr. arrived about a
month early, but I guess he's doing fine and so is Eddie's
wife.*

*A few weeks ago Eddie managed to get his hands on a
box of American cigars. He's been saving them for this
occasion. He passed them out to the boys in the squadron.
Somebody else had a quart of whiskey, so those who cared
to imbibe did so, even though there wasn't a lot to go
around.*

*With the way they all carried on, you'd have thought
Eddie was the one who did the hard work of bringing that
baby into the world. And Eddie, well, he acted plum loco.
You never saw a guy so delirious with joy. Maybe they're
all still celebrating, but I had to get off by myself.*

*Lucy, I'd sure like a chance to be a father to our babies.
I must have told the Lord that a hundred times. Did I
ever say the same thing to you? Do you know how much
I'd like to see you cradling our son or daughter in your
arms? I can imagine you sometimes, sitting by the window
in a rocking chair with a soft blue or pink blanket falling
over your shoulder, your head tipped down as you stare at*

the bundle in your arms. I can imagine it so clearly it makes my chest hurt.

I remember reading—I think it was in Psalm—that the children born to a young man are like sharp arrows in a warrior's hands, and that the man whose quiver is full of them is joyful. I was too young, I guess, to appreciate the truth of that verse. But today, when the flak and shells hit our bomber and I knew we were in bad shape and I wasn't sure we'd make it back, well, I had to wonder if I'd ever have even one in my quiver. I had to wonder if God was saying no to my prayers to come home to you.

Maybe this is nerves talking. Maybe it's that with each mission I fly and each time I see another plane drop out of the sky, I know the odds are growing that my plane could be next.

Paul said, "For to me, living means living for Christ, and dying is even better." In my head, I know what he meant. Dying means an end to the troubles we have in this world. Dying means never seeing a comrade in arms shot and bleeding and suffering. It means never seeing another plane going down in flames. Dying means no more tears or sorrows or wars. But, Lucy, dying also means not seeing you again. At least not in this earthly life. I know I'd see you again someday in heaven, but I'm selfish enough to want to see you here, now.

I'm selfish enough to want to raise our children together, to grow old together, and bounce our grandkids on our knees together. I imagine myself sitting on a front porch with you. Your face is soft and creased and your hair is gray. You wear glasses on the tip of your nose and there's a quilt wrapped around your legs to keep off the chill while the sun sets.

Can you imagine that, too, Lucy? I want that future so bad I can taste it.

It won't be long now before the Allies invade Europe. With the North African campaign ended a week ago, that gives us a base near the toe of Italy's boot. The bombing of strategic sites in Europe will increase now. The bombers will be able to fly farther than we could before. I don't think I'm breaching anything classified to say that, although the censors wouldn't like me doing it. Still, it's got to be common knowledge, even in the States. The Germans and the Italians won't be surprised when we push across the Mediterranean. They're preparing for it. Any fool could look at a map and see what's coming next. The months ahead are going to be unlike anything any of us, friend or foe, have seen yet.

Lucy, please forgive me if I die over here. Sound crazy? I suppose so. Still, I'm asking. Don't be mad at me if I don't make it home. It won't be because I don't love you. I love you with everything I am, everything I ever hope to be.

Maybe you're feeling these same sorts of things. Your letters lately have seemed different. I hope you're okay. I want you to be okay. I want you to be happy. I pray that God will give you joy, Lucy. No matter what comes, I pray that God will give you joy.

I'll love you always,
Richard

To: 1st Lt. Richard Anderson, APO, N.Y.P.E.
From: Lucy Anderson
Saturday, June 12, 1943

My dearest darling,
Today the postman delivered your long letter. I was so excited to get an envelope rather than a single sheet of paper. The letter came to me with every word intact. The censors cut nothing out.

But there are tears in my eyes as I begin to write this reply. My heart is full of too many emotions—pain, fear, love, and more love. I miss you so much, and I wish I had words to write that would encourage you and bring you peace and comfort. Or perhaps make you laugh. But all I can do is tell you what's happening to me and around me and inside me. I hope that's enough, darling.

A week ago, Stuart Maxfield challenged me with a question about God's will, and all week, I've been pondering terms like <u>predestination</u>, <u>God's sovereignty</u>, and mankind's <u>free will</u>. I've tried to find understanding by reading the Scriptures and asking the Holy Spirit for illumination.

All week, I have felt like Jacob of the Old Testament, like I was wrestling with an angel of God. "I won't let you go until you bless me with understanding!" I cried to the Lord. Jacob got his blessing when he wrestled. His name became Israel because he struggled with both God and man. And he won. But I haven't won. I don't understand any better the complexities of war and death and evil and senseless loss.

I suppose I hoped, in answer to my prayer, to become suddenly theologically profound. That didn't happen. I still have questions. There are so many things about the Bible and about God Almighty that I do not understand and will <u>never</u> understand.

But perhaps I did get a few answers through my wrestling and questioning. His word is true, and my lack of understanding doesn't change that. God is good, and the awful things that happen in this world don't change that. He doesn't mind my questioning. He can handle my "Why, God?" He loves you and He loves me, and whether you and I live into old age or not won't change that.

In Revelation, Jesus says, "I will ask nothing more of you except that you hold tightly to what you have until I come."

I only need to hold tightly to the truth I have now, today, this moment. He's asking nothing more of me than that.

My darling, I let fear have too much room in my life in recent months. I regret that lapse of faith more than I can say. I've feared that you wouldn't return to me from this war. I still fear it sometimes, and a letter like the one you wrote wrings tears from my heart. I want you, Richard. I want you as my husband for all of my life. I want your quiver to be full of children, too.

But I swear to you, darling, I will not let fear make me forget the truth that He's given me.

You asked me to forgive you if you die in Europe. Oh, my beloved, my tears make it hard to see this page. How do I answer that? I would forgive you anything. I would forgive you even that. But I pray God won't ask it of me. I would forgive, but could I live?

And that's when I must face God's sovereignty once again, isn't it? You will not die if it's God's will for you to live. The Nazi Luftwaffe cannot shoot you out of the sky apart from God allowing them to do so. "What purpose would it serve if that happened?" I ask. Is war His will? He is a God of love. How can it be? Why must evil remain a moment longer on this earth?

I don't know, but I will hold on to the Truth that I do know. I know Jesus and Him crucified. That's what I know. I know that God said we will have trials and heartaches and difficulties as long as we live on this mortal earth, but no matter what, He is worthy of my praise. He is God and I am not.

Here are two verses I found last night as I sought refuge in His Word.

Psalm 73 says: "My health may fail, and my spirit may grow weak, but God remains the strength of my heart." Daniel 3 says: "The God whom we serve is able to save us. He will rescue us from your power, Your Majesty. But even if he doesn't, we want to make it clear, Your Majesty, that we will never serve your gods or worship the gold statue you have set up."

There is more, of course. So much more.

Forgive me, my love, for this letter. My falling tears have stained the paper and caused the ink to run in places. And perhaps my words make no sense, for I have written quickly, pouring out whatever came to me without stopping to wonder if I should. My thoughts race and my heart weeps, and I long for you with every breath I take.

Richard, dearest, night has fallen and a nearly full moon is on the rise. It isn't the same full moon you sat beneath when you wrote the letter that lies on the table near my hand. Eddie's son is nearly a month old, and you and your squadron have flown more missions since you put that pen to paper. How many missions, I don't know. Even now, in the early predawn hours of England, you could be preparing to leave on another one. If so, I hope you know I'm praying for you. I'm asking God's protection for you. Nothing could stop me from nightly asking Jesus to spare you.

I, too, am selfish. I, too, want to grow old with you. I want to see your face wrinkled with age and your black hair turned white. I want to see you bouncing a grandchild on your knee. Or even two or three grandchildren. I want to listen as you repeat one more time the stories of when you fought in the war.

I love you, Richard. No matter what happens, I will love you always. And no matter what, I have set my heart to praise the Lord. Those two things I know to be true. Those two.

You're always in my heart,
Lucy

53

Margo set her purchases from Payless Drugstore on the kitchen table: four rolls of Safetex toilet tissue, fifteen cents; four bars of Woodbury's facial soap, twenty-five cents; a package of stationery and envelopes, nineteen cents; and a roll of Diamond wax paper, fifteen cents. Oh, how quickly her weekly salary disappeared. Twelve dollars didn't stretch as far as it used to, not with higher prices due to the war and the 5 percent Victory Tax that was withheld from her paycheck each week. It would soon get worse, with the enactment of Congress's income tax plan.

Somewhere in the New Testament, Paul wrote that he'd learned to be content with much and with little. Margo suspected it was easier to be content with much, but she was vastly more experienced with the little.

Sighing, she walked down the hall to her bedroom to change from her work clothes. The house was quiet tonight. Greg and Dottie were having supper with friends and afterward they were going to a movie.

Greg at a movie? Why? Imagine someone paying forty cents to go to something he couldn't see. Now *there* was a waste of good money. But when she'd said as much to Dottie, her daughter explained that Greg wanted to *feel* normal.

Maybe there's something to that, Margo thought as she kicked off her shoes near the chest of drawers.

She unbuttoned the tailored top of her summer suit, then unfastened the clasp and lowered the zipper of the matching skirt. After hanging the suit in her closet, she donned a cotton blouse, a pair of slacks, and her old, very comfy house slippers, and returned to the kitchen.

A glass of iced tea was her first priority. She even sweetened it with a little of their precious sugar supply. After taking a sip, she released a sigh of pleasure as she carried the glass onto the back porch, where she settled onto a padded chair.

She felt bone weary. There had been so much bad news lately, coming in waves. Four more families at church had lost sons or grandsons overseas. And an unusually large number of airmen who'd trained at Gowen Field were shot down in recent weeks.

The bad news didn't come only from the front lines.

Race riots had erupted in Detroit this past Sunday. The news reports said the influx of some three hundred thousand people—whites and blacks—to work in the war plants led to the violence. By Tuesday, thirty-five people were dead and another five hundred injured. And Detroit's wasn't the first riot. The same thing had happened in Mobile, Alabama, in May and in Los Angeles, California, and Beaumont, Texas, earlier this month.

"Father, send us peace." Margo stared toward the sky through the lacy tree branches that sheltered the backyard. "Peace in Europe. Peace in Asia. Peace here at home."

She took another sip of iced tea, then leaned her head against the high back of the chair and closed her eyes. It was warm but not uncomfortably so. The quiet of the neighborhood was soothing after the busyness of her day. For a time, she thought of nothing. But eventually, her mind wandered back to her prayer for peace.

"Why *do* You tarry, Lord?"

With so many of God's children praying for peace—faithfully

praying, without ceasing—why didn't He end this bloody conflict and let the young men and women of America come home? Why did any more have to die? Why didn't God stomp out evil once and for all? Why couldn't there be peace on earth and goodwill toward men?

These things I plan won't happen right away.

Margo's heart quickened. She opened her eyes, half expecting to find someone with her on the back porch.

Slowly, steadily, surely, the time approaches when the vision will be fulfilled. If it seems slow in coming, wait patiently, for it will surely take place. It will not be delayed.

The Shepherd's voice. She knew it and found reassurance as it washed over her. God had a plan. His plan was in place from the foundation of the earth. It was *His* vision, and it would be fulfilled. She believed that with every fiber of her being. Even if it didn't fit *her* timing . . . or *her* plans.

"But it does seem slow, Lord," she whispered, glancing upward again, "and it's hard to be patient. Sometimes it feels like You've looked away and are missing what's happening on earth. I'm in a hurry for peace in our time. How long must we wait?"

A wry smile curved her lips. She sounded like King David: "O LORD, how long will you forget me? . . . How long will my enemy have the upper hand? . . . How long, O LORD, will you look on and do nothing? . . . O LORD, how long will this go on? Will you hide yourself forever?"

It seemed to Margo that the ancient king of Israel whined and complained a great deal about his lot in life, but she noted something else, too. David, a man after God's own heart, might begin a psalm in moaning, but he ended in praise and expressions of trust in the God of his salvation.

"I want to be like that, Lord." She closed her eyes a second time, allowing calm to settle over her. "Let me be open and honest with my feelings, but help me always end in words of praise and trust in You."

54

THE IDAHO
DAILY STATESMAN

Boise, Idaho
Wednesday Morning
June 23, 1943

Flying Fortresses
Set Huge Fire
in Nazi Rubber Center

LONDON (AP) — Formations of R.A.F. heavy bombers thundered over the southeast coast toward the continent early today after American Flying Fortresses, completing round-the-clock smashes on the German Ruhr for the first time, kindled a square mile of blazes that raged through the German synthetic rubber town of Huls Tuesday. . . . But the raids took a heavy toll—20 U.S. Bombers and four fighters Tuesday and 44 British bombers and one fighter Monday night. . . .

✶ ✶ ✶

Boise, Idaho
Thursday Morning
June 24, 1943

Italy Writhes Under Smashing Air Attacks While Crushing of Ruhr Extends to Muelheim

ALLIED   HEADQUARTERS, North Africa (U.P.) — For the fourth time in 24 hours, Allied bombers have lashed the Neapolitan industrial area, striking at railway targets around Salerno while fires from earlier raids still smoldered amid the gaping ruins of war works in Naples itself, it was announced Wednesday. . . . It began Sunday night with a Wellington block-buster raid serving as "interference" for two waves of American Flying Fortresses, totaling 100 planes, which plastered military targets in the heart of Naples and at nearby Cancello by daylight. . . .

✶ ✶ ✶

Boise, Idaho
Monday Morning
July 5, 1943

Fortresses Pick Targets
Over France

LONDON (AP) — The R.A.F. rocked the already devastated city of Cologne for 45 minutes Saturday night and also pounded Hamburg, while large formations of American Flying Fortresses took over the daylight offensive Sunday by laying a destructive bomb pattern across three important Axis targets— Nantes, Le Mans and La Pallice in France. The co-ordinated sky assaults cost the R.A.F. 32 planes and the U.S. air force eight Fortresses . . . .

✫ ✫ ✫

Boise, Idaho
Saturday Morning
July 10, 1943

Fliers Clear Landing Path

By Associated Press — Countless bombings of key cities, airfields and fortifications softened Sicily for the assault which carried Allied troops to the front door of the Italian mainland early today. . . .

✫ ✫ ✫

Boise, Idaho
Monday Morning
July 19, 1943

500 Bombers Blast,
Burn Italian Port

ALLIED HEADQUARTERS in North Africa (AP) — More than 500 Allied bombers blasted the vital Italian port of Naples from dawn to dusk Saturday in the most shattering aerial attack ever carried out in the Mediterranean war theater. . . Four-engined Flying Fortresses followed the night-flying Wellingtons over Naples to open the mammoth daylight assault. . . .

✫ ✫ ✫

Boise, Idaho
Tuesday Morning
July 20, 1943

Fortresses Lead Way
Along Tiber

ALLIED HEADQUARTERS in North Africa (AP) — Special trained American precision airmen dropped hundreds of tons of bombs on rail and airfield installations at Rome Monday in the first attack of the war on the Eternal City. The first "bombs away" call of Flying Fortress bombardiers came at 11:13 a.m. (5:13 a.m. EWT). Leaflets first were dropped, advising the inhabitants why certain sections of the city were military objectives. Tons of explosives then smashed the San Lorenzo railway yards four miles east of Vatican City.

August
1943

WESTERN UNION

1943 AUG 6

MRS LUCY ANDERSON=

✯✯ 1602 JEFFERSON ST BOISE, ID=

THE SECRETARY OF WAR DESIRES ME TO
EXPRESS HIS DEEP REGRET THAT YOUR
HUSBAND FIRST LIEUTENANT RICHARD L
ANDERSON HAS BEEN REPORTED MISSING IN
ACTION SINCE NINETEEN JULY OVER ITALY
IF FURTHER DETAILS OR OTHER INFORMATION
IS RECEIVED YOU WILL BE PROMPTLY
NOTIFIED=

M. R. JOHNSON ACTING THE ADJUTANT GENERAL

55

There was a slight whirring sound in Lucy's ears as she lifted her gaze from the telegram in her hand to the uniformed woman standing on the stoop.

"I'm sorry, Mrs. Anderson," the stranger said softly. She seemed poised beyond her years, and her eyes and voice were filled with compassion.

How many such telegrams had this girl delivered? That's all she was, really. A girl. No more than nineteen or twenty years old. Had she delivered ten? thirty? one hundred? more? Did it get easier with each one? or did she dread going to work in the morning?

"If there's anything—," the young woman began.

Lucy closed the door and turned her back to it.

Mere minutes before, she'd been preparing her supper when she heard the knock on the door. Now the precious, hard-to-come-by meat was scorching in the skillet. Smoke filled the kitchen, stinging her eyes and throat. She should turn off the burner. She knew she should, but she couldn't make her feet move. She stood there, frozen in place, her body numb, her heart growing cold.

Missing in action.

"No."

She wouldn't accept it. It wasn't true. She wouldn't let it be true. She would will it away. Refuse it. She would make herself awaken from this nightmare.

Missing in action.

She recalled the April day when she and others painted the Hinkle house. She remembered the look on Dottie's face when she learned Greg had been wounded in Africa. She remembered returning to this apartment and weeping, afraid something would happen to Richard.

And now something *had* happened to Richard.

Something worse.

Missing in action . . .

Missing in action since nineteen July . . .

Missing in action since nineteen July over Italy . . .

"No. No, it can't be true." She looked toward the ceiling and shouted, "Don't let it be true!"

V···–Mail

To: 1st Lt. Richard Anderson, APO, N.Y.P.E.

From: Lucy Anderson

Saturday, August 7, 1943

Richard darling,

Where are you? I cannot sleep, and so I write this in the wee hours of the morning. Where are you?

"Missing in action," the telegram says.

What does that mean?

You were over Italy when your plane went down, and you are missing. Are you a prisoner of war? Or did you manage to escape capture? Did some kindly Italian woman put you in her barn or attic to hide you from the enemy? Are you alone or with others of your crew? Were you injured? Are you in pain? Would I feel it in my heart if you were dead?

I like to think I would feel the absence of your life at the exact moment it left your body. But I don't feel it. Does that mean you're alive?

Richard, you cannot be dead. You cannot be. Don't be dead, Richard. Live. Wherever you are, live. Live for me.

Lucy

56

"Lucy?" Dottie rapped on the door again, Greg standing beside her on the stoop. "Lucy, are you in there? Please let us in." She glanced over her shoulder at her mother. "Do you think she went out?"

Margo shook her head. "No. She's in there. I'm certain of it. Keep knocking."

Dottie did as her mother said, striking the door harder this time. "Lucy, please open up."

At last she saw the flutter of the curtain at the window. Then she heard the click of the lock a second before the door creaked open. Lucy, clad in her pajamas, turned and headed back to the living room without a word to acknowledge her visitors.

Holding Greg's hand, Dottie drew him into the apartment, her mother following right behind.

"How did you find out?" Lucy sank onto an overstuffed chair and drew her knees to her chest, clutching them with her arms.

"Mrs. Hilburn. She saw the woman delivering the telegram yesterday, and she called Mother this morning." Dottie didn't have to explain further. Everyone knew wartime telegrams rarely brought good news. "What did it say?"

Lucy pointed to a slip of paper on the coffee table. The telegram looked as if it had been crumpled into a wad, then flattened again. "Missing in action." She pressed her forehead against her knees, muffling her voice. "He went down over Italy last month."

Dottie gave Greg's hand a squeeze as she guided him to the sofa.

As they sat down, Greg said, "Don't give up hope, Lucy. I know plenty of guys who survived their planes going down."

Plenty? Dottie thought he exaggerated. How many men actually survived a plane crash in the middle of a war? *Please, Father. Let Richard be one of them.*

Margo sat on the arm of Lucy's chair. "Greg's right, dear. You mustn't give up hope." She placed a hand on Lucy's head and gently stroked her hair. "Haven't we prayed for God's protection and guidance for Richard? Haven't we asked all these months for God to give us personal victory over our fears? Of course we have. Now we must hold on to hope. We serve a mighty God."

"But what if—" Lucy lifted her tearstained face from her knees—"what if God says no?" Her voice was pencil-thin. "Margo, what if He's already said no? What if Richard is dead?"

Dottie held her breath, thankful Lucy hadn't asked her that question. What would she have answered? She might simply have wept.

As if sensing Dottie's despair, Greg put an arm around her shoulders and drew her close against his side. She did begin to cry then, silently.

"Lucy," Margo said at last, "I don't know what the answer is. At least, not an answer that will make the hurt go away." She leaned down and kissed the crown of Lucy's head. "I'm not going to offer platitudes. I've done that too often in my life. Whatever comes, we'll walk through it with you, dear. No matter what comes."

57

Penelope Maxfield stood on the sidewalk, staring at her home.

Or was it her home? She'd been gone four months. Four months without a letter or a phone call to Stuart. Four months without one inquiry about her children. To be honest, she'd scarcely given any of them a thought. Not until she ran out of options.

Her stomach cramped, and she wondered if she would be sick. She'd thrown up twice this morning in the bus depot restroom. Not that there was anything in her stomach. She hadn't eaten in two days, other than a couple of crackers. At least she wasn't pregnant. Last week she was afraid she might be. Then what would she have done?

Kill myself. That's what.

Penelope had wanted an adventure, and she got one. At first it was all she'd hoped for. At first she reveled in her newfound freedom. It was intoxicating. Sure, she had to go to work, but the rest of the time, she did exactly as she pleased. She was young and attractive. The sailors in San Diego wined and dined her on a nightly basis.

When did it stop being fun? When she lost her job because of coming in to work late one time too often? When her landlady kicked her out because she couldn't pay her rent? When she awakened one morning and didn't know where she was or the name of the man lying beside her in bed?

Her stomach turned again. Her knees felt unsteady, and she didn't think they would hold her much longer.

"Go home, Pen," Frances had told her weeks ago. "Go back to Stuart and make things right."

But her sister didn't understand. Frances was single and living in England and had no obligations except to the WAACs. Frances didn't have an ever-present husband and small children who constantly demanded her attention, wanting things from her, needing things from her.

"You used to have a good marriage," Frances had said. "You used to love Stuart."

Had she loved him? Penelope wasn't sure. She used to think so, and she'd blamed the change in her feelings on his cowardly reaction to the war, on his supposed back injury, on a host of things she couldn't remember any longer.

But what did that matter? She was here. She was tired, hungry, and she had nowhere else to go. Her father wouldn't let her stay in his house, even if her mother would. No, this was her only port in the storm.

Drawing a steadying breath, she headed for the door. She had a key. Should she use it? Would it be right to just walk in? No, she supposed not.

Her rap on the door echoed the hollowness in her soul.

It seemed an eternity before her knock was answered. Stuart's expression when he saw her went from shock to disgust to aloof in a heartbeat. It made her wish he hadn't been home.

"Hello, Stuart." His name came out scratchy and weak.

"Pen."

"May I . . . may I come in?"

He pushed open the screen without a word.

She stepped past him, pausing in the hall, listening for the sounds of children. She heard none.

Stuart said, "They're with your folks for the weekend."

"Oh."

He didn't move, didn't say anything more, didn't try to make it easier for her. His coldness surprised her. Despite everything, she'd expected more of a welcome.

She cleared her throat. "Is there . . . is there any coffee? I could use a cup." That was a lie. She was certain coffee—especially what passed for it these days—would come right back up if she swallowed any. But it was the only thing she could think to say; the silence was too awful to bear.

"Yeah." He jerked his head toward the kitchen. "Help yourself. You know where it is."

Penelope hesitated a moment more, wondering if he would lead the way. He didn't. He stood there, like a stone statue. Swallowing her nausea, she walked toward the kitchen.

The distinctive crisp scent of Pine-Sol filled the air. A bucket and mop were near the back door. The counters and floor shined. Dishes were stacked in the dish drain to the left of the sink. Her husband had been busy this morning.

Penelope crossed to the stove, picked up the coffeepot with her right hand, and reached for a cup with her left.

"There's some milk in the fridge," Stuart said, "but we're out of sugar."

Normally, she would want both. She added neither.

Full cup clasped tightly, she turned toward her husband. She hoped he couldn't see the way her hands shook. Silence stretched between them, awkward and heavy.

Slowly, she became aware of changes in his appearance. His golden blond hair was shorter than he used to wear it; she liked it. The sleeves of his T-shirt were rolled up, revealing arms more muscular than she remembered, and his skin had been bronzed by the sun. He looked . . . healthy . . . handsome . . . vigorous.

Stuart frowned, as if he'd read her thoughts. "What are you doing here, Pen?"

"I—" her stomach churned—"I wanted to see the children . . . and you, of course."

"Really." The word oozed sarcasm.

"Yes."

Stuart made a sound of frustration as he sat on one of the kitchen chairs. His eyes downcast, he raked the fingers of both hands through his short hair. She felt his loathing from across the room.

What if he sent her away? What if he threw her out, the same way the landlady in San Diego had?

Dizziness washed over her. She had to sit before she fell down. Hurriedly, she moved to a chair opposite Stuart. Coffee sloshed onto the table as she set the cup in front of her.

"I'm sorry," she whispered.

"It'll wipe up."

"No." The desperate lie came easily. It wasn't the first lie she'd told and would undoubtedly not be the last. "No. I'm sorry I left you the way I did." She lifted her gaze and found him watching her again. "I made a mistake."

"A mistake? Is that what you call it?" He chuckled, a humorless sound. "What do you expect from me, Pen? To welcome you home with open arms?"

"I . . . I don't know what I expected. I . . . I just had to come. I had to try." She pushed her hair back from her forehead. "It was wrong to leave, but I was strangling under the weight of everything. So I ran."

Stuart took a deep breath and let it out slowly. "Things're different now, Pen. *I'm* different."

Black dots danced before her eyes. "You used to love me enough to forgive me anything."

"Yeah—" a long pause sucked the oxygen from the room—"I used to."

It was the last thing Penelope heard before the black dots converged and blessed darkness engulfed her.

V··· —MAIL

To: Corporal Clark King, APO, N.Y.P.E.
From: Margo Clark
Sunday, August 8, 1943

Dear Clark,

I haven't received a letter from you in more than a week. The last one was written prior to the Allies' taking of Sicily. But I must assume you are there, and I pray you are well.

Everyone here is holding their collective breath, waiting to hear of the invasion of Italy's mainland by our forces. I don't know whether to want it because it will hasten the end of the war, or dread it because it means you will continue to be in situations of danger as you drive the enemy back toward Germany.

I feel that my work is ever more important as the young officers I tutor prepare to move into occupied territory. I will say no more about that, lest the censors cut holes in my letter.

Your sister and her husband are doing well, all things considered. There remains only slight hope that Greg's eyesight will be restored, but he is in good spirits. He has decided to apply for a Seeing Eye dog. I've come to admire Greg a great deal.

As for Dottie, she grows more round every day. She positively glows with happiness, a baby on the way and her husband by her side. These two are truly in love. I'm blessed to be a part of their happiness until they are able to afford a place of their own. Although where we will fit a dog and a baby and three adults in this small house, I haven't a clue.

Now I must share some distressing news. Lucy's husband, Richard, was shot down over Italy several weeks ago. He is officially listed as missing in action. I've tried to encourage her to hold on to hope. It isn't unheard of for flyers to be reported missing after their planes go down, and then to learn that they are prisoners of war (God forbid that

Richard is in the hands of the enemy) or even that they make it out of enemy territory on their own. But I also know—or at least, I think I know—how I would feel if I were to receive such a telegram about you.

So we wait and we pray and we trust in God's mercy and grace. We trust He will give us the strength we need to endure whatever comes.

I do have good news. Stuart called Dottie and told her that Penelope returned to Boise yesterday. He said they talked for a few minutes, and then she fainted dead away. Turns out she hadn't eaten for a couple of days. Stuart thinks it's because she had no money after buying her bus ticket home from San Diego. Heaven knows why she was destitute or what caused her to come to her senses and return to her family.

Poor Stuart. Dottie says that man doesn't know if he's coming or going. She promised him we would come to see Penelope in a few days, once she's rested. Dottie suggested that Stuart and Penelope join us for church this morning, but he declined. Same as he always does. All I can say is, God help those two. Without the Lord, I don't see how they'll salvage this broken marriage.

Oh, one more thing about that family. Penelope's sister, Frances, has been posted to England. (I'm sure you remember me telling you that she's a WAAC.) She wrote to Dottie and said she's fallen in love with London. She says the devastation from the bombing is wretched, but that the resolve of the British is strong.

I hope the resolve of the people in <u>all</u> of the occupied countries is equally as strong. My heart breaks for them and what they must be suffering. May God grant you the strength and grace to render them aid as you are able, my son.

With much love,
Mom

58

Lucy was grateful for her friends and church family. They rallied around her in many ways, offering food, comfort, a shoulder to cry on. She was particularly thankful for their prayers, for she was unable to pray herself. She couldn't make her mind or heart form the words. She spent long, sleepless nights, curled on her bed, crying, her face pressed against a pillow.

"But the Holy Spirit prays for us with groanings that cannot be expressed in words."

Groanings that cannot be expressed in words. Yes, that was all she could do—groan—and hope God heard and understood and would answer.

Her supervisor offered Lucy time off from work, but she didn't take it. She needed to stay busy. She needed to think of something other than the words *missing in action*. Not that her work achieved that goal. No matter what she did, her thoughts turned to Richard.

Was he alive? Was he injured? Was he in pain? Was he in captivity?

Lucy's soul continued to groan.

On the following Friday, she received a letter from the War Department:

Dear Mrs. Anderson:

This letter is to confirm my recent telegram in which you were regretfully informed that your husband, First Lieutenant Richard L. Anderson, 0530530, Air Corps, has been reported missing in action over Italy since 19 July 1943.

I know that added distress is caused by failure to receive more information or details. Therefore, I wish to assure you that at any time additional information is received it will be transmitted to you without delay, and, if in the meantime no additional information is received, I will again communicate with you at the expiration of three months. Also, it is the policy of the Commanding General of the Army Air Forces upon receipt of the Missing Air Crew Report to convey to you any details that might be contained in that report.

The term missing in action is used only to indicate that the whereabouts or status of an individual is not immediately known. It is not intended to convey the impression that the case is closed. I wish to emphasize that every effort is exerted continuously to clear up the status of our personnel. Under war conditions this is a difficult task as you must readily realize. Experience has shown that many persons reported missing in action are subsequently reported as prisoners of war, but as this information is furnished by countries with which we are at war, the War Department is helpless to expedite such reports.

The personal effects of an individual missing overseas are held by his unit for a period of time and are then sent to the Effects Quartermaster, Kansas City, Missouri, for disposition as designated by the soldier.

Permit me to extend to you my heartfelt sympathy during this period of uncertainty.

Sincerely yours . . .

Lucy stood on the edge of her Victory Garden, looking at the abundance of produce, the fruits of her labor. Soon, she could harvest tomatoes, along with beets, okra, and cucumbers. The rows of corn grew taller every day. Only last week, she was excited about picking, eating, and canning all of these wonderful foods. But now . . .

She walked away from the garden, away from her apartment, away from that wretched letter from the War Department. She paid no attention to where she went. She simply wanted to keep moving, as if she could out-walk her fears and her heartache. She wandered up one street and down another until dusk brought some relief from the August heat.

That was when she found herself outside the Bannock Street Market. She had avoided this corner for the past three months, and seeing it now sent a shock wave through her body.

Had she arrived at this place by chance or did she have a subconscious desire to be here? Did she come hoping to speak to Howard again? He'd comforted her before. Did she want that again? Was she really that weak? Would she misuse his friendship a second time?

She pondered those questions as she stared at the storefront, pondered them until she knew with certainty—in this regard, at least—her conscience was clear. She didn't want to see Howard again. She only wanted Richard.

She started to walk away, then stopped when she realized the store wore a dismal, deserted look. Something wasn't right. She stepped closer to the window and peered inside. A light was on in the rear of the building, and she could just make out the empty aisles. Not a single grocery item on the shelves. Not a can. Not a bag. Not a package.

What happened? Howard always did a brisk business. People in the neighborhood loved this market because the proprietor took such good care of them.

She saw movement at the back of the store. Before she could stop herself, she knocked on the window and called, "Howard?" She knocked again.

But it wasn't Howard. She knew that even before the stranger stepped into the light and she saw his face clearly. She took a step back from the window as the white-haired man headed toward the front door.

Opening it, he said, "Sorry, ma'am. This store's out of business. I'm only here to do some final sweeping up so they can sell the building. There's a Safeway over on—"

"Is Mr. Baxter here?"

The man shook his head. "Nope. He moved away. Been gone more than a month now." He squinted as he looked at her. "You wouldn't be Mrs. Anderson, would you?"

Her mouth dry, Lucy nodded.

"He left somethin' for you, in case you chanced to come by. Wait here and I'll get it." He disappeared from view.

What would Howard leave for her? She wasn't sure she wanted to know. She considered walking away before the old man returned. But she didn't. She was still there when he stepped into the doorway a second time.

"Here you go." He held out an envelope.

Reluctantly, she took it.

"Good day to you, Mrs. Anderson." He gave her a nod, then closed the door.

Lucy drew a deep breath to steady herself. Could she bear to read another piece of bad news? She felt battered by words already. However, she couldn't *not* read it. She had misused his friendship. When she'd recognized they were entering danger-ous emotional waters, she hadn't steered away. Whatever Howard's blame for loving a married woman, Lucy's blame was greater. She had spent time with him so that he *could* love her.

Whatever Howard had written to her inside this envelope, she felt she owed it to him to read it.

5 July 1943

Dear Lucy,

It's been two months since you decided you couldn't see me anymore and said good-bye. For a time, I tried to tell myself I could hate you. I tried to hate you. I couldn't. Then for a time, I hoped you'd come back. I hoped you'd realize you were wrong and that you loved me after all. Every time the door to the store opened, I looked to see if it was you. Every time the door opened, the wrong customer stepped through.

I loved you, Lucy. I still do. You've got a husband serving overseas, and I shouldn't wish he was out of the picture. I can't say I like myself much, wishing that.

So I'm closing the store and moving back to the Midwest, where my family came from. Starting over won't be nearly as hard as staying here, near you but not having you in my life.

There's a part of me that loves you even more because you're the kind of woman who remained true to her husband. I hope somehow you'll know that.

I'm going to leave this letter in the store. An old friend will finish closing things down after I'm gone and get the building ready to sell after the last of the stock is gone. I'll ask him to give this letter to you if you ever come by. If you don't, I'll tell him to burn it.

As I close this letter, I think I can honestly write that I hope the God you believe in gives you what you want most—Richard and his children and a good life together.

Howard Baxter

59

Dottie handed Stuart a glass of lemonade, then sat on the sofa beside Greg.

"I really appreciate you still looking after Alan and Evelyn at night." Stuart stared into the glass. There were dark half-moons under his eyes, and his face had an unhealthy pallor. "Pen says she's not strong enough to be responsible for the kids yet."

"We're glad to do it, Stuart."

He lifted his gaze, meeting Dottie's. "It was easier when she was gone."

"Oh, Stuart." Her heart ached for him.

"She's indifferent to the kids. I can understand that she and I've got problems, but why can't she show them some affection?" He rubbed his forehead. "I wish she hadn't come back."

Greg found Dottie's hand and gave it a squeeze. "Give it some time, Stu. She hasn't been back all that long."

The sound of children's laughter drifted to them through the back screen door. Stuart straightened on his chair and turned his head in the direction of the kitchen. "They don't laugh like that at home. Pen snaps at them if they make a sound." He took a quick gulp of lemonade. "She snaps at me, too."

"Do you think it would help if I went to see her?" Dottie asked. Penelope hadn't exactly welcomed her earlier in the week, but Dottie was willing to try again if Stuart thought it would do any good.

"I don't know. I'm not sure anything will help what ails her." Stuart set his glass on the coffee table, then stood. "I'll be by to get the kids in the morning."

"Why don't you sleep in?" Dottie suggested. "We'll take them to church with us and bring them home afterward." She pushed herself up from the sofa. "Is that all right with you?"

"Sure. They like your Sunday school." He gave her a weary wave. "I'll let myself out. See you tomorrow."

After Stuart left, Dottie and Greg went out to the backyard to watch the children playing in the sandbox. Greg settled onto one of the loungers. At nearly eight months pregnant, Dottie preferred the height and stability of the wooden deck chair beside it.

"If only Pen and Stuart knew the Lord," she said softly, more to herself than to Greg.

"No one comes to Jesus unless the Father draws them. That's what the book of John says."

"But it's also the Father's will that none should perish." She leaned her head against the back of the lawn chair and stared at the blue August sky. "If I was smarter, I'd know the right thing to say to them both."

"Dottie, you can't coerce someone into faith with the excellence of your words. They have to want it in their hearts."

"I know. But Penelope is so hurt, so lost and confused. More so now than before she ran off. Something awful must have happened to her in San Diego." She sighed deeply. "Stuart's a wonderful father and a good man. How can she not see that? With faith and love, they might be able to salvage their marriage, but if they go on the way they are now . . ." She left the sentence unfinished, ending it with another sigh.

"Dottie Wallace, you have a tender heart." Greg's soft-spoken words caressed her. "It's one of the things I love about you."

A smile curved her lips as she looked over at him. He wore dark glasses to hide his sightless eyes. She thought they made him look like a movie star. Even the scar on his face gave him a rakish look that she found appealing. "What else do you love about me?" she asked.

He chuckled. "Fishing for compliments, are we?"

"Uh-huh."

"Come over here, beautiful. Sit with me, and I'll tell you all the things I love about you." He waved her closer with his hand.

It was her turn to laugh. "We'd break that lounger if I did. I'm getting too fat."

"Hey, that's one of the things I love about you."

"Are you *agreeing* that I'm fat?" She playfully slapped his hand. "Creep."

"Angel cake."

"Stooge."

"Butterfly."

"Gooney drip."

"Princess."

It was his pet name for her that brought the banter to a halt. She couldn't resist him any longer. She pushed herself up from the chair and stepped to the lounger.

"Scoot over," she said, her voice husky.

Greg turned on his side to give her more room. When she reclined beside him, he draped his arm over her belly and patted it.

"Reasons why I love you. You're beautiful. I thought so the first minute I laid eyes on you."

"And?"

"You're the mother of my baby."

"And?"

"You have a tender heart."

"And?"

He kissed the curve of her neck. "You love me back. No matter what I've done, you always love me back."

"I couldn't help it if I wanted to."

Greg put his mouth next to her ear and whispered, "Just what I wanted to hear."

As if in response, the baby moved within, trailing an elbow or a knee from one side of Dottie's belly to the other. Greg laughed when he felt it.

A frisson of joy raced through Dottie. *Thank You, Lord. Thank You for blessing me so.*

60

Saturday evening. Stuart was at work. The children were with Dottie. Penelope was alone and bored.

Restlessly, she walked from the bedroom to the living room. All was tidy. There wasn't even any sign of the bedding Stuart used to sleep on the sofa every night when he got home from the theater.

She wasn't sure if she should be relieved or insulted that her husband preferred to sleep on that lumpy sofa rather than to share a bed with her. The arrangement was her idea at first, but she thought he would object. He didn't.

When Penelope had returned, things were different between them, and she didn't know what to do about it. Or if she wanted to do anything about it.

Stuart didn't need her the way he once had. She used to hate the way he hung around, wanting to be near her, saying he loved her. She felt as if his words were smothering her. Now he said nothing, and that didn't seem right either.

As for the children, while they seemed glad to have her at home, it was their father they went to when they wanted or needed something. She was more guest in the house than mother.

Her friends were different, too. Dottie was married and large in her eighth month of pregnancy. Margo seemed softer around the edges in some indefinable way. And then there was Lucy. Penelope hadn't seen Lucy yet, but she'd heard about Richard.

Stuart had suggested more than once that Penelope should pay a visit to Lucy. "She'd like to see you. She needs her friends."

"She hasn't come to see me, has she?"

Although he answered softly, there was a hard edge to his words. "Her husband's missing in action, Pen. He could be dead. Maybe you should think about her instead of yourself for a change."

That's totally unfair, Penelope thought as she went into the kitchen. *I* do *think about others*.

She walked to the counter near the telephone and picked up the shopping list and ration book Stuart had left for her. He'd not only written down the foods she was to buy but also the color of stamps and the points each item required: One pound of butter, eight points, red stamps. A twelve-ounce can of whole-kernel corn, twelve points, blue stamps. One can Morrell's pork loaf, five points, red stamps. Point free: one box Wheaties, two cans preserves, one jar peanut butter, two loaves sliced bread.

She supposed she should go to Safeway before it got any later. Besides, she had nothing better to do.

"Saturday night," she muttered, still staring at the list, "and nothing better to do than go grocery shopping."

What a sad state of affairs.

☆ ☆ ☆

"Hello, beautiful."

The stranger who slid onto the bar stool next to Penelope was good-looking in a dangerous kind of way. His dark gaze slid down the length of her and back again.

"What's your name, sweetheart?" He sounded like Bogie when he said that.

She met his gaze, waiting a few moments before answering, "Penny." No one had called her that since she was twelve. But she was tired of being Penelope. Tired of being Pen. She wanted to be someone different.

The stranger reached out and fingered a lock of her red hair. "Not quite a copper penny, huh?" His smile sent a quiver through her. "Do you come here often, Penny?"

"No." She took a cigarette from her purse and held it to her lips, waiting for him to light it, which he did with practiced ease. After taking a drag and blowing it out, she asked, "How about you? Is this your regular watering hole?"

"First time, actually. I'm just passing through Idaho on my way to the coast."

He was about thirty-five or so. He had all of his limbs. No obvious injuries. She wondered why he wasn't in uniform, then decided it didn't matter. She'd met plenty of sailors while in San Diego, and they weren't always a lot of fun. They had to follow too many orders.

"Lucky you," she replied. "I'd like to be just passing through, too." Penelope hadn't found happiness in California, but she was convinced she would never find it in Boise either. There had to be some place better than this. There had to be a better life than the one she was stuck in now.

As if reading her thoughts, the stranger leaned a little closer. "Really? Maybe we could pass through Boise together."

Her pulse quickened. Her mouth went dry. A rush of adrenaline caused her hands to tremble as she took another drag on the cigarette.

"My name's Ned. Ned Carter." He pointed at her drink. "Can I buy you another one, sweetheart?"

Penelope had stopped in the bar after doing the grocery shopping. The two shopping bags—with their pound of butter, can of corn, pork loaf, cereal, bread, preserves, and peanut butter— were on the floor beneath her stool. She should take those bags, leave this smoky bar, and go home. Only she didn't want to go home. Not yet. Not while Ned Carter was looking at her that way, his eyes promising excitement and adventure.

"Sure," she said. "You can buy me another drink, Ned. The evening's young."

V··· —MAIL

To: Mrs. Richard Anderson, Boise, Idaho, U.S.A.
From: 1st Lt. Richard Anderson
Monday, July 19, 1943

My beloved Lucy,

My location has changed since I wrote my last letter to you. We are getting ready for a major push, and by the time you receive this letter, you'll have read about it in the newspapers. It will long since be over. I have no doubt of the ultimate outcome, but I know many will be laying down their lives. That's the way it is in war. It's pitch-black outside, hours before the dawn, but there's a lot of activity going on at this base. Mechanics are working to get planes ready for the flights we'll be taking soon enough. I should be sleeping, getting what rest I can while I can, yet here I am, wanting to put these words on paper. Needing to put them on paper. Honey, I love you, and whatever the next day or days bring, whatever happens to me now or in the future, that will still be true. Some believers say those who've gone on to heaven can see us down here on earth. But how could there be no sorrow or tears in heaven if those who have passed on can see all the horror and heartbreak down here? I don't know. But, Lucy, I hope it's true. I hope if I die that I'll be able to see you from heaven so I can pray for you. And if I don't come back, I want you to make a new life for yourself. You'll grieve, but don't stay there, Lucy. "Weeping may last through the night, but joy comes with the morning." It's time for me to close. When you read these words, Lucy, remember that I held you in my heart as I wrote them.

Always,
Richard

61

Limbo, Lucy had read, came from a Latin word that literally meant "on the border of hell."

Truly, that's how she felt. She didn't know if Richard was dead or alive, and therefore, she didn't know whether to hope and rejoice or despair and mourn.

Standing before the bedroom closet, she pressed one of her husband's shirts against her face and breathed deeply, hoping to find Richard's scent trapped in the fabric. But it was gone. It had been too long since he wore these clothes. It had been too long since he was with her, since he held her in his arms, since she inhaled his combined scents of soap and woodsy cologne.

"Richard," she whispered, dropping slowly to her knees. "Richard."

She couldn't remember his voice. Once she'd known the deep, warm sound of it better than her own. Now it was gone, lost in a mist of distant memories.

"Richard."

Outside this bedroom, outside this apartment, there were people going on with their lives as if there were no war, no hurt and dying, no soldiers missing in action, no innocent civilians trapped in a world of bombs and invaders and terror. In Boise on this Saturday night, there were young men courting young women, wooing and winning hearts. Even with the news, these men, these boys, believed—at least subconsciously—that they were invincible, that they would be among the survivors.

But here, inside this apartment, inside this room, Lucy knew different.

Lying on her side, curled into a ball, the shirt still pressed against her face, she prayed the only way she could. "Oh, God, please."

62

When Margo got out of the shower early Monday morning, she was met by the enticing scent of bacon frying in the skillet. She was surprised because neither Dottie nor Greg was usually up at this hour.

Half an hour later, dressed in a short-sleeved, two-piece rayon suit, she walked into the kitchen. Dottie was setting breakfast on the table as she entered.

"Hi, Mom." Dottie pulled out a kitchen chair. "I hope you're hungry. I made bacon and waffles."

Margo kissed her daughter's cheek. "I am hungry, dear. Thank you." She sat. "What has you out of bed at this hour?"

"The baby wouldn't let me sleep. Whenever I recline, he thinks it's time for athletic exercises." She patted her belly as she turned toward the stove.

Margo smiled. "I remember what that's like."

Indeed, she did. It seemed only yesterday that she awaited the births of her children, and now one of them was about to make her a grandmother.

Lord, how brief my time on earth will be. An entire lifetime is just a moment to You, God. Human existence is but a breath. Lord, help me treasure every moment I have with those I love.

"Penny for your thoughts," Dottie said as she set a breakfast plate and a glass of orange juice on the table.

Drawn from her reverie, Margo looked up. "Just that I'm glad you and Greg are staying with me. You won't live here always. No married couple should live with their parents if they can help it. But I'm selfishly glad you're with me now."

"Me, too." Dottie sank onto a chair next to her. "I . . . I'm glad things have . . . changed. You know. Between us."

"So am I," she whispered.

Someday she would tell her daughter how God's extreme grace had softened her heart, how He'd lifted her sense of guilt and condemnation and, in so doing, she'd been able to stop judging others, including Dottie and Greg. Someday, but not yet. This daring way of walking in faith, this freedom in the Lord, was too new, and Margo was still finding her way.

Mother and daughter smiled at each other, and it was enough.

In a comfortable silence—so different from those that used to stretch between them—Margo ate her breakfast, then carried her syrupy plate and empty juice glass to the sink.

"Just leave the dishes, Mom. I'll take care of them after Greg's eaten."

Margo glanced at her watch. "Thanks, honey. I am running late. I'll have to dash for the bus as it is."

"When you see Lucy," Dottie said, "send her my love, will you?"

She gave her daughter a sad smile of understanding. *Lord, show us how we might help our dear Lucy.* "Of course I will."

The prayer stayed in her heart as Margo brushed her teeth. It stayed with her as she hurried to the bus stop, pocketbook clasped beneath her arm and lunch pail in hand. It stayed with her as she bid good morning to Jeb Pratt. And it was still there, several stops later, when Lucy climbed aboard the bus, looking pale and wan.

A lump formed in Margo's throat. "How are you, dear?" she asked as her young friend settled onto the seat beside her.

Lucy gave a pathetic shrug. "I'm not sure." She looked at her hands folded in her lap. "I received a letter from Richard on Saturday."

Empathy stabbed Margo's heart.

"He wrote it the day . . . the same morning he . . . the morning his plane went down." She lifted her gaze. "I want to believe it means he's still alive, Margo. Do you suppose it does?"

Not knowing what to say, Margo put an arm around Lucy's shoulders and gave her a gentle squeeze.

"God willing," Lucy said softly, answering her own question. "God willing, he's still alive."

Tears stung Margo's eyes, and rather than let Lucy see them, she turned to stare out the bus window. Whenever trouble came, a Christian was to let it be an opportunity for joy, an opportunity to develop endurance and a strong Christlike character. How hard that was to put into action.

Trouble came to everyone on earth at one time or another. Margo had allowed trials to build high walls in her life. She hoped Lucy wouldn't do the same. Margo would do everything she could to help her friend avoid the same mistakes she'd made.

She turned her gaze from the window. "Trust God, Lucy. Just keep trusting Him, no matter what."

63

Lucy sat on the front pew of the base chapel, staring at the gold cross on the altar. She'd sat here for the past hour, waiting. Waiting for what, she couldn't say. Just waiting.

Trust Me.

Ah. This was why she waited. To hear His inaudible but unmistakable voice.

She bowed her head. *I do trust You, Lord.*

Trust Me with Richard.

She stared at her clenched hands and realized she clenched her husband's memory in the same way. God couldn't give her anything, not even an answer to her prayers, until she opened her hands—and her heart—in trust. She must let go before she could receive.

"Faith," she whispered, quoting the familiar verse, "is the confidence that what we hope for will actually happen."

But what I want to believe is that Richard's coming home. Lord, will You promise me he's coming home?

She strained to hear God's answer. She willed Him to tell her what she wanted to hear. She willed Him to tell her that her husband would be all right, that He would restore Richard to her.

Trust Me, beloved.

God's will and not her own. Did she want her way or God's

way? She knew the answer. As much as she loved Richard and wanted him back in her arms, she wanted God's way more. Truly, she did.

But at what cost?

Air rushed out of her lungs as she slipped from the pew to her knees. "Help me choose Your way, Lord." She squeezed her eyes closed and pressed folded hands to her forehead. "No matter the cost, let me choose You."

On the runway, airplane engines roared to life. A vehicle rumbled past the chapel. Men's voices rose and fell in the distance.

But those sounds could not compete with the voice of Love: *Take delight in Me, beloved, and I will place My desires into your heart and make them yours.*

She grew still. Not simply her body. Everything. Her mind. Her soul. Her spirit.

All was still. She was at peace in the midst of her turmoil.

She would be all right, Lucy realized. She would be all right because no matter what tomorrow brought with it—even if it was more heartache—she would stubbornly, determinedly, and with God's help, choose to delight in the Lord.

64

Margo turned off the classroom lights before stepping into the hallway and closing the door behind her. The bundle of exams she clutched to her chest weighed a ton. The heat of the afternoon was oppressive, zapping the last iota of strength from her body.

Releasing a deep breath, she headed toward the exit.

"Mrs. King?"

She swallowed a groan at the sound of Colonel Rhodes' voice. Not that she minded talking to her boss. But if he asked her to take on another class or special pupil . . .

She turned around.

The colonel smiled as he strode toward her from the far end of the corridor. "I've heard from Travis. He's back in England."

"Oh, Colonel. That's wonderful news. I'm so glad."

"My son said to tell you—" his expression sobered, and his gaze was intense—"he found your French lessons *most* helpful."

"Thank God."

"Yes," Colonel Rhodes said with a nod. After a short hesitation, he continued, "You must be headed home. Mind if I walk with you? I'm headed in that general direction myself."

She was surprised by the request but answered, "Not at all."

"Good." He motioned for Margo to proceed, then fell into step beside her, shortening his stride to match hers. When they reached the outside door, he held it open for her.

As she moved past him into the hazy light of the August afternoon, Margo felt her heart flutter and her knees go weak. Good gracious. How odd. What was wrong with her? She hoped she wasn't about to experience heatstroke.

"It's a scorcher," Colonel Rhodes said, as if reading her mind.

Margo was relieved to discover that her legs held her upright. It would be embarrassing to crumple to the ground in front of this man.

"I've been meaning to ask how your daughter is faring."

"Dottie's well. Fat and happy and eagerly awaiting the arrival of the baby."

"When's it due?"

"The end of September or early October." She wondered if he did some quick calculations in his head, coming up short a few months.

If he did, he gave no indication. "And how's her husband? Any change in his vision?"

"He can make out some light and shadows, but that's all. The doctors finally told him that's as good as it will ever be. But Greg is a courageous young man. I think he accepted the facts long before the doctors confirmed them." She smiled to herself, thinking how much she enjoyed being with her son-in-law. "He's scheduled to get a Seeing Eye dog later this fall, and he's even looking into taking some courses at the college."

They walked in silence for a short while before the colonel spoke again. "Mrs. King, I need to tell you something. You'll have a new supervisor as of next week."

"You're leaving Gowen Field?"

"No. I'll still be on this base. I'm being reassigned."

Margo's relief was out of proportion to the importance of his announcement. Officers were often reassigned in the military.

She cast a sideways glance in Colonel Rhodes' direction and found him watching her. When their gazes met, he grinned.

There was that silly flutter in her chest again.

Colonel Rhodes touched her elbow, bringing both of them to a halt. "Mrs. King, now that I'll no longer be your supervisor, I wondered if you would have dinner with me some evening."

"Dinner?" she echoed.

"Yes."

"Well, I—"

"Please, Mrs. King. I'm tired of eating alone or with the other officers. It would be nice to sit at the table and see an attractive woman across from me."

He thought her attractive?

"Here comes your bus." There was a teasing twinkle in his eyes as he added, "You'd better say yes before you miss it."

Breathlessly, she said, "Yes, Colonel Rhodes. I . . . I'd like to have dinner with you."

"Wonderful." His smile broadened. "I'll call you at home and we can pick an evening that's good for you." He took a step back. "And I hope you'll call me Vance from now on."

She nodded.

He tugged the brim of his hat—a kind of mini salute of respect—then turned and strode away.

She stared after him, feeling dazed. Did what she think just happened *really* happen? Did she, Margo King, actually have a *date* after all these years?

Laughter bubbled up inside her as she turned her gaze toward the sky.

It would seem, Lord, that You still work miracles in our time.

65

Lucy observed Colonel Rhodes as he walked away from Margo. Margo, however, didn't budge.

Lucy cupped one hand to the side of her mouth and called, "Margo, you're going to miss the bus! Hurry!"

Her friend turned, and the bemused look on her face caused Lucy to wonder what had transpired between the officer and his civilian employee.

The bus door whooshed open. "Afternoon, Mrs. Anderson," Jeb said. "How was your day?"

"It was good, Mr. Pratt. And yours?"

"Can't complain, although I'll be glad to see cooler weather get here."

Lucy glanced in Margo's direction and saw her friend walking swiftly toward the stop. Then she climbed onto the bus. Moments later, Margo sat on the seat next to her.

"What's up with you?" Lucy asked softly as the bus jerked into motion.

The corners of Margo's mouth curved into a wry grin. "Colonel Rhodes asked me out to dinner."

"I thought he was married. Didn't you tutor his son last spring?"

"He's a widower."

Lucy smiled. "So what did you tell him? Did you accept?"

"I . . . I said . . . yes."

"Well, hallelujah! It's about time."

Margo's grin vanished, and her brows drew together in a frown. "I haven't gone out with a man in . . . in *years*. I won't know what to say or how to act." She gave her head a slight shake. "I'm no spring chicken, Lucy, and I'm no raving beauty. I don't know why he asked me."

"Don't be silly." Lucy put an arm around her friend's shoulders and gave her a hug. "It's obvious Colonel Rhodes realizes how special you are. You'll both have a wonderful time."

"I wish I was as sure as you seem to be," Margo mumbled under her breath.

Lucy laughed. "Have a little faith."

They rode in silence for a while—a worried silence, if her friend's continued frown meant anything—before Lucy introduced a new topic for discussion.

"Margo, I'd like to give Dottie a baby shower. Would you mind? All I'll need is a guest list from Dottie."

The distressed expression left Margo's face, replaced by a look of tenderness. "You always think of others, Lucy. You're the kindest woman I know."

She shook her head. "I can be as selfish and thoughtless as anyone else."

"Well, my dear, I've seen no such evidence."

God has, Lucy thought as she glanced out the bus window. But then she recalled His whispered *Trust Me*, and she felt His grace wash over her once again. Yes, God knew her faults. He knew her every thought. Before she spoke, He knew what she would say. Yet He loved her.

"Amazing," she whispered.

"I'm sorry?"

Lucy gave her head another small shake. "Nothing. Just talking to myself."

The bus slowed to a stop and Margo stood. "I'll ask Dottie who she'd like at her shower. I'll bring the list in the morning."

"A *short* list," Lucy said with a laugh. "Remember, my apartment isn't large."

"Will do." Margo waved her hand, then stepped off the bus.

Lucy leaned back on the seat, closed her eyes, and began making plans. Dottie was . . . hmm . . . about six weeks from delivery so the shower needed to be soon. A Saturday afternoon would be the best day and time for Lucy. Or maybe they should have it in the morning, instead, before the day got too warm. Then, if there were many guests, they could have the party outside on the lawn.

"Comin' up on your stop, Mrs. Anderson."

Lucy opened her eyes, surprised to find she'd been lost in thought so long. "Thanks, Mr. Pratt."

The walk home from the bus stop was a short one, and Lucy was glad of it. The August sun was brutal. As she followed the narrow sidewalk around to her back entrance, her gaze fell on her Victory Garden. It was in need of weeding. She hadn't given it the attention it required. Maybe later this evening she would get to it, after the sun fell lower in the western sky and the earth cooled.

She turned the corner and was reaching for her house key when she saw Penelope Maxfield rise from the stoop. "Pen?"

"Hi, Luce. Hope you don't mind me dropping by like this."

"Of course not. I'm glad you came." She stepped toward the door. "How are you?"

Penelope shrugged. "Okay." But she didn't look okay. There was something sad and hopeless about the expression in her eyes and in the downward turn of her mouth. But the resolute set of her shoulders spoke of something different—something hard and unyielding.

Lucy wondered what Penelope wanted. If she'd learned anything over the course of the past year, it was that Penelope always thought of herself before others. At one time, Lucy had hoped she could be an agent of God's peace to this troubled young woman. Lucy had tried to befriend her, as had Dottie and Margo. Had they failed completely?

"Come inside," Lucy invited, "and I'll get us a cold drink."

Penelope followed Lucy into the apartment. "Stuart told me about Richard. I'm sorry."

"Thank you."

In the ten days since Lucy had received the telegram, she'd learned the best response to other people's expressions of sympathy was a simple one. Best for them. Best for her.

She set her purse on the kitchen counter, then opened the refrigerator and removed the pitcher of tea. "I'm glad you're home again, Pen. I'm planning a baby shower for Dottie, and you'll want to be there."

"When are you having it?"

"I'm not sure." Lucy put ice into two tall glasses and filled them with tea. "Two or three weeks. Can't wait much longer. The baby will be here soon." She turned, glasses in hand.

Penelope stood looking out the window. "I'm not sure I'll be here in two or three weeks."

"Why not? Where are you going?"

"I've made up my mind. I . . . I can't stay with Stuart. I want out." She turned from the window at last.

Lucy caught a glimpse of such emptiness of the soul, such despair, it made her sick at heart. The look was replaced a moment later with one of bitterness.

"I hate who I am when I'm here, Luce. I hate who I am when I'm with Stuart. I'm unhappy, and I make everybody else unhappy, too."

Lucy tried to think of something to say. She tried to think of the *right* thing to say.

"I want a divorce."

"Oh, Pen, no." Lucy sank onto a chair at the table. "Surely it isn't as bad as that."

Penelope sat, too. "It *is* that bad. Stuart and I . . . we don't love each other. I dislike him. No. Worse than that. I hate him, and my hate is stronger than my love ever was. If I ever *did* love him." She shrugged. "I can't stay with things like that between us. I'm too young to be miserable for the rest of my life, married to the wrong guy. I deserve to be happy. Everybody does. I only came back because I lost my job and didn't have a place to live. I didn't know where else to go. But it was a mistake to come back. I don't belong here, and I sure don't belong with him."

Lucy felt sick to her stomach. "What about the children?"

"They don't need me. They've got Stuart."

"But they *do* need you, Pen. You're their mother, and children always need their mother."

Penelope stood. "Being a mom's not all it's cracked up to be. Snotty noses and skinned knees and all the whining." She blew out a breath as she walked across the kitchen, her agitation obvious. "You don't know what it's like, always having somebody demanding your attention. I never have time to do what I want."

Lucy felt an overwhelming desire to slap Penelope. *Does she have any idea how selfish she is?*

Penelope lowered her voice as she returned to the table. "I met this guy the other night. Ned. He's handsome and single, and he's a lot of fun. He's asked me to go away with him, and I'm going."

"Don't do this, Pen. It's wrong. You'll regret it. Don't throw away your family for—"

"Are you going to tell me it's wrong to want to be happy? Stuart's never going to make me happy. All he wants is a home and the kids. He's never going to have a job where he makes enough money. Besides, he's an old stick-in-the-mud. I don't like him, can't stand to be around him, and he sure doesn't like me." Penelope motioned toward Lucy with her right hand, a challenge in her gesture. "Ned likes me. He likes me just like I am. We have fun when we're together." She released an exasperated sigh. "Why do I bother? You'll never understand."

Lucy almost said Penelope was right. She felt angry and frustrated with Penelope's attitude and thoughtlessness, and she wanted to tell her so.

Do you love Me, beloved?

Lucy caught her breath, sensing the Lord had something important to say to her. And she was certain it wouldn't include giving Penelope an angry piece of her mind.

For I, the Lord, cause everything to work together for the good of those who love Me.

All things working together for good. . . . All things working together for good. . . . All things . . .

A tiny shiver followed on the heels of understanding. *You'll use even my mistakes, won't You, Lord? You'll use my sins to help others if I give them to You and don't try to keep them hidden.*

Lucy looked up. "Pen, I've made some bad choices this past year. I'd like to keep you from doing the same."

Penelope cocked an eyebrow.

"I ... I was so lonely I almost . . . I almost betrayed Richard. I *did* betray him in my heart."

"You? Miss Goody Two-shoes, unfaithful to her husband?"

Lucy ignored the barb. God wanted her to love Penelope, no matter what. "I shared that so you'd know I understand some of what you're feeling. I've experienced the temptations that are out there." She drew a deep breath and released it. "But I also know God's awesome power and His great love for us. He'll help us overcome the temptations if we let Him. He helped me."

"Spare me the sermonizing, Lucy. I've had all of that I can stomach from Dottie and Margo." She turned toward the door. "I was afraid it would be a mistake to come here, and I was right. Nobody cares about my happiness but me."

Lucy rose. "You're so wrong. God cares."

Penelope groaned as she yanked open the door.

"Pen, don't throw away your family. You'll live to regret it if you do."

But Penelope didn't listen. She didn't hesitate an instant. She walked out of the apartment without a backward glance.

Lucy followed as far as the stoop. She stopped there, knowing it was futile to chase after Penelope. "Why couldn't she hear me, Lord? I thought I was doing what You wanted me to do, but she didn't hear. I don't understand."

In answer, she recalled what Jesus told His disciples: *One person plants and someone else harvests.*

Trust Him. That's what God had asked of her earlier today in the base chapel. That's what He asked of her now. Trust Him with Penelope. Trust Him with Richard. Trust Him with her future.

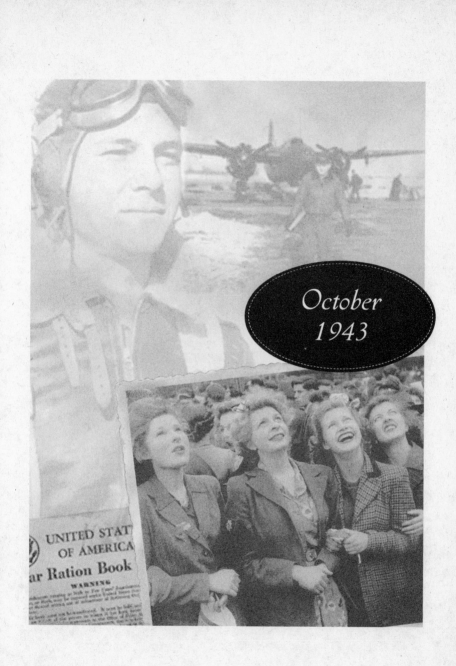

October
1943

To: 1st Lt. Richard Anderson, APO, N.Y.P.E.
From: Lucy Anderson
Saturday, October 2, 1943

My darling Richard,

Once again I sit down to write a letter that I cannot mail. It is almost two months since I received the telegram telling me you were missing in action. Two months and still no word and still I write. There are a stack of letters for you in a shoe box now; a stack of letters that I pray God will allow you to read one day.

I am just now back from the hospital. Dottie gave birth this morning to a baby boy. Rudolph Wallace. Rudy for short. Oh, he is beautiful and squalling and a joy to behold. He has a shock of black hair like his father's, and he will undoubtedly have brown eyes like both of his parents. I was with Margo and Greg in the waiting room for the final four hours of Dottie's labor. (Her labor was about twenty hours in all.) Greg nearly wore a groove into the floor, pacing back and forth.

There is more good news for Dottie and Margo besides the baby. At least, we all believe it is good news. Clark King and his unit are to remain in North Africa for the foreseeable future, maintaining order around the new Allied bases there. That should mean he is out of harm's way.

And speaking of good news, I think this applies. Margo has gone out several times with Colonel Rhodes, and I do believe things are becoming serious between them. I have to laugh. Margo walks around with a half-dazed expression much of the time, and I feel certain it is directly related to thoughts of the colonel.

As for me, my darling, I am well. I miss you. I pray for you. I wonder about you. Sometimes I fear for you. But God sustains me each day.

I love you, and I long for the day when you will read these letters. Soon, Richard. Let it be soon.

Lucy

November
1943

UNITED STAT
OF AMERICA
ar Ration Book
WARNING

WESTERN UNION

1943 NOV 30
MRS LUCY ANDERSON=
☆☆ 1602 JEFFERSON ST BOISE, ID=
REPORT JUST RECEIVED THROUGH THE
INTERNATIONAL RED CROSS STATES THAT YOUR
HUSBAND FIRST LIEUTENANT RICHARD L
ANDERSON PREVIOUSLY REPORTED MISSING IN
ACTION IS NOW WITH ALLIED FORCES IN ITALY
IF FURTHER DETAILS OR OTHER INFORMATION IS
RECEIVED YOU WILL BE PROMPTLY NOTIFIED=
M. R. JOHNSON ACTING THE ADJUTANT GENERAL

*December
1943*

UNITED STAT
OF AMERICA

ar Ration Book

WARNING

66

For four weeks after receiving that miraculous, marvelous, wonderful telegram, Lucy waited to hear something more. *Anything* more. A letter, another telegram, a phone call. Anything at all.

She waited in vain.

✷ ✷ ✷

Lucy clutched the collar of her coat close about her neck before descending the bus steps.

"I hope there's a letter awaitin' you, Mrs. Anderson," Jeb said. "You have a Merry Christmas, and I'll see you on Monday."

She glanced over her shoulder, smiled the best she could, and nodded. "Thanks, Mr. Pratt. Merry Christmas to you, too."

The door closed, the engine roared, and the bus pulled away from the curb.

Why, Lucy wondered, was it as hard—perhaps even harder—to wait for news now, knowing Richard was alive, as it had been when he was reported missing in action and might have been either dead or a captive? Shouldn't it be easier?

Maybe. But it wasn't.

A cold winter wind buffeted her back as she walked toward

her apartment, pushing her along the sidewalk, quickening her pace. Not that she was in any hurry to get home. It was so silent, and the evening hours dragged by, minute by painful minute. She missed Richard. She longed for news. Any scrap of news that might tell her how he was, that he was truly safe, where he was stationed, what he was doing.

Another Christmas without Richard. If only she would hear *something*.

When she looked back over the past year, it seemed to Lucy that she'd been on one very long roller-coaster ride. One moment she was at the top, and then she was plummeting to the depths. Up, down, up, down, up, down.

Sorry, Lord. I always mean to be strong, to keep the faith, but somehow I end up weak and faithless again.

She sighed.

As she followed the narrow sidewalk around the house to her apartment entrance, she glanced toward the corner of the yard where her Victory Garden had flourished in the summer months. It was dormant now, forlorn looking with its skeleton remains of tomato plants and cornstalks. The jars of tomatoes, pickles, beets, and more that lined her shelves were a more pleasant reminder of the success of her first garden.

Whatever is good, think on these things, she reminded herself.

She put her key in the lock and opened the door. As always, her gaze fell first to the floor, looking for mail. Hoping against hope.

Nothing.

She sighed again and closed the door. "I'm home, Empress." She placed her purse on the kitchen counter. "Want some milk?"

Her cat always came quickly, if not at Lucy's call then at the sound of the refrigerator door opening.

Lucy poured milk from the glass bottle into a bowl, expecting to feel Empress rubbing against her leg as she placed the bowl on

the floor. Loud purring told her the cat was near, yet the milk remained untouched.

"Hey, kitty." She turned. "Don't you—" The remainder of the
sentence died in her throat. Her entire body stilled. She dared
not even breathe.

Richard stood in the archway between kitchen and living
room, holding a contented Empress in his arms. His thick black
hair had been trimmed recently. His jaw was dark with a day's
growth of beard. And his marvelous, wonderful, gold-flecked
hazel eyes watched her with the tenderest of gazes. He looked
healthy. Strong. Whole.

"Is it you?" she whispered, disbelieving. "Is it really you?"

He set the cat on its feet. "It's really me, darling."

Feeling returned to Lucy's limbs, and she launched herself
across the room and into his waiting embrace. "Richard. Oh,
Richard. It's you. It's you!"

His mouth captured hers in a kiss, long and deep. All the sen-
sations that she'd longed to remember when she believed him
lost forever—the scent of him, the taste of him, the feel of him—
came rushing back in a flood.

Richard . . . Richard . . . Richard . . .

At last, the kiss ended. Breathless, Lucy leaned back, cradled
her husband's face between her hands, and stared at him, memorizing every new line on his beloved face. He looked older.
More than tired. But wonderful. So wonderful.

"You're home," she whispered.

"I'm home." He brushed his lips across her forehead. "Honey,
I've been posted to Gowen Field. I'm going to be training pilots
for combat."

She couldn't believe it. She must be hearing things. "Gowen
Field? You're home to stay?"

He grinned. "That's what it looks like."

"Oh, Richard. Oh, Richard." She trailed her hands from his
shoulders to his wrists and back again, confirming that he was

whole, making certain he was real and not a dream. "No one told me you were coming. Why didn't I know you were coming?"

"I pulled a few strings to get here before you were notified." He brushed her hair back from her face, hooking it behind her ear. With the same hunger she felt, he studied her. "I wanted to surprise you for Christmas."

She laughed, gladness bubbling up from some deep place in her spirit. "You did. You did surprise me."

They kissed again, Lucy melting into his embrace, wanting never to leave it.

She didn't know what tomorrow held in store for them. Only God knew. So she would treasure today, every day, moment by moment, blessing by blessing. No longer would she borrow trouble from tomorrow. Instead, she would be thankful for answered prayers—and the warmth and joy found in her husband's arms.

February
1944

Tuesday, February 15, 1944

It's late at night as I begin this entry in my diary. Richard is fast asleep in our bedroom, but my thoughts are too full, my mind too busy, for me to find rest.

Today is, in a way, the anniversary of the birth of the Victory Club. One year ago, we heard the news of the battle in North Africa that took so many lives. I remember how gloomy and beaten in spirit we were as we sat together at lunch. That was the day I declared I would pray for victory, not just for the Allies but for each woman in that circle of friends and for those they loved. That was the day I promised to pray for victory over our fears.

One year already, and how different we are, how much we have gone through to get to this day.

Dottie is a loving mother to Rudy, whom she believes to be the most perfect, happy, good-natured baby in the world, and a devoted wife to Greg, who is doing so well now. He's learning to read Braille, and he and his dog Buster go all around town together. I'm amazed by what Greg is achieving. He plans to start college next fall.

As for Margo, she is head over heels in love with Vance Rhodes. I haven't seen her look so radiant since I've known her. (I'm sure it helps that Clark remains stationed in North Africa rather than being in the thick of battle in Europe.) Although Margo hasn't said so, I think Vance has proposed and she said yes.

No one has heard from Penelope in more than two months. Her mother told me she got a divorce in Nevada last fall and married that man she left town with before the ink was dry on the divorce decree. I can understand why she wouldn't contact me. I tried to talk her out of leaving Stuart, and she didn't like my interference. But I can't understand why she makes no attempt to contact her children. I'll never understand that. My heart breaks for her and all she's thrown away.

It's difficult to know how Stuart feels. Mostly, I think he's relieved. Yet there is a great sadness in him, too. We are all praying for him, just as we continue to pray for Penelope.

As for me, I am blessed. Richard works hard every day, training crews for what they will face overseas, but he comes home to me each night. We are happy and well. There were difficult times to work through after I confessed my moral failure to him. But he forgave me, and our union is stronger than ever, forged as it was through that time of testing.

"The LORD is my strength and my song; he has given me victory." That's what Psalm 118 says. I've learned over the past year that, in the end, Christ is the <u>only</u> victory that counts. Trials will come. Battles will be fought. But Christ alone is my victory. I want to live each and every day in Him and in His victory.

L.

A Note to Readers

Dear Friends,

We live in perilous times. The news blasts those perils at us 24/7. Terrorists blow up buildings and buses. Wars rage. Famine and drought wreak havoc. Epidemics ravage nations. Earthquakes shake the foundations of our world.

But God is not surprised by what happens. He doesn't look away, then find us in trouble when He looks back again. He knows the beginning and the end and every moment in between. What the devil means for evil, God can and does turn to good in the lives of those who love Him. Nothing enters the life of a follower of Jesus that is not caused or allowed by God the Father as a means of changing our character to be more Christlike. Nothing. God is in control. He has a grand design, a master plan. We see only a tiny speck of time. He sees eternity.

Prior to His crucifixion, Jesus prayed to the Father on behalf of those who trusted in Him then and those who would trust in Him in the future: "I'm not asking you to take them out of the world, but to keep them safe from the evil one. They do not belong to this world any more than I do. Make them holy by your truth; teach them your word, which is truth. Just as you sent me into the world, I am sending them into the world. And I give myself as a holy sacrifice for them so they can be made holy by your truth" (John 17).

No matter what perils swirl around you today, remember that He loves you and He will see you through if you put your trust in

Him. Jesus doesn't just bring victory into our lives in the midst of troubles. He *is* the victory.

In the grip of His grace,

Robin Lee Hatcher

From her heart . . . to yours.
www.robinleehatcher.com

About the Author

Robin Lee Hatcher discovered her vocation as a novelist after many years of reading everything she could put her hands on, including the backs of cereal boxes and ketchup bottles. However, she's certain there are better plots and fewer calories in her books than in puffed rice and hamburgers. The winner of the Christy Award for Excellence in Christian Fiction, the RITA Award for Best Inspirational Romance, and the RWA Lifetime Achievement Award, Robin is the author of over 45 novels, including *Catching Katie* (Tyndale), named one of the Best Books of 2004 by the Library Journal.

A mother of two and "extremely young" grandmother of five, Robin enjoys the beautiful Idaho outdoors, books that make her cry, and romantic movies. She is passionate about the theater, and several nights every summer, she can be found at the outdoor amphitheater of the Idaho Shakespeare Festival, enjoying Shakespeare under the stars. She and her husband, Jerry, make their home in Boise, sharing it with one persnickety cat and three dogs, including Poppet the Papillon, also known as "Robin's obsession."

Robin loves to hear from readers. You can contact her via her web site at www.robinleehatcher.com or by mail at PO Box 190407, Boise, ID 83719-0407.

The Victory Club

For your book group's free discussion guide, visit
www.robinleehatcher.com or www.christianbookguides.com.

From her heart...
to yours

*Visit your local bookstore to find these and other
heartwarming books by Robin Lee Hatcher.*

www.tyndalefiction.com